What a Girl Needs

By Kristin Billerbeck

What a Girl Needs By Kristin Billerbeck Copyright © 2014

Print Edition

Chapter 1

"MARRIAGE WON'T SOLVE your problems. It will only highlight them." My mom used to tell me that and I'd laugh. I mean, *seriously*, she married my dad. What did she expect? Roses and serenades from the balcony? One can hardly expect romance from a man who grunts the vast majority of his words. Let's not even bring up the fact that he thinks it's appropriate to unzip his pants after a big meal—regardless of who is present. Clearly, romance wasn't a priority to my mother, so I wasn't inclined to take her advice in this arena.

"You'll see," she'd say, then grin at me like I didn't possess a brain cell. Her condescension infuriated me, and I'd follow her into the kitchen, determined to tell her my future didn't look anything like hers.

"I won't marry a man who isn't romantic. You won't catch us reading the paper at the breakfast table. That's so depressing when couples do that, like they're just not interested in one another at all!" At this point, I'd get a little heated. I'll admit it; I took it personally when she'd tell me romance was a myth.

"Well, I hope you meet this Prince Charming, Ashley. May the enchantment and lingering gazes over the scrambled eggs last forever." Mom would then roll her eyes and set the breakfast dishes in the sink.

As I'm about to celebrate my second anniversary to Prince Charming, I have to admit, there may have been a little truth in my mother's words. Just a smidgen. We still don't read the paper over breakfast, but I'd be lying if I said my expectations weren't the slightest bit dashed. I thought the daily rejection that was my single-life existence would end at marriage. I mean, someone basically signed a contract to not reject you, am I right? Three years ago, I wanted nothing more than to be married. And now? Now I just want a husband who is home once in a while...

✦   ✦   ✦

I, ASHLEY STOCKINGDALE NOVAK, did marry my real-life Prince Charming. Amazingly, he was available in human form: Dr. Kevin Novak, Resident Pediatric Surgeon. I *used* to be a leading patent attorney working on the latest technologies in Silicon Valley. We left the area, and my career behind, for Philadelphia, so that my husband could further his profession in the renowned neonatal surgical unit with preemies.

Patents on the latest integrated circuit seemed insignificant by comparison. I mean, Kevin isn't just a doctor, he's like Superman and Mother Teresa rolled into one amazingly hot package... And I'm...well, outside of patents, good at shopping. If I have other skills, I have yet to discover them.

It certainly isn't cooking.

When I dwell on the humanity chasm that looms between my husband and me, it becomes overwhelming. While he disappears off to the hospital to save someone's precious child, I tell myself that it's enough to be at home as his support system. I tell myself that it's a godly thing to be satisfied with being his helpmate, that there's honor in being Robin to his Batman. Or am I Alfred the butler?

Every day I start with prayer and good intentions. Today I'm going to bake cupcakes and have a three-course meal on the table when Kevin returns from his arduous day. Only, I'm not such a great cook, and while shopping may be a specialty, grocery shopping is like browsing for a casket. You might HAVE to do it, but does anyone really want to? Maybe foodies who watch the Food Network. But two channels over on QVC they're selling Chi hair straighteners on EasyPay. I ask you, where would your attention go?

When you're lacking a set schedule, the day begins to get away from you, and before you know it, you've lost an entire day and can't account for it. Being unemployed, for me is like being on a drunken binge. At least, what I imagine a drunken binge to be like.

I'm in Philadelphia, but my life is still back in Silicon Valley, where I left my job, my friends, my family and my church. It all seemed so reasonable and self-sacrificing for love—it was romantic. Except the reality is that I'm bored out of my skull. I should be content. The operative word being *should*, but I'm bored out of my skull.

I still have my patent license, but I'm not legally allowed to work for a law firm in Pennsylvania without passing the bar. So I *can* do my job, but no one will actually hire me to do it. In this state, I'm only qualified to be a patent agent, so I'm relegated to consulting occasionally on patents for the kind of chintzy gadgets sold on late-night television. *A monkey could write these patents.*

"You're an intellectual snob," my friend Brea told me. "You're not the belle of the ball in Philadelphia and you can't handle it."

Perhaps, but eventually, you have to own your truth. And here it is: I need more mental stimulation than writing patents for the "finger-mounted fly swatter" and making dinner every night.

At some time in the last two years, I stopped finding joy in shoes and that's when I knew I was in trouble. As a patent consultant, I rarely had reason to leave the house. Let's face it, you don't need schematics and design engineers to describe "The ABC Banana Peeler" in graphic detail. Forget the fact that this is what opposable thumbs are for. This kind of patent work can be done over the phone or by email. Or in crayon scribbled on a piece of binder paper.

There was intrigue in the fact that patents I worked on were at risk of being stolen by foreign countries—it brought this whole espionage thing to the table that made me feel like a female 007. Countries that are tempted to steal the next iPhone design couldn't care less about Junko's latest weight-loss gimmick. Without an office and a steady stream of work and compliments on my shoes, my joy in fashion lost its power.

And in essence, so have I.

It appears, and this totally surprised me, but it appears as though I am not all that good at sacrificial living. I may even be…gasp…slightly selfish. However, after two years of living in this interim mode, I've finally worked up the courage to tell Kevin that I need more from life. California doesn't share reciprocity with Pennsylvania, so I either need to get licensed as an attorney in Pennsylvania, or find meaningful work to do while Kevin saves lives. Since Kevin's position wasn't permanent, it seemed silly to get licensed when we might move again soon. So I waited. And I bought more shoes. And I became this cardboard cutout of myself.

No more.

Ashley Stockingdale Novak is back, and I plan to be better than ever and rekindle the romance of life that makes it worth living.

Kevin's and my second anniversary falls on a Monday night, and I plan to use the occasion to tell him my truth. I smooth my electric blue skirt in the mirror and practice what I'll tell him. "I'm so proud of you Kevin, with all you do to save babies who wouldn't stand a chance without you. You're so selfless and awesome, but—"

And this is where I stop. But what? But I'm too shallow to sit home while you save babies all day? I must write patents the way Dickens had to churn out words, what?

The doorbell rings, and I slide into my strappy, silver sparkle Sergio Rossi heels. There's a lot of money in Philly. So much money in fact, that you can buy designer heels for nothing at consignment shops. I never saw myself as a "used" shoe kind of girl, but when what I could afford on Kevin's salary became obvious, I became frugal.

Giving up my job didn't prepare me for what I'd actually have to surrender: Shoes, clothes, coffee shop soy lattes on a regular basis…it's like being in college without the work to take your mind off the sacrifice.

I open our front door, and Kevin is standing in a charcoal suit with a cobalt-and-red tie I bought him back when I had a job. He looks as if he's stepped out of a Nordstrom window and I'm taken aback by the warmth in his eyes. He holds up a bouquet of red roses. "Happy Anniversary." He puts the flowers on the table by the doorway and envelops me in a hug. He kisses my neck and whispers, "I love you." With a small growl, he suggests, "We don't really need to eat *now*, do we?"

"You made reservations. We're going to be late," I say in obligatory fashion, but the idea of a quiet evening at home sounds like absolute bliss. His work is constantly on his mind, and the notion of having his full attention burrows in deep and finds a warm spot in my heart.

"I did make reservations." He helps me with my coat and opens the door wider and leads me outside. "C'mon, sexy. The sooner we go to dinner, the sooner we'll get home—"

I hang onto his solid bicep as he shows me to his waiting white horse: A Dodge Stratus. He tells me about his day and the surgery he performed until we arrive at the Society Hill restaurant. He pays for valet, which thrills me, since the Sergio shoes are not comfortable, and I'm out of practice in heels. I'm fumbling about like Bambi getting the feel for new legs. Gone is the confidence dressing up once gave me—now it's as if I'm wearing my mother's heels and padding about awkwardly. If, in fact, I had a mother who ever wore heels.

Kevin places his hand at the small of my back, and we enter into the romantic dim lighting. The restaurant is everything I do love about Philadelphia. It is filled with history, from its beamed ceilings and exposed brick walls to its underground tunnels. Everything in the city seems to have a story, and running my hand along the brick wall I wonder what it could tell me if it could speak.

Kevin checks in with the maître d' and we are seated at an intimate table in the wine cellar, which is candlelit and ours alone. The music from the piano bar above wafts in and echoes off the brick walls, and the ambiance is everything I might possibly hope for.

"I knew my mother was wrong about romance ending." I smile across the table.

Kevin is as gorgeous as the day I married him as he looks deeply into my eyes. "Are you happy, Ashley?"

"Do you think anyone was Shanghaied in these tunnels?"

He gives me that look. "Really Ashley?"

And I feel slightly ashamed of myself for missing the moment, but I'm captivated by the arched concrete over our heads. Or maybe I just don't want to answer his question. Because if you can't say anything nice…

"Well, it's totally romantic for us, but don't you wonder what happened here in another era? I mean, someone could have been captured and held hostage down here, and we're preparing for a culinary feast and feeling romantic. But what if they got sent through the tunnel to a boat waiting offshore and were taken from the only life they'd ever known?"

"Correction," Kevin says. "It *was* romantic." He clasps his beautiful, knotty surgeon's hands on the table, and his slightly narrowed eyes tell me he knows I'm trying to divert his attention. "I asked you if you're happy."

"Happy?" I close my eyes for a moment and contemplate that perhaps it is me who turned into my father. What if I'm the one doing the Stockingdale male equivalent of sitting at the table with my pants unbuttoned? "All right. Reset." I stare at him and try to forget the neurotic voices in my head. "I love you, sweetheart. It's been two years, but it seems like yesterday that I walked down the aisle toward you. I remember it was near impossible to walk slowly because all I wanted to do was get to you, for fear you'd run off before I reached the altar."

"I would have waited an eternity."

"The beat of that wedding march is ridiculous. They should speed it up."

"But are you happy?" he repeats.

Notice, I didn't quite answer the question. I don't know how to answer because Kevin delights me. I regret nothing, and I'd marry him over and over again, but my current life is not enough – and for that reason, I feel like I've betrayed him. I search for the words to tell him that I need more, and that it has little to do with him.

"I feel like a failure," I say.

"A failure? Ashley, you accomplished more in your short career than most people accomplish in a lifetime. How many patents did you secure?"

"*Accomplished.* Past tense. As in, I'm over. Finished. Shouldn't I have something to look forward to at this age? I mean, I'm too young to be looking backwards, am I right? You're just getting started in your career. You have so many babies to save, and I have—what? Another pair of shoes to buy?"

Kevin's expression drops, and once again I've changed the mood—just like my dad taking it one portion of his zipper at a time.

"I didn't realize that's how you felt. I knew you weren't your bubbly self, but I suppose I didn't fully realize how miserable you really were."

My shoulders slump as I see how I've let him down. "I'm a failure as a Christian wife, Kevin, don't you see? Cooking, caring for others—it should make me happy and fulfill me, but it doesn't. What's wrong with me? I make dinner, and I try to find pleasure in it like Nigella Lawson does—"

"Who?"

"She's a famous chef. But she puts love and joy into her food. I feel like I put bitterness with a side of resentment into it. I abhor cooking and I want to find pleasure in it." I frown. "But I don't."

Kevin taps his finger on the dark table as if searching for the answer to the universe. I pick up the scents of Italian food between us. There's the pungent odor of garlic mixed with the heady scent of red wine and the sweet wax from the candle at our table. My husband is silenced. I've silenced Kevin. I have that ability to shut people down because they don't know how to answer me. I don't know when to be quiet. Just like my father doesn't know when to keep his pants zipped.

"I'm ruining the romance. I shouldn't have said anything,"

The waiter comes and brings us waters with lemon in it. He reads off the specials, but I'm not listening. My eyes are trained on my husband who wants to fix my mess that isn't his to fix. It's not his job to put me back together again.

"May I get you started on some beverages?" The waiter rattles off wine selections, but Kevin and I don't drink. Nobody wants his or her surgeon to drink, and me? Well, it goes without saying that I don't need alcohol. I'm more than enough for most people perfectly sober.

The waiter finally leaves us alone in the wine cellar, and rather than romance, there's this heavy air hanging between us. Kevin takes my hands in his.

"Just because you don't find fulfillment in darning my socks doesn't mean there's anything wrong with you, Ashley. This may be hard for you to believe, but I never imagined you as much of a housewife."

I grimace. "I could do it if I wanted to."

"Domesticity is not your strong suit, honey. That's why you lived with Kay."

"It is not!" But I slink a bit in my chair. "Okay, it probably is, but there's nothing wrong with taking pleasure in what Kay enjoyed. She enjoyed the house as her castle." *Why do I feel like my anniversary is suddenly a critique on everything I'm not?*

"There's our house," he says. "It doesn't feel like home to you and I know that's true because when you lived with Kay you made the parts of it that were yours, truly yours. You decorated. You bought a fancy bedspread that matched the curtains—"

Kevin's parents bought our house. It was a wedding gift. A really crappy wedding gift, if you ask me. Because people, no matter what their budget, should have a choice in the kind of life they want to live. I didn't, and every time I enter the house, I think of it as Kevin's mother's house – not my own.

"I knew who I was then. I was the woman who liked 500-thread count sheets and Sheridan bedding with bright colors to match my mood. I'm not about anything anymore." The realization hits me like strong drink. "I used to sing in the choir and help Kay organize parties for the singles' group. I used to write patents and travel all over the world. Now, I can't get a job. The new church choir is full with singers, and our house is a dump that I don't have the energy to fix because even when it's done, it will just be lipstick on a pig."

As all of these truths spew out of me, Kevin's face looks more horrified, and he understands that he may be married to a curmudgeon. A young, well-dressed curmudgeon.

"I'm a has-been."

"Maybe this is a good time to give you my anniversary present." He drops my hands and reaches into his jacket pocket.

"I wish I could take back everything I've said tonight, Kevin. I've ruined our anniversary." I look down at the linen napkin in my lap. "I've become my father."

"Not at all, Ash." There's an edge to his voice, something I don't recognize. "In fact, you've only confirmed that I bought you just the right gift to cure what ails you." He looks at me expectantly while he hands me an envelope. "Happy Anniversary, baby."

Kevin's a terrible gift buyer, I confess. He gets so excited to watch me open things, and I have to really work to act excited over a desk lamp—"Oh my goodness, just what I needed!" I'll squeal. Or there was the time he bought me a silver toilet bowl brush. He was so proud of himself that he'd bought me something that would match the bathroom; I didn't have the heart to point out the obvious—that *anything* involving scrubbing a toilet is not a great gift.

So it is with trepidation that I slice open the card with my freshly manicured nail. (Nails I gave up Saturday lattes for!) "I can't imagine what it could be!" Tears flood my eyes when I see it. "An airline ticket?" I can barely speak. "We're going on a trip? I get actual time with my h-husband?" I stammer. "Oh, Kevin!" I scramble out of my seat to his side where I hold his strong jaw in my hands and kiss him. (This was supposed to be like one of those Bachelor moments, on the hometown dates, but it comes off as more of a thwarted mugging.) "Kevin, really? We're going to have time together?" My throat is tight as I process how much he cares and I have that prickly, stinging feeling in my nose. "When are we going? Kevin, when?"

He clears his throat and tugs at his tie. I notice as he does so that I missed a crease in his shirt. (Strike ironing off the list of things I do well—actually, let's just go with anything domestic, full stop.) My arms are clasped around his neck in an awkward position, and instinctively, I know the news isn't good. The sorrow in his eyes should be a warning sign. But I am so zealous at the idea of a hotel room with my husband in it; I believe he's just shy about my reaction. I mean, a waiter could enter at any moment, and Kevin isn't big on public displays of affection.

I tend to be, what Kevin calls, *enthusiastic*. Read: Obnoxious. I rise from the floor and sit back down in my chair as if the last few seconds had never taken place. He faces me. I drink in his eyes. Every time I stare into his eyes, I fall for him all over again because they are dripping with love for me. There is no question how he feels about me. Toilet brush notwithstanding. He wants to give me the world. He just has other priorities. However, the road to you-know-where is paved with good intentions.

"Ashley," he says while looking down at his blood-red linen napkin. "I'm not going with you on this trip. I've got those two huge cases right now." He clears his throat. "And I don't think I'm what you need."

Not what I need? My heart sinks. I try to keep up the smile, but I'm disheartened in a way I haven't felt since I was single and hit with the sting of dating rejection.

He goes on, "I can't leave town right now, but I can't have you sitting alone in the house waiting for me to come home. I need for you to be happy."

I know I shouldn't doubt his words, but he needs for me to be happy, so he's propelling me out of town like a rock from a slingshot? "I've never made you feel like you had to entertain me, have I? I don't expect for you to be my world."

"No, no. It's not that."

"How did you afford this?"

"My Dad gave me his frequent flyer miles."

His dad. So not only am I being sent away, but on someone else's dime?

I hold up the card he's given me and try to decipher what he's telling me. "So this gift is a trip by myself? For our anniversary?" I don't care what marriage book you're reading, that can't be good.

"I think, Ashley," Kevin says in his sweetest southern drawl, "you should go home to the Bay Area for a visit. Figure out what will make you happy again, and then do what you must to make it happen when you return. I don't want you to resent me or my work."

"I don't resent you." *I resented the toilet brush. I may resent this weird "gift"—but I don't resent him.*

"I'd like to keep it that way." Kevin shakes his head. "I was selfish to get married when I knew what I was facing in this residency and then the fellowship."

The lump in my throat swells and my eyes sting. "So what you're saying is that you wish you weren't married? That's a stellar anniversary gift."

"Not for a second. That's what makes me feel so badly. I'd do it again in a hot minute, but there was a price to pay, Ashley, and you're paying it and I'm feeling it. No real man lets his wife take the fall. It's not lost on me that you're taking the fall."

"So you're sending me away? That's your answer?"

"I'm not putting this well, I'm—"

The waiter enters the wine cellar, takes one look at me and my quivering lower lip, and makes a mad dash exit.

"Brea knows you're coming," Kevin adds, as if I've won some kind of anniversary lottery.

Brea's my best friend. She has been for an eternity and she knows me like the back of her hand. Maybe better, because she has two boys under five, so I don't think she actually ever gets to look at her own hand. She's been so busy, I barely hear from her, so maybe Kevin is right. Maybe building back old friendships is the key to figuring out my future.

"When do I leave?" I ask, as if I'm headed for the gallows. It's one thing to win a vacation, it's another when you get a lone ticket across the country for your two-year anniversary.

"Wednesday. You'll have tomorrow to pack and then you'll be on your way. I have that big study going on and I'm not going to be home much anyway." He says this like it was some kind of anomaly. He's never home, but when he is, it's worth all the trouble. Doesn't he understand that? It's like getting a guilt offering rather than an anniversary gift.

I suddenly remember what I wanted to tell him about my future, and I don't have to, because it's as if he's read my mind. It feels like breaking up with someone when you don't want him or her to do it first so that you can maintain a shred of dignity.

"Here, I thought we were going to discuss our future family."

Kevin gives a mild shrug. "Is that what you want to discuss?"

I suddenly feel like I'm talking to a stranger. My throat goes dry. "Seems a moot point now."

When I first got married, I thought I wanted a family right away. Thirty-three is no Spring Chicken for having babies, no matter what Hollywood tries to tell us, but my ticking clock started to slow when

I visited Kevin at work. Seeing all those preemies, so pink, delicate and the size of gerbils, bringing new life into this world didn't seem as simple. A fear developed. It's hard to take the miracle of life for granted, or believe that a healthy baby ever arrives, after you witness so many of them struggling to hang onto life. It sucks a bit of the joy out of the idea, if I'm honest. Fear is the antithesis of faith, I get that, but with a visual reminder fear is also very real.

Naturally, Kevin's mother thinks I'm barren and manages to mention it every time she calls. She seems to think comparing my eggs to "dehydrated fruit" is appropriate conversation. I'll tell you one thing, when Elaine Novak comes to visit, there isn't a box of Raisin Bran within fifty feet of the house.

I finally find my voice. "Your mother will think we're having trouble if I go to California alone. It's bad enough she thinks I'm barren."

Kevin's eyes go wide. "She doesn't think you're barren!" he says, as if I'm a total drama queen and his mother hasn't implied that very thing from day one.

It also doesn't help that my sister-in-law Emily is pregnant. Not married or in a serious relationship, but pregnant. Mrs.-Novak-the-First thinks this is appalling behavior, but rather than say so, she focuses on the fact that I'm *not* pregnant rather than find any error with her own offspring. Kevin, bless his heart, tries to maintain the peace between the women he loves.

"Don't take it personally, Ash," he tells me. "My mom's just upset about my sister and doesn't know how to deal with it. This vacation is for you, and I really put thought into this gift—I know you were disappointed with the silver toilet brush."

Well, that's good. *Progress.* It seems obvious though, doesn't it? Toilet brush equals unacceptable gift.

"If you don't want to go, you don't have to, but you need to find your focus again. I think California and your family and friends can help with that." He meets my gaze with those devastating eyes of his.

"I miss your sparkle."

I'm still on his mother's comment. "So it's acceptable that your mother compares my girl parts to dried-up fruit because your sister's pregnant?"

"Of course it's not," Kevin says, dropping his head in his hands. "But if I tell her it bothers you, she'll only find a way to say it differently. You *know* my mother. That's why we live three states away." Kevin reaches over the table and kisses me on the forehead. I temporarily forget about his mother and the future. "We'll have a baby when we're ready to have a baby. For now, go enjoy yourself back home."

Home? Before this *romantic* anniversary dinner—a mere hour ago—I thought "home" was wherever Kevin would be. My thoughts are swirling too fast. *Deep breaths.* I tilt my chin and look straight into Kevin's eyes.

"Will you eat while I'm gone?" My voice is robotic because I'm calculating how much this trip cost us, and how the forthcoming bill will probably serve to remind me how useless I feel without a job. "If your mother comes, she's going to yell at me for not feeding you."

"I'll eat."

And there it is. Before we even order drinks in our fancy Italian wine cellar, I've been sent off alone on a mystery trip just like the Railway children. Happy anniversary to me.

He takes my hand and folds it into his own. "The next move will be permanent, Ashley. Then, you can go back to your work. I'm so sorry I brought you along on this roller coaster ride. I've been very selfish."

"I'm not sorry." I reach over to touch his jaw, and as he comes closer I inhale deeply. *I'm too reliant on him. He feels it, and the pressure will break us. I need work. I need a purpose that isn't an unhealthy attachment to my husband, who doesn't really need me. I'm just a nicer diversion.* I inhale again. Deeper this time.

He pulls away. "What are you doing?"

"I don't want to forget what you smell like when I leave. It's the most powerful memory-inducer, you know."

"Ashley, you sound like a dog sniffing my ear. Would you cut that out?" He's shooing me as the waiter comes to take our orders.

"This is a first. A one-way trip alone for my anniversary. You know, a lot of *Dateline* shows begin like this."

"It's not one-way." He raises his brow. "Don't give me any ideas."

I smirk.

"Ash, you'll be back in two weeks, and by then I should know if we're staying in Philadelphia. We'll have a decision to make. This vacation is nothing to get dramatic about."

"Uh, have we met? I get dramatic about everything. And you'll forgive me if I mention that giving a single ticket vacation to your wife is not exactly the pinnacle of romance." I pause. "But it is better than a silver toilet brush."

"See? I'm improving with time – like a fine wine."

"Two weeks, you say?" I stare at the ticket again, calculating what I'll do for two weeks. I still won't have a job in California, and my dad will be over my visit in about two hours. "Any idea where we might live permanently yet? You have to have some idea. Which programs have you looked at seriously?"

"We'll have to discuss it, but if I can't get back to Stanford or UCSF, where I know you'd prefer, and if Philly doesn't want me, Atlanta might be the best place for us."

My eyes nearly pop out of their sockets. "Atlanta!" I guzzle the water that's set before me. "It may have escaped your attention, but your mother lives in Atlanta. And didn't you just get through telling me why we lived three states away from her?"

"Atlanta is a nice place to raise a family."

Correction. It would be a nice place to raise a family if the mother-in-law from the dark side didn't reside there. With her little minion, Emily. And soon, a minionette in the form of a grandchild.

"I know it's a nice place to raise a family," I tell Kevin. "Luckily, your sister seems to be taking care of that and your mother will have a grandchild close by." I clamp my teeth over my bottom lip. This is not how I want my husband to remember me while I'm gone. I want there to be longing—gnashing of teeth while he waits for me to return and all that. But Atlanta?

"It's nothing tangible yet. Go enjoy your vacation."

"It's just—I never knew it was a consideration." First he says, we have a decision to make, then I hear the word, *Atlanta*. My trust issues are coming out to play.

"It might not be from the look on your face." Kevin cups my jaw with his hands and kisses me deeply over the table, which sends our waiter with our iced tea right back where he came from. "Stop worrying, Ashley. Go engage your mind in Silicon Valley. You'll come back to me with all the latest and I'll see that spark in your eye again."

Not if he mentions Atlanta again, he won't. He'll see sparks all right, but they won't be in my eyes.

As I gaze at the ticket, I can't help but wonder what his mother will say to this. Kevin sending me away for our anniversary—allowing my eggs to shrivel further while Princess Emily can have a baby all on her own.

"Besides, Kay needs you there," Kevin says about my old roommate. "She says she has a big decision to make and she needs you there for it."

"Well, if Kay needs me..." I let my voice trail off. It would be good to feel useful again.

Maybe Kevin wants to send me back to "The Reasons"—which is what I called my singles' group—as in "we all had our reasons we weren't married." This way I might find the "reason" for my discontent in Philly. Though the weather, my lack of interesting work, and a schlumpy house might have something to do with it. I've clearly got as many Reasons as I started with before marriage—now I just have another half named Kevin.

Chapter 2

WEDNESDAY ARRIVES LIKE an unwelcome Visa bill—too quickly and it includes a whole bunch of details that I'd forgotten. As Kevin drives me to the airport, I start to panic about his future job offers for his next fellowship. A specialty like his requires years and years of study. I worry that my future may be decided for me before I return and any work I do to plan the next stage of my career may be pointless.

Selfish. But still true.

"What do you think about Jersey?" I ask Kevin, as we set out on the turnpike.

He turns toward me, shakes his head and focuses again on the road. "New Jersey?"

"Yeah. We just take the Ben Franklin Bridge and we're home, so it wouldn't be a hard move. There must be children's hospitals in Jersey. I mean, look at all those kids on the *Real Housewives*. Kids equal children's hospitals, right?"

"It doesn't work quite like that. South Jersey is a far cry from North Jersey – I don't think you want to live with the cows, Ashley."

"Do they have a Wawa?" I sigh dreamily. "I do love a Wawa," I say about my cheaper version of Starbucks, which I've grown to love after living on one salary.

He cocks his eyebrow. "Trust me, I'm going to do a lot of research before we consider moving for the fellowship, and that research won't include anecdotes, or offspring from the *Real House-*

wives."

"I could totally handle living in a place where sparkly, blingy clothing and animal prints are perfectly acceptable. I think people bold enough to wear sequins are happier, but that's just me."

Kevin grimaces. "Yeah. That's not going to happen. The last thing your wardrobe needs to do is grab more attention."

I stare out the window and sigh deeply. I feel like a dog being taken to the vet when it actually thinks it's going to the beach. *Yes, I get that I'm actually going to the beach in California, but that's hardly the point here.*

"Kevin, you make it sound like I have tacky taste. I *don't* have tacky taste, but mark my words, women who shun the sequin are less happy. There has to be a study somewhere."

"Yeah. Probably in Jersey, sponsored by the Bedazzled Company."

I laugh. "Kevin made a funny! And you know what a Bedazzler is. I'm totally impressed."

"Some days, I cannot believe you got through law school."

"Magna cum laude, baby!" Granted. Maybe I was better at school than actual life, but I'm grabbing at straws here.

"You need meaningful work, Ashley." He taps the steering wheel nervously. "If you're still obsessing about us moving to Atlanta, what more can I tell you? You have my word that we're not moving to Atlanta. We're not going anywhere until you decide what's going to happen with you next. It's your turn, Ashley."

"Well, that came out of nowhere. Is that your way of telling me to get a job?"

"What?" Kevin slaps the steering wheel. "No! Are we having the same conversation?"

I can't let up. A surprise vacation…a surprise anything isn't like my husband. I'm right to be suspicious. "We're going to Atlanta aren't we? That's what this is all about. You need further training, and Atlanta is in my future." I'm mentally preparing myself for southern belles and laser-focused subtext. I can already hear, *bless your heart...*

"We could stay in Philly for it. You can pass the bar here if that's what you want. I just need you to know what you want, without my influence."

"Right. So you're sending me away to solve the great mysteries of the universe."

"This is a vacation for you, Ash, but our future is about *us*. I'm not making any decisions without you. I made that mistake once and I've anguished over it ever since."

Every time he says something like that, I hear that he's regretted marrying me. I'm sure he doesn't mean it that way, but it doesn't prevent my mind from going to all sorts of dark places. I mean, I should have a life by now. I've been in Philadelphia for nearly two years. When did I become a sloth?

"I went from being a cheetah to a sloth," I muse.

"What? Ashley, what goes on in that head of yours? You didn't try to pass the bar here because we were getting settled, and you knew we probably weren't staying. There's no shame in that."

"So why do I feel it? Like I've been wasting the precious time God gave me."

"You know what Albert Einstein says about inertia..."

"I totally don't." I shrug. "Should I? Because they don't teach that in law school."

"Einstein said, 'Nothing happens until something moves.' I'm just giving you the push you need to get moving again because I feel like my precious Ashley is slipping away from me."

This should give me comfort. He's giving me a little push—but seriously, all the way to California? "You think I knew that we were leaving Philadelphia? I'm psychic now? Because if this were true, I would definitely not have coats in my closet to last me into the next millennium."

"Nothing has seemed to work out for you here, and as your husband, I have to take that as a sign. I want the woman I married back."

"A sign? Kevin, if I didn't have bad luck, I wouldn't have any luck at all. This has nothing to do with Philly. I simply don't know what my purpose is since I've left patent law."

"Then maybe you shouldn't have left it," he says plainly.

The practical reality is my patent certification works anywhere in the United States. The reality is, no state outside California will hire me to do patent work until I pass their individual state bar or it's a state where California's bar is transferrable. *Catch-22*. The mantra of my life.

"What about when you volunteered at the Career Closet? I thought clothes, people who are less fortunate, you'd forget about the law for a while, but it didn't work out."

I see disappointment etched on his handsome face; the realization that I am not his mother, nor will I be leading Junior League committees anytime in the near future.

My casual stroll into philanthropy lasted a month. The Greater Philadelphia Career Closet asked me to step down for refusing polyester blend suits from donors. These women, many of them single moms who hadn't worked in years, were trying to get back on their feet. Someone expects them to do that in puckering polyester? (FYI, the answer to that question is yes. *Go figure.*)

Long story, short: I was fired from volunteering, but not before I donated all of the silk and wool suits I could spare.

"That was not my fault!" I pull my attention from Kevin, cross my arms and stare out the side window. "Those women needed to feel good about themselves, and they were taking crap clothes. How is a woman supposed to feel human in a polyester suit, much less have the confidence to go out and land a job?" Suddenly I'm choked up. "Poor women left there looking like they were extras on *The Mary Tyler Moore Show*. That's just not right. I had a moral obligation to those women. They would have been better off selling that garbage and buying them some nice, fashionable things at Target. That's all I tried to say."

Lesson Learned: People often don't want the truth. They want the easiest path. *You know, the road I can never seem to take.*

"I'm not placing blame, Ash. I'm basically saying the same thing you are, that it didn't work. Maybe it's part of a bigger master plan."

I exhale. "Maybe you're right. Maybe I'm not meant for the world outside of Silicon Valley. I mean, you can take a girl out of the Reasons, but you can't take the Reason out of the girl."

"Excuse me," Kevin says. "I did take the Reason out of the girl. Or have you forgotten?"

I grin at him as we pass a road sign for the Philly Airport. But yeah, he totally did take the reason for being single out of the girl.

"Philadelphia…the city of brotherly love," I say as we pass a road sign. "Do you think they call it that because it's freezing half the year and proximity plus fuzzy socks are necessary for survival?"

"I do not think so. I do think it's early and your brain isn't quite engaged."

"You're probably right. I'm focusing on winter, when brotherly love is possible. I'm forgetting about the rest of the year. When it gets so hot and sticky that I feel like an abandoned lollipop glued to the sidewalk. Like if you pulled me up, I'd make that terrible sucking sound like a cleaner fish in a tank. *Ah, Philly.* The smog-soaked, history-heavy city that holds one attraction for me: You, Dr. Kevin Novak."

"I'm honored." Somehow, he doesn't sound honored.

As we get off the Interstate, I have this sick feeling in my stomach. "But it's still one hundred times better than Atlanta."

"You've made your point. Atlanta is not an option."

Somehow, I don't think I have. I know Kevin's mother, and she's going to use my absence. Somehow. It's just how she rolls.

"Do you think I'm slow?" He cocks his eyebrow and beams those beautiful eyes at me.

"No, I think your family is…persuasive."

He winks at me. "You have one advantage over them."

"Only one?"

Kevin finally parks the car and cuts off the motor. He turns to me and looks into my eyes in that captivating way that he has, as if I'm the only person on the planet. The very same look that makes his family worth enduring. It's as if he can see inside my very soul and comfort me with a glance.

He shakes his head. "I don't know what I was thinking to send you away. I can't imagine what it's going to be like to come home to an empty house."

"It's not empty," I remind him. "Rhett is there. You're not going to forget to feed my dog, are you?"

"Emily will feed the dog."

"Emily?" My stomach lunges. "Emily, your sister?"

"She's coming to stay with me while you're gone."

"In our house?"

"Ashley, would you rather my sister visit while you were there?"

Truthfully, I'd rather she not visit at all. "Rhett doesn't like Emily." Translation: I don't like Emily and my dog is an equally good judge of character.

"The dog will be fine. Kay needs you. Have you forgotten?"

"Doesn't Emily have a baby to baste? What's she doing traveling all over the country when she's pregnant?"

"My sister isn't exactly following God. Do you want my nephew or niece raised in the kind of environment Emily will currently provide?"

"Is that a trick question?" My breathing is coming too fast. I'm going to lose the filter between my brain and my mouth, and that's never a good thing. "I'm wondering, when did you and your mother and Emily plan all this...behind my back?" See? It came out as an accusation and I didn't mean it that way!

Kevin's jaw tightens. "I'll work on a timeline for you." He rubs his eyes. "I'm not up to this now."

My fingers and toes are tingling, like I'm losing my grip. "I just find it interesting that she's coming while I'm in California. Is that why you're sending me?"

"Of course not! You're welcome to stay home and visit with Emily if you'd like."

I'd rather wear cheap shoes that were a size too small. "No, thank you." I clasp my fidgety hands in my lap. "Kevin, she's going to tell you about a job in Atlanta. I know this is going to happen as sure as I sit here. I can feel it. It's like the more I resist it, the more I am going to become a transplant Scarlett O'Hara."

Kevin pulls in a noisy breath. "Ashley, you already are a transplant Scarlett. No matter where you live." Another shake of his head. "And my sister didn't plan this. She just called yesterday and said she needed to get away."

"*We* need to get away. Alone. You and I."

"We can make that happen, Ash, but not right now."

Fear bubbles to the surface again, like I'm losing the man I love. "Just…keep your sister out of my shoes."

Kevin tilts his head. "Your shoes? She's not going to wear your shoes."

See, how he makes me sound totally ridiculous while I know Emily's going to be stuffing her fat, expectant, swollen tootsies into my Donald Pliners, and then saying something like, *if they don't fit you anymore, Ashley, I'll take them.*

"I'm not going." I cross my arms in front of me. If I'm going to take the blame for us not having a family yet, I may as well take it in person.

"Well, that's good. Stay. My sister said she wanted to see the City. Maybe you can take her to see the Liberty Bell while I'm at work. Introduce her to all the delightful sugary, caffeinated goodness that is Wawa."

He called my bluff. Kevin knows I'd head to Tunisia rather than spend time with my sister-in-law – and I don't even know where

Tunisia is. While this doesn't make me the best Christian on the planet, it does make me sane. Kevin hops out of the car, walks around the car to open my side. He swings the car door open with a bit too much vigor.

He kisses me as I stand up. "I promise. I won't let my sister manipulate me."

I've got no choice but to believe him. As we walk across the pedestrian bridge to the terminal, I'm reminded how love has no rhyme or reason.

As a single woman—or "reason" as I liked to call myself, I tried so hard for a man's attention. Lesser men than Kevin, and I just scared them off like I was some kind of bunny boiler. In contrast, Kevin simply loved me. To see him, one would think he belongs with a darling petite blonde, who has shampoo commercial hair and one of those tiny waists you're tempted to try to fit your hands around. But he's with me, and while I may question it every day, I wish someone told me: You don't have to work that hard for real love. God just makes it happen. It might have spared me heartache, and a few cringe-worthy moments. Maybe even a brush or two with the law while I was overreacting.

"Emily won't be here when I return, right? Because I'm not sure I can glimpse my gorgeous, golden California Mountains and find the stamina to get on the plane to come back to my sister-in-law. No offense."

Kevin smirks at me. "I'm here in Philly. Don't you want to come back to me?"

Darn it. He's got me there, and he knows it.

I gaze into Kevin's green eyes, and I know that it isn't really a concern that I'd never return to him. He's stuck with me. He promised in front of the minister and everything. However, I don't want to covet, and I covet my old job and my old life in countless ways. I wrap my arms around him tightly and press myself against his chest, fighting back the tears.

"Ashley, you're only going for a visit. I'll be working on the study for long hours. That's why this is the best time. Quit acting like you'll never see me again."

I nod as I pull away. It's not Kevin's fault that I have no life in Philadelphia. It's mine. And I fear if I don't find one before we move elsewhere, this might be my lot in life. Saint Paul was content in jail, so what's wrong with me? To be a washed-up patent attorney who *used* to dress well, who *used* to sing at church and who *used* to host parties and Bible studies?

"Emily may look after Rhett, but don't just ignore him when you get home. He'll be so excited to see you at the end of the day. Be sure and let him give you his version of a hug."

Kevin nods. "I hate when that dog licks me. Can't you train him?"

"I have trained him. Rhett loves you, that's his sign of affection."

"Hmm."

We walk into the Philadelphia airport, which is white, bright and open—as if you're entering the Promised Land. My bright pink luggage stands out like a neon jumpsuit at an Amish gathering. I scan my license and check my luggage. As I hand it off to the attendant, I hike my laptop case over my shoulder and gaze longingly at my husband.

"Really? You can't even come with me for a few days?"

"The next move will be permanent, honey. I promise. Go and think about where you'd like to live. I'll send you a list of my top choices for the fellowship and we'll vote when you come home."

I reach up to kiss his jaw and inhale deeply.

He pulls away. "Would you stop that?"

"I'm taking one last sniff. I told you, scent is the most powerful memory-inducer."

"And what kind of memory is my wife as a bloodhound going to give me? Do you see anyone else sniffing their significant others?"

"Maybe they don't smell as good as you do."

"Sometimes, Ashley—"

"I also stole a T-shirt of yours to sniff while I'm gone," I admit. "So if you're looking for that Boston Marathon T-shirt, don't bother."

"Check. When you get back in two weeks, the study will be over. I'll narrow down the programs and we'll decide if we're staying."

My heart sinks just a little when he says it. *Staying.* I didn't know how much more I could take of Philadelphia. There is an energy to it that simply doesn't agree with mine. And it's a great city, so I feel guilty for not loving it, but Philly simply never felt like home. Not mine anyway.

I'm a left-coast kind of girl.

Kevin cups my jaw and kisses me deeply. "Stop worrying. Silicon Valley is waiting, go remember your life before you became a real housewife of Philadelphia."

I nod absently with images in my head of Atlanta. I can see my sister-in-law Emily in an antebellum gown dancing a Virginia reel without a partner. My sister-in-law is certifiable. I know people always say that about their in-laws, but in my case, it's true. She once canceled my wedding dress (a Vera Wang) and had one made exactly for a Civil War bride. Who does that? Someone without proper boundaries, or obviously, fashion sense.

Kevin's soothing voice interrupts my daytime nightmare. "You'll come back to me with that spark in your eye again and we'll plan our next step." His gaze holds expectation and I don't want to let him down. Clearly, I need a life, and getting perspective must be tantamount to that.

What happens if I return with no more direction than I'm leaving with now? If I don't have a direction, my compass could be pointed south. I enter into the security detail of the airport and wave goodbye to my gorgeous husband through the glass planes. Kevin briefly glances over his shoulder then turns and quickly walks away.

I thoroughly reject the thought that my mother was right.

Silicon Valley, get ready, Ashley Stockingdale Novak, like the Governator, *will be back.*

Chapter 3

AS I LAND in San Jose, it's like that scene in *The Wizard of Oz* when everything turns colorful, and I shiver at the beautiful sight of *home*. The sky is bluer, the mountains seem to be shimmering gold and the view is sharp and crisp. My body relaxes as the plane touches ground and my heart is fluttering with excitement. All I want to do is get off this plane, and I nearly shout, "Amateurs, get out of my way!"

I mean, I'm home. I'm not expecting a parade or anything, but let's be honest, I wouldn't turn one down.

It's these days that I wish I were Moses. I could stamp my staff to the floor and the aisle would clear, giving me a straight path to sunshine and my destiny. I will find my purpose again. I feel it.

Once in the wide, open terminal, I want to dance with my arms outstretched, but I catch sight of all the travelers in their tech T-shirts, and grin. I forgot that no one in Silicon Valley actually purchases clothing. They simply go to trade shows and stock up on nerd-wear that advertise some new gadget. Is it any wonder I miss standing out? It really took very little effort here—which makes me wonder if maybe I wasn't the fashionista I thought I was—maybe I was just slightly better than the tech nerds in free semiconductor T-shirts.

That's a disconcerting thought.

The new terminal in San Jose is extensively long, and there are none of those mobile staircases, so I practically sprint to get to my ride and the new future that awaits me. This is just what I needed: Clarity. Home.

Some guy in a Nvidia T-shirt practically runs me down to reach the escalator down to baggage claim before me. *Classy.* And typical. *It makes me feel like I'm home!* Chivalry is completely dead in the Valley and I do not miss that. Men in Philly grew up with proper mothers and manners! Men in the Valley grew up racing girls and tripping said girls when they passed them up.

Brea stands at baggage claim with her two boys—I should say she's *trying* to stand near baggage claim, but she's actually running around chasing her little monkeys as they run through the airport like standing still would cause spontaneous human combustion.

I stop for a moment and gaze over the balcony that hangs suspended over baggage claim. Sunlight streams in everywhere and illuminates the entire building. Brea seems older than when I left her—less put together, which is completely out of her character. I always thought she'd handle motherhood like a Real Housewife: In a clingy, barely-appropriate dress and heels, with a proper handbag slung over her elbow. Today, she's wearing an army green skirt, a pale yellow tank top and black flats.

Maybe it's just a bad day. I run down the escalator and envelop her in a hug. "Brea! Oh my gosh, I've missed you!"

We cling together for far too long and there's something in her grip that feels desperate. Not the calm, cool, collected Brea that I left. The boys stop in their tracks to stare at this strange women hugging their mother. If they only knew how strange!

Miles and Jonathan, in contrast to Brea's tired look, could be two Gymboree models ready for their close-up. They're wearing matching plaid, short-sleeve shirts, navy shorts and matching blue sandals, and she quickly takes them by their hands. They're so much like twins; it's unbelievable that one of them is adopted and the other, not. They could not appear more like brothers.

Miles is the older of the two, and he was adopted. Jonathan is their birth child, not that Brea differentiates them at all, but it's the reason they are three months apart. Which is physically impossible without an adoption. At least the last time I checked. But as my mother-in-law will tell you as often as you're willing to listen, I'm not a mother.

I kneel down. "Do you remember your Auntie Ashley?"

The boys blink their wide eyes and stare at me as if I'm a serial killer.

"I brought presents!"

The boys toddle toward me like two little minions caught in an alien's tractor beam. "What you get us?" Miles asks me. "My brudder likes twains."

"Well, I think your brother is going to be very happy then."

"Where our pwesents?" Jonathan stares up at me with huge, brown eyes, and I melt a little.

"They're in my luggage, sweetie. When this machine starts," I say, pointing to the luggage carousel, "it will bring out my bright pink suitcase. Do you think you can help me find the pink suitcase?"

Both boys walk to the edge of the crowd that has clustered tightly around the carousel.

"Boys, don't touch that belt. You might get your hands stuck." Brea yanks the boys back by one shoulder each. "We can look with our eyes."

"Brea." I narrow my eyes. "They're fine, I've got them. Why don't you go sit down for a minute?" I point at a bench near the Starbucks. It's not like this is a crowded terminal. It's enormous, open, and the only cluster of people is right around us.

It's hard to see Brea looking so haggard, she could be an extra on *The Walking Dead*. Brea was always the woman that troubles skirted. If there was one lonely house standing amidst a raging forest fire, it would have been Brea's, and it's disconcerting to see life hit her and take a toll.

"I'm all right," Brea says and hovers over the boys.

"You're really not. I can feel the anxiety coming off of you. Go sit down."

She glares at me and I glare right back.

"My dog is still alive. I kept your boys and your dogs alive while you were gone. I can handle them for, twenty feet from you. I promise."

"I'm fine," she snaps. "I've got the key to drop you off at Kay's on the way home." She holds up a familiar key.

Kay's my old roommate. She's obsessive-compulsive and organized to a fault. I'm...not. You can imagine how that roommate situation went. "I'm not going to your house?" I hold firmly onto the boys' chubby hands. "Kevin told me I'd be staying with you. You're dumping me already?"

I'll admit, I can be a handful, but Brea knows this. She's known this since we were four years' old, and I really don't need the rejection, quite frankly.

"I'm not dumping you." Brea purses her lips. "Kay has a dinner party planned for you."

"A dinner party? Not with the *Reasons?*" I say, referring to my old church group.

"That, and the boys have a doctor's appointment this afternoon. Tonight, John is getting home from Korea and he'll be exhausted, and I didn't know how to break it to him that you'd be coming. I thought we could have more quality time together later in the week."

"So my husband sends me across the country. My mom has houseguests and can't"—I lift my quote fingers up—"'Accommodate' me, and you've got plans. It's like a game of Hot Potato, and I'm the potato!"

"Ever the drama queen. It's just a busy time, that's all." Brea's not telling me something. I can feel it. I want to ask her so many things, to get caught up and hear everything that's happened at church since I've been gone, but the kids and their needs come first. Maybe that is her issue, who knows? I used to simply *know* what was the matter with Brea, but she feels a million miles away and it's like I'm in the deep canyon unable to get to her.

Philly may not be home, but life in Silicon Valley has gone on without me, and finding my place here may not be any easier.

The crowd gathers tighter around the snaking metal belt as the luggage starts to trickle out of the back room and I wonder if I haven't made a mistake. Maybe I should have just figured things out at home with my husband. Like a normal person.

"I should warn you. Dinner *is* the old *Reasons*. Kay is having Arin and Seth over to dinner tonight."

"Stellar." Seth is my ex-boyfriend. Arin is my husband's ex-girlfriend. "That's not awkward at all."

Isn't that cozy how we all up and switched partners? It would be really awkward if we all weren't living the celibate Christian life. Well, I can't say Arin was living that life as Seth married her when she was pregnant. Not by Kevin, but she'd gone on a missionary trip and come back in, shall we say, less than a missionary position. Seth, needing someone to rescue, married her, and from what I hear, they're pregnant with another child now.

"It will be fun. Pastor Max and Kelly are coming and Sam. I wish John and I could be there. Kay thought it was best to get it over with. You know, rip the Band-Aid of awkwardness off right away."

"Or not at all." I watch the different luggage pass by. "You can always match a person with their luggage. That guy right there, basic black." The engineer who cut me off at the escalator grabs his black bag and rushes out of the terminal.

"I should warn you that your mother's convinced you're here because you're pregnant and you want to tell her in person," Brea says.

"She's going to be vastly disappointed then. I'll add her to the list. Kevin's mom is convinced it's not possible, that I'm too old."

"Kevin's mom is a psycho."

"That's more true than I'd like it to be. Kevin needs to get a per-

31

manent job and we need to settle before we start a family." I say this so calmly, no one would ever know I'm not completely freaking out that I will get old and haggard and unable to have a child. But Brea knows. I see it in her downturned eyes.

"I see it!" Miles jumps up and down and points to my pink suitcase.

"You do see it, good eyes, Miles."

"I see it, too," Jonathan says.

"You both have incredible vision. It's so far away still!" I lower my voice. "Tell me the truth. Are you both related to Superman?"

"No!" they scream in unison.

As we wait for the conveyor belt filled with luggage to snake towards us, Brea asks me, "Is it going to be weird seeing Seth and Arin pregnant?"

I blink a few times. "I don't know if I'll see them."

"I still don't like that woman, missionary or not. There's something cunning about her."

Arin, my ex-boyfriend's wife, was one of those sick sorts who looked like they swallowed a cantaloupe but had no other visible signs of pregnancy; no gnarly skin changes, no bum the size of circus pachyderm's, not even a double chin. Just a yoga body with a baby basketball in front. I'm sure she will be the same this time.

"Well," I say, after imagining Seth having a child at all. "It's going to be hard to see her if she's thinner than me while pregnant, but Seth?" I shrug. "I can't say I'm looking forward to it, but I'm not nervous about it. It wasn't weird seeing him at my wedding."

"No, you're right. Why would it be weird?" Brea shrugs. "I didn't really think you'd be nervous about it, only that it wouldn't be on your top ten list of things to do. Kind of somewhere up there with shopping at Kmart."

"Kay's a creature of habit," I say about my old roommate. "Arin and Seth will be on the invite list, simply because they're always on the invite list. Kay doesn't think it should be awkward, because she believes we're all adults and should suck it up."

"I suppose she's right," Brea says. "Kay's practical ways are the only thing that has kept that singles' group together all these years. She amazes me. I would have lost patience for the lot of 'em years ago."

"I'm sure Arin will look fabulous, and I'll rethink dessert. My sister-in-law is still tiny, and she's five months into her pregnancy. At least from what I see on Facebook with her daily quota of bathroom selfies."

We both giggle—it comes out cattier than we'd like.

"Did Emily tell anyone who the father of the baby is yet?" The boys are starting to squirm, and Brea lifts Miles onto her hip and takes Jonathan's hand. Miles wriggles out of her grasp and runs to my pink hard-shell bag and plucks it off the conveyor belt.

"Got it!" he says as he uses all of his strength in his tiny arms to yank off the suitcase. Brea is freaking out and whisks him up as if he's just plunged from a moving airplane. He drops my suitcase with the brisk movement.

"Miles, you could have been hurt! Do you know how many shoes Auntie probably packed?" She grimaces at me.

"I'm strong!" Miles says and stops to pose.

"Yes, you are," I tell him as I grab my bag. "Brea, chill out. He grabbed a suitcase. He didn't jump off a third-floor balcony."

"Shh! Don't give him any ideas."

Brea herds her boys with all the expertise of a seasoned cattle dog, and takes them both by the hand and we walk past the Starbucks toward the parking garage. We have to cross the street to get there, and Brea is panicked, though there's no traffic to be seen. I push the walk button and we wait to cross. We could easily cross without the light, but with Brea so tightly wound, I know better than to suggest such a sin.

"Kay's so excited you're coming."

I try not to react. "Are you going to take me to your house first?

Before Kay's house?"

"Shh. Wait until we cross the street."

We manage to get across the street unscathed. Brea seems to think this is akin to neonatal surgery in the dark.

"My house is a disaster," Brea says as we get to her car and she's flustered in a way that confuses me.

"Brea, we had slumber parties on your filthy floor. I can handle your mess now." Admittedly, I'm feeling a little beggarly. My two favorite people in the entire world have rejected me today. That's not exactly cause for celebration.

"Kay will have everything set up for you from the luggage rack in your room to a few emptied drawers for your convenience. She lives for visitors. I thought Kevin would have told you. This is best for your high-maintenance self."

"People deciding what's best for me has become my norm. Is this some kind of mental breakdown intervention?" I try to conceal my disappointment. "I want to spend time with you, Brea. I don't care what your house looks like. Mine probably looks worse, and I don't have two kids as an excuse."

"It's not a good time, Ash. Really. You don't want to see it in its present state. We'll get time together when John gets home from Korea."

"Auntie, we want our presents!" Miles says.

"Boys, that's rude," Brea says.

She should talk.

"It's not rude." I kiss each boy on his cheek. "Buckle them into their carseats, I'll get the gifts. You've been so patient! The last time I saw you, you could never wait this long!"

"You're spoiling them worse than their grandmother!"

"Brea, your mother never spoiled a thing in her life—except maybe a good time."

"True."

I unzip my bag as I listen to Brea with her boys. She was always such a calm mother before I left—the kind who did everything so naturally—and now, she's like me as a mother—well, how I imagine myself anyway. Nervous. Second-guessing everything she does, worrying herself into a frenzy. The fact is, the world doesn't need two Ashley Stockingdale Novaks. Some might argue that it doesn't even need one.

I grab the presents from my bag and hand the boys their wrapped packages. I zip up my luggage and toss it in the back of the minivan. Miles and Jonathan don't waste a second before tearing into their packages.

"Legos!" Miles shouts.

"Trains!" Jonathan shouts.

I grin at Brea. "My work is done here."

Brea sits in the driver's seat and stares at me. "Good job, Auntie. That ought to give me some quiet time after their appointments, but I'll never get them down for a nap now."

"Brea, seriously. Let them have some joy. You're wound tighter than a drum and I don't even know how to say this, but you're acting like your mother."

Brea gasps. "Take that back!"

How can I take it back? We used to call Brea's mom "the fun sucker" because she could take any given situation and drain the fun out of it like an inflatable pool toy with a giant hole in it. I know for certain that the world only needs one Mrs. Browning.

Brea's lower lip begins to tremble, but she says nothing and starts up the car. I've never known my best friend to keep anything from me, and now the distance between us feels like it is far more than simple geography.

"Something is wrong, Brea. Since when did you become the stoic type and suck it all up? Let it out before you explode! You're making me feel like I'm in an alternative universe!"

A small whimper escapes and I sense the first sign of true emotion. "I don't want to talk about it in front of the boys. I'm fine. John is fine. Our family is fine, that's all that matters. You're here for a good time, not to worry about me." She smiles brightly, though falsely.

This offends me. I'm a fixer. Granted, I may screw things up while trying to fix them, but I want a shot. "Brea, you're ticking me off. You're treating me like I'm some random stranger. What's wrong?"

"Quit being such a drama queen." She clicks her seatbelt into place. "I'm not ready to talk about it just yet. We'll connect later. I promise."

As we emerge from the parking garage into the dazzling San Jose sunlight, the boys are quiet except for the boy "noises" they're emanating. Miles has his teeth tight as he spits out Star Wars' light saber sounds while Jonathan emits choo-choo whistles while pushing his train across his legs.

Brea's got a hair clip clamped in her mouth as she steers the minivan with her knees. She shakes her curly mop of hair and clips it in a high ponytail. She's the poster child for distracted-driving.

So I'm shut down, just like that. Brea always was the one who could handle everyone's drama and keep the remote coolness of Martha Stewart with a dash of Rachael Ray's enthusiasm. I've always been too much for some people to take, and I can't help but wonder if my absence has made my best friend one of those people. Maybe the boundaries people create are necessary walls to keep me away. Maybe I've gotten worse being in Philadelphia and spending most days talking to the dog and random strangers in Starbucks.

Before we hit Highway 101, the boys have dozed off in their carseats, with their toys clutched to their hearts. We drive up the Peninsula toward San Francisco to the town of Palo Alto and the home I used to share with Kay. I use the term *share* loosely because Kay had a certain way of doing everything. Ways, which I will never understand in this lifetime, but that involve a lot of order that makes no sense to my brain. Everything has a place and everything is in its place. Unless I was there. *I tried*, I really did, but things just didn't come naturally to me the way they did for Kay. She taught me a lot though, about entertaining, about cleaning up as you went along, and that life was just always going to be harder for a mind like mine. In essence, it was Kay's world. I just lived in it.

After a few short minutes of casual church updates that keep real issues at bay, Brea pulls alongside the curb outside Kay's house on Channing Street and waits for me to exit.

"Aren't you coming in?" I ask her.

"The boys are napping. I don't want to wake them before their appointments." She shrugs and unsnaps her clip, unleashing her wild curls. "Kay never was much into kids. I doubt she'd appreciate them tearing through her house."

"Kids are messy." I laugh. "It's the same reason Kay never had much use for me."

She gives me a half-grin. "So text me and let me know your plans or if you need a ride over to your mom's."

"You're the one with the life here, Brea. When can we get together? I'd like to have more than the trip home from the airport."

She looks at her watch. "I'll text you."

"Where have I heard that before?" I grin. "I have a gift for you too, not just the boys."

"I'll get it later." Brea presses a button and the hatchback yawns open and I hear my suitcase tumble to the street below. "Sorry about that. It must have shifted."

I get out of the car, take a glance at the angelic boys with their grips tightly on their gifts, and smile toward Brea. "Well, thanks for the ride."

I walk to the back of the van and pick my case off the asphalt. By the time, I stand up again, Brea has pressed a button, closed up her car and driven off—as if she's just abandoned an unwanted puppy. I watch her taillights glow as she turns off the street. Looking at Kay's bungalow, I wonder if it's true what Thomas Wolfe wrote, *you can't go home again.*

I guess that you can go home again—after all, I am here. The question is, will anyone want you once you get there?

Chapter 4

Kay's bungalow is a quaint little house on a tree-lined street in one of Palo Alto's most sought-after neighborhoods near Stanford University. Everything about its simplicity and familiarity makes me feel as if I've stepped back in time and as if Philly never happened. I'm suddenly a single girl dreading the latest Friday "open mic night" at a local coffee shop with the rest of the church singles' group. The thought makes me shudder and I have to remind myself it's all a flashback.

I'm married. I'm married. Seth and rejection are in my past.

If only that were true. I lift my suitcase across the grass, rather than drag it across the stepping-stones that lead to the small, brick porch. There's a single white iron chair – a symbol for all things lonely, and the irony is not lost on me.

I sit down, when the chair buckles underneath me. I nearly bang my head against the wall when I realize the chair is just for show—it's not strong enough to actually hold someone, a fact I'd clearly forgotten.

Let's just say no one has rolled out the welcome mat for me just yet. I call Kevin before I knock on the door.

It wasn't terrible being single. In fact, I wish I'd taken more advantage of it and truly relished the time with myself. I'm not *that* bad. So why do only the hard memories come bubbling up to the surface from my subconscious? I had value when I was single. Isn't that what being married taught me?

Kevin's assistant answers and tells me he's in surgery. Typical.

"Would you tell Kevin that I arrived safely in California when he's finished?" I ask her.

"Of course, Ashley. Have a great time! Bring home some sunshine—without this awful humidity, would you?"

"I'll do my best." It's terrible that I'm upset Kevin's in surgery because I can't whine to him about Brea tossing me out of her car like the morning newspaper. Sometimes, whining is my favorite sport, which probably doesn't make me the most pleasant person to be around. I toss my phone into my Burberry bag (a leftover from my working days) and try to figure out what's missing from the sorry, lonesome concrete stoop.

The Fourth of July decorations aren't up, for one thing. Kay's more accurate than the Mayan calendar, which I'm sure isn't saying much now that their calendar did not end in our destruction. The point is the same. Kay's fastidious about flying the individual flags of celebration. She's so obsessed in fact, that she usually sucks the fun out of any holiday. The porch is bare and I have to check the house numbers to ensure I'm in the right spot. I am; so I stand up and press the doorbell. Heavy footsteps approach.

I'm completely caught off-guard when Matt Callaway opens the door, in nothing more than khaki shorts, a tool belt and his bare chest. *Um, yuck.* He's a hulking figure who is still handsome despite rapidly passing middle age and having the personality of the smarmiest pyramid salesman. Silicon Valley ages a person. The hours are brutal—but then again, Matt could be looking at me and thinking Philly and joblessness ages a person. Matt possesses a dark, full head of hair graying at the temples and a wicked sense of mischief that I never could understand. He and Kay were dating at my wedding, but that was years ago, and I assumed he'd faded away like the brown from his head. The only thing Matt had ever been consistent at was dating inappropriate women. Kay did not fall under that heading.

"Matt?"

His gaze travels up and down my person critically before he speaks. "I thought you weren't coming until tomorrow."

"Nope. It's today."

We stare at each other awkwardly and it's clear neither one of us wants to make small talk. We're both authentic enough to know we needn't pretend we like one another.

"What are you doing here?" I ask. "Aren't you still practicing patent law? Or is this your shot at being a Chippendale dancer?"

"Very funny. Still the same ol' charming Ashley, I see." He stands in the doorway preventing my entrance. "I'm helping out Kay with some handyman work in the backyard."

"Why?" I clear my throat. "I mean, when did you suddenly become handy?"

"I'm that kind of man and I've always been handy, not that you ever bothered to notice."

"I noticed you were dating a large cache of my friends back in the day. I guess I missed the part about you being handy." *I was too busy noticing you being a jerk.* I inhale and try to reset my attitude. Anyone can change. I would hope I've evolved since we last met.

"You're supposed to be here tomorrow," he repeats.

"Nope. Pretty sure it's today. I know because the plane wouldn't have let me board if I had the wrong date on the ticket." I stare around him, into the backyard and notice a mess of boards in the backyard blocking the doorway. "What kind of handiwork are you doing? Kay approved that mess?"

"Just little stuff. She had a fan out in the bathroom and I'm building a pergola in the back. She'd like to host more barbecues, and it gets hot back there without a cover."

I raise my eyebrows. "You're building a pergola? Is the patent business that slow?"

"No, why? You looking for a job? My office could use someone. When my partner found out you were coming, he was ecstatic. We've found this new niche, and we're on fire. Where are you working?"

My heart flames with excitement at his words and I forget all about the pergola. I want to ask him everything about business, but my pride prevents me from saying a word. "I'm not really looking for anything," I lie. My words surprise even me. Pride's an ugly trait.

"Too bad. The patent business is fast and furious with all the software and social media sites popping up right and left. It's like another Dot Com bubble for us patent attorneys. I can't believe you're not in on it. There are these trolls buying up patents left and right, then they sue small start-ups for patent infringement and put these companies right out of business."

"No kidding? That's new. They're buying the patents?"

"Which, as you know, means they can put them into use that day. They buy them, start litigation and the battle for intellectual property is on."

My teeth clench at the injustice and I want to jump out of my skin with questions, but I put my game face on. "What's the patent office doing about it?"

"Nothing yet." Matt adjusts his tool belt then steps out onto the porch, like I'm a Jehovah's Witness and he's trying to keep me out of Kay's house. "You know how well they understand the technology. It will take them time to catch up."

I ball my hands into small, tight fists. His words bring everything out in me that made me want to be a patent attorney. The rights. The doing battle for inventors and creators. I'm practically foaming at the mouth to get in on it, but I know if I'm overeager, Matt will drop the subject like yesterday's news. "Have you been to court with any of them yet?"

"It takes less than an hour of the judge's time for these morons to get shut down." He steps back and opens the door wide enough for me to step over the threshold. "So what are you working on now?" He glances at my suitcase. "Besides your shoe collection, I mean."

"Oh, you know."

"You shouldn't have sold your share of this house to Seth." Matt shakes his head. "You burned the ships. Lot of people make that mistake, and then there's no getting back into Bay Area real estate."

"I did burn the ships."

"You're not the kind of woman who just becomes a housewife. Hadn't you noticed that?"

"What's that supposed to mean?"

"It's not a criticism. It's just you don't bake or cook, you're sloppier than me from what I remember, and Kay mothered you when you lived here. All I am saying is if I were going to recommend a patent attorney, you'd top my list. But a housewife? We can't just change who we are by moving."

"How is that not a criticism?"

"Maybe it is, but my motive is pure."

I cross my arms. "I doubt that. Let's not forget you are a lawyer."

"As are you, Ashley. You always seem to attribute every piece of ugliness about the law to me, without taking any credit for it being your own profession."

My eyes scan the room behind him, and the loss of this house looms large for me. Matt's tossed-aside T-shirt and flip-flops are strewn across Kay's pristine floor and it seems I've been replaced.

Matt goes on, "My brain is in constant motion. That's why I love the busy work around Kay's place. It gives my brain time to ruminate on how to beat these monsters at their own game. You need that downtime, you know? To strategize."

I sigh. He may as well have said he's getting free Prada with each paycheck. "The timing's all wrong for me. I've been out of the game too long."

Admittedly, I want him to say it's not true. But looking to Matt Callaway for comfort is the first sign I've completely lost my mind.

I should mention that Matt and I have a dark history. He hurt Kay once. And let's just say she's more forgiving than I am. If I had my way, he'd never darken her doorway again. Kay thought they were a couple back when, but he began dating my sister-in-law Emily while she was here for my wedding.

I never forgave him for making Kay look like a fool, not that I was his biggest fan in the first place. It didn't help that Matt's ancient next to Emily. She's just twenty-nine now, and Matt's rapidly flirting with fifty. The fact that he's still in Kay's universe doesn't add up. It's hard to meet people in the Valley, so I chalk it up to Kay's insane level of patience for people. Maybe she's just throwing him a bone as a friend. But it doesn't add up.

Kay's so...practical. Matt is smooth. Smarmy even. He's a patent attorney, what else does she need to know? Didn't she have enough of that with me?

"I've got to get to the office," Matt tells me, as he lifts my suitcase into the foyer.

Wow. Chivalry. Go figure.

"Come on in and get settled. Kay's got you in your old room, I suppose." He smirks at me. "Just don't get too comfortable in there. It's my office when there are no guests here."

"Your office? You have an office, not to mention a house. What gives?"

"Just don't get too comfortable, all I'm saying."

"You're just going to leave that mess?" I stare out the back door at the stacks of two-by-fours.

He follows my gaze. "Does it bother you?" He sneers. "Isn't that rich?"

"Maybe," I tell him. *He bothers me.* "What kind of patent attorney gets to be home in the middle of the afternoon these days? Did Silicon Valley go on hiatus?"

"The kind of patent attorney that's sought-after and whose services are in demand." He tucks his chin and stares at me with a wicked eyebrow raised. "You, if you were around to get in on the action. I haven't seen your name on any tech patents since you left."

He may as well have struck me. "Below the belt."

"Maybe, but it was your choice to follow the good doctor and not think about yourself. Very self-sacrificing and noble, I'll admit, but not very bright." He lifts his shirt off the hardwood floor and puts it on over his tool belt. He buttons a few buttons and flicks the cuff on the long sleeve. "I make my own rules now. My own schedule." He cocks one eyebrow, yanks open the front door fully and passes me with a swift breeze. "Think about what I said."

The door slams behind him, and I'm left wondering how Matt always seems to get the better of me.

Kay's living room is still much the same. The hardwood floors shines like a Minwax commercial. The house has always looked staged—as though a realtor placed furniture in all the right places to make it appear lived in—but never really had the feeling of warmth or home.

The small bungalow is decorated sparsely with only black, white and beige in a neutral palette that lacks personality and any hint of excitement. Walking through the house, I peek into Kay's master bedroom. It's spotless as usual and this gives me peace. Something is as it should be. She has the same bedspread as when I left (who can live that long with the same bedspread? Doesn't she get bored?)

In my old bedroom I'm flooded by desperate memories. How many restless nights were spent in this room, pining over elusive men and reasons I thought I'd never get married? Most notably, Seth Greenwood. I feel the aura of sadness in the room, like the imprint of that obsessive, hopeful single girl is still here. I'm almost glad no one is renting the room, lest they pick up on the pathetic, husband-hungry air. Seth didn't want me. Why didn't I get it? *Why did I think I could make him love me? Looking back on my younger self really makes me wonder how I had the brain cell count to get through law school.*

The minuscule corner shower, the only one in the house, is flanked on one side by the toilet, and the sink on the other. It's a bathroom of togetherness. These 40's bungalows were made for business. You weren't supposed to be spending all morning on your beauty regiment. And the builders made sure that you wouldn't. It was a male conspiracy, I'm certain of it.

In the mirrored medicine cabinet, I find an old box of "Scarlet Copper" hair color that I decided I'd try on one particularly desperate night when I thought maybe red hair would make me irresistible. Its $3.99 clearance price tag makes me laugh—*who was I?* Kay probably couldn't bear to throw it away at that price, so she left it in case I returned for it.

I always thought that a new hair color would define me, make people take notice of me. It dawns on me that maybe that's what is missing from my life. No one notices me anymore. I've become invisible.

I need to go back to Philly with a plan. I need to prove to Kevin that he didn't make a mistake in marrying me, and I will find something to do with my days.

I lift the box and stare into the mirror at my dark brown, boring hair. I study the box for a few seconds and check my watch. "Why not?" I ask my reflection. "If I happen to get a job interview while I'm here, they're more likely to remember a redhead."

Chapter 5

MY HAIR IS red. Not highlights of copper mahogany as the box promised, but Ronald McDonald red with undertones of my dark color. It's not even. So it's kind of like a tie-dye summer camp experience gone wrong with various shades of brown, fuchsia and garnet. I shake my head. Maybe a bit of salmon pink, too, if I'm honest.

It's the house. I thought it was me, but clearly, this house brings out the stupid in me—because what sane, thinking person would dye their hair without testing the color, right before a dinner with their ex-boyfriend and his spritely, perfect wife? It's not like I want to impress Seth or Arin, but I seriously don't want to give him a sense of relief for dodging a bullet, either. No one wants to send their ex into a happy dance over the way they've let themselves go, am I right?

I wrap a towel around my head and emerge from the bathroom just in time to hear the front door unlatch. "Kay?" I grasp the towel and wonder if it's possible to make a beanie look fashionable in the middle of the California summer.

Kay is at the front door, bogged down by several bags of groceries. She keeps them snug to her chest—and her mouth drops open. "Seriously, what did you do to your hair? I mean, Ashley, it's so awesome to see you. You look great!"

Kay's like the strictest mother on the block. She notices everything.

I yank the towel off for her full reaction, and Kay gasps. *It's obviously bad, as Kay is not a drama queen like myself.*

"I found an old box of color," I explain. "I thought it might be a nice change and maybe light a new passion in me."

"It lit something, but I'm not sure it's passion." She wrestles with the groceries, uncertain if she should hug me or show some sign of warmth.

I pat my head. "I needed a change. That's why I'm here to begin with." I straighten my shoulders and try to own it. "I can fix it when I get home." I move toward her and give her a one-armed hug so as not to make her too uncomfortable.

She bristles at my touch. "Have you had your eyes checked lately? It's really bright, Ashley." Then, she sets the bags down and swallows me in an awkward, engineer hug. "I so missed your crazy self! If by 'nice change' you were meaning an ode to clowns…did you by chance arrive in a tiny car with lots of others?" She looks outside.

"It can't be that bad?" I feel my hair, and it's a wee bit crispy. The way you'd like your chicken, not your hair.

"It's much worse than you think it is, but I never was a fan of hair color that doesn't exist in the real world. Well, this planet anyway."

"Is this your way of telling me how much you love me?"

"If the lawyer thing doesn't work out, you could apply at the local tattoo parlor in Philadelphia."

I sigh. "I got sucked into this *48 Hours* on the OWN channel and had to find out who killed the woman and I kind of forgot to set the timer for my hair."

Kay gives me a look of pity. "Well, if you had to know who killed her…"

"I don't have time to fix it, do I?"

Kay shakes her head. "You should stick to your bad reality shows. This is proof. It's God's way of telling you that you don't have the attention span for serious television."

Kay made a funny.

"I thought maybe I was more adventurous when I was single and living here. I thought it was time to take a risk. Then, maybe I wouldn't feel as invisible in Philly."

"Oh, you are definitely not invisible. Cal-trans wants to hire your head for their 'Men Working' road sign."

"Rude! When did you get such an attitude?"

She ignores my question. "The dinner guests will be here soon. I'm making a fresh shrimp salad, so preparation won't take long. I'm assuming you don't have any hair dye to fix this disaster anyway?" Kay bites her bottom lip for a second as she contemplates my current disaster. "That might take a professional."

I grin sheepishly. She knows me too well. "Do you have a summer hat I can borrow?"

"A summer hat?" Kay laughs. "Have we met? You've seen my closet, and even if I did have a summer hat—it's not going to fix that. I could see it through the towel. You know what it reminds me of?"

"Dare I ask?"

"When you're a little kid and you mix all the ice cream flavors together and then it ceases to be appetizing. It's like a lump of brown with swirls of color in odd places?"

"I get it," I snap. "It's awful. Could you just – not? I need a break, Kay. I came here for a respite, and I really need one. I need to understand that I'm not the biggest loser on the planet. Just for today, all right?"

Kay's expression softens and she picks up the grocery bags. "Come help me put the bags away. People will be too happy to see you to notice your hair anyway. One crisis at a time."

Kay's an engineer and has the typical engineering personality with a side of obsessive-compulsive disorder. So I'm certain she's exaggerating about my hair. At least, that's what I'm going with to get through the next few hours where I get to play third wheel to my ex-boyfriend Seth and his wife Arin—again.

As Kay walks into the kitchen away from me, I'm shocked at how thin she's gotten. "Kay, what have you been doing? You're so tiny!"

"I've been running. I've found it's a good way to get my mind clear. You know, take my mind off all of the stuff that needs to be done around here."

"Nothing needs to be done around here. You just can't sit still."

She turns and faces me, a slight blush across her cheeks. "Did you see the pergola I'm building in the backyard?"

"I saw Matt Callaway building your pergola." I raise my brows, but she turns without giving me a reaction. "When were you planning to tell me he's still hanging around? I think we missed that topic on Skype."

"Matt's a friend. Since when is that news?"

"He answered the door looking like a member of the Village People. That seems like more than friends."

"We're friends." She opens the refrigerator and disappears behind the door.

Kay, because she's so straitforward, is a terrible liar.

"Close friends," she mumbles. Kay peers at me from over the fridge door. "You were here dyeing your hair in my bathroom. People make themselves at home here. Can I help that?" She continues to unpack the grocery bags. Unlike me, Kay isn't big on sharing. *Curse her private nature!*

"You don't have your Fourth of July decorations up. Of all the things I hadn't expected to change around here, it was you, Kay. What is the world coming to if you're suddenly, haphazard?"

"I'd hardly call getting my Independence Day decorations out late, *haphazard.* You need to get a job, Ashley. You're watching too much ID Network. Not everything warrants a police investigation."

"I'm just curious why you didn't mention him to me?"

"You tend to be excitable. I didn't want to excite you. You and your Cinderella dreams. You think everything is a step toward happily ever after."

"Regular? You're saying that I'm like a housewife, instead of a *Real Housewife.*" It's worse than I thought. *Much worse. My lack of motivation is showing up in my daywear. What happened to Ashley Stockingdale?*

Kay stares at me. "I have no idea what that means. I assume the housewife reference has something to do with your shallow entertainment choices, which I may remind you would have saved you from that horrific hair color."

"Never mind." I'm not in the mood to explain Bravo. "Seriously, do I look that different from when I left?" Maybe my appearance holds the key to what's wrong with me. "Maybe I left my style ability here in California and I've turned into a beige chick from Philly. Am I beige?"

"Are you what? Ashley, you still make no sense." Kay's eyes drift to the remnants Matt left on the back porch, which includes a tool chest, and she rolls her eyes.

"Thank goodness! His mess bothers you!" I accuse. "I worried that you didn't even see it."

"I wouldn't say it bothers me, so much as I notice it."

"Well, if I seem less me, you seem less you, Kay. Why aren't the Fourth of July decorations up yet?"

"Enough with the decorations. Work's been busy. The house is always a mess when I get home from work after Matt's been here. I guess I just didn't feel like rummaging through the garage for the right season."

"Rummaging? Please. You don't have to rummage. It's all labeled and in calendar order. Give me a break already." I cross my arms ever tighter, trying to look menacing, but Kay just swishes by me with some pasta and opens the pantry cabinet. "You would have never let me get away with that." I point to Matt's mound.

She looks over her shoulder and into the cozy living room where the building remnants lay. "Matt's a slob like you, Ashley. You should understand that and I can't imagine why it would bother you. What's got you so upset about Matt?"

"I come here to find my single, chaste friend—who likes everything just so—with a half-naked man in her house wielding power tools. It's disconcerting. Have you forgotten what he did to you?"

"Apparently, you haven't." Kay looks genuinely hurt. Once again, I've said too much, but I'm only trying to help. "Ashley, everyone makes mistakes. How many mistakes did Seth make and you welcomed him back with open arms time and time again? Until he finally broke your heart once and for all."

Kay's right and I know it. But this is not about me. "Stop changing the subject. Matt Callaway, that's the subject."

"I thought it was you being beige."

"I'm not beige!" I stamp my foot childishly. "So, if you're comparing him to Seth, how many times are you going to allow Matt to break your heart before it's once and for all? I mean, seriously, do you want to take your romantic lessons from me? If anyone was the long-suffering, pathetic girlfriend, it was me with Seth."

"I suppose that's up to me, isn't it?" She slips an apron on over her head. "Are you going to help me get dinner on the table or berate me for my social life? I should remind you that you used to berate me for my lack of social life."

"Watching sci-fi movies with engineers is not a social life."

"In Silicon Valley, it's absolutely the only one that matters. Except for maybe, gaming."

She throws an apron at me and grimaces. "Change the subject." Her tone is foreboding.

I'm less concerned with my hair than I am that Kay noticed my fashion choices were lacking. Changing the subject suits me.

"Is it true you invited Seth and Arin for dinner?" I set the apron on the counter.

"Come on, Ashley, he and Arin have been married for a long time. You and Kevin have been married a long time. They have their second child on the way, and you used to be friends. We're all Christians and I wanted the old group back together. You dated Seth. Kevin dated Arin, so what? You can't let the past bother you."

"No, because that would be weird, right?" *I mean, is it me?*

"You don't have to be so melodramatic about it. So you dated the guy. It's over. Life moves on."

"I get this. I've moved on, but hanging out with Seth and Arin just feels...I don't know, forced. Awkward."

"Well, it's Seth. It felt awkward when you were dating him." Kay shrugs. "It was like that at first with Matt after, you know, he went out with your prepubescent sister-in-law, but eventually, I realized I could obsess on Matt's one mistake, or look to the good he brought into my life."

"Matt brings good into you life?" I pop a grape into my mouth. "I'm intrigued."

"If Matt hadn't taken Emily out that time, would you still feel the way you do about him?"

"It wasn't taking my sister-in-law out that bothered me, it was the way he lied about it and sort of dated the two of you at the same time. I just don't trust him."

"Luckily, you don't have to trust him. At the time, no one was exclusive. That's what people do when they're dating. They test the waters."

Uh, Matt tested the waters, all right. Like an ocean full.

"If it doesn't bother me, Ashley, I fail to see why it bugs you. Your life would be so much easier if you would just move on."

"I think you're better than him, that's why."

"I thought you were better than Seth. Did you ever listen to me?" Kay pulls out a bag of carrots and dumps them into a silver colander in the sink. "In the words of a famous creepy director, 'the heart wants what it wants.'"

"Are you really going to quote a creeper to make your point on love? Because...just eww."

"He may be a pervert, but he's right in the sense that the heart isn't logical. Of course, I know better. It's like people telling you God's enough—that He can fill all your needs. And He can, I understand that, but it doesn't mean that I don't get lonely. That I don't stare at couples in church longingly."

"I know, but Kay being alone beats being in a—"

She cuts me off. "Do you know with all my years in the singles' group, how many of you I've seen coupled together like they're getting on Noah's ark? All that time, I sat at the base of the gangplank and forty years came and went."

"So that's why Matt's hovering? You're lonely? Get another roommate! Remember how fun I was?"

"You never faced that, Ashley. Not really, not the fear that you'd be alone in the nursing home and that you'd never have a child. It's hard to come home to an empty house every night unless you take the time and effort to plan a dinner party."

"I think that's why people get cats."

"Ashley!"

"I didn't mean it the way it came out. I only meant—"

"Just never mind. If I want to spend time with Matt, it's really none of your business. Can we talk about something else?"

I'm lost in my thoughts as I ponder the depth of what she's said. It's true. God *should* be enough. Being married *should* be enough, but life can still be lonely. *Really lonely.* And sometimes, God feels intensely absent. And the worst of it is when some well-meaning Christian tells you that you're a terrible Christian on top of it all; otherwise, you wouldn't feel that way.

"I get it, Kay, I really do. Sometimes Kevin is so tired when he gets home, he doesn't even say hello before he drops into bed. Marriage is lonely sometimes, too."

"Perhaps it is, but you can't compare your situation to mine. A man loved you enough to put a ring on your finger and marry you, Ashley. Kevin spoke vows in front of God and everyone and pledged his love to you."

"I didn't know you wanted that, Kay."

"I may not express myself as vehemently as you do, but I still have feelings. Rejection still hurts."

The expression that crosses her face is exactly the one I remember when Matt was in her life the last time. It's exactly why my feelings against Matt run so deep.

"I just don't want you to be rejected by Matt again. I don't want you to run on that relationship treadmill like I did with Seth."

She draws in a deep breath and nods.

"What are you making for dinner again?" I change the subject.

"A fresh shrimp salad. It's got lime juice, cilantro, jalapenos, fresh basil and this light dressing." She pulls out a lime to offer proof. "Perfect for summer. I got everything at the Farmer's Market after work, so it's all totally fresh. Even the shrimp."

"You're no different than me, Kay. Not really," I tease. "You just put all your effort into color-coordinating your food and your table instead of your clothes."

Kay stops chopping veggies and looks at me with those serious eyes of hers. She always had the air of a judge, the kind of woman who could shut you down with a look while she took her time to gather her thoughts. Somehow, others drew silent and waited for her to make a statement of stealth importance.

"I need you to get out of my way while I cook," Kay says. She never did like anyone in her kitchen, but especially me. Things tend to spill when I'm in the kitchen.

"I need to go rinse my hair anyway and see if I can get some of this color out." I move to the doorway, out of her lair.

I slog to the bathroom with rapt anticipation that my hair color is not as bad as Kay makes it out to be. If Kay noticed how boring I've become, how far behind can Kevin be? Maybe my husband has already noticed. Didn't he say I'd lost my sparkle? The pressure mounts for me to find my passion again. Somehow, I know dinner with Seth isn't going to help that. Did Kevin realize he was sending me to the wolves?

Chapter 6

I AM TURNING beige. This can only mean one thing. I have peaked, and it's all downhill from here. I kick off my flats, and opt for summery, strappy wedges. They're Kate Spade and I got them on clearance, so they didn't break the bank. They have tiny daisies on the heel and they scream, *Notice Me. I am not beige. I am colorful and full of life.*

Kicking off my shoe, it sails under the bed, so I drop to my hands and knees and clamber under the guest bed—which incidentally is covered in clutter. Clutter that wouldn't have been allowed when I lived here. Under-the-bed clutter was under the same jurisdiction and rules as the rest of the house. *Hiding it does no good, Ashley. It's there. God knows it's still there, even if I don't. Clear out the clutter and you'll clear your mind,* I hear Kay preaching at me.

My teeth clench, as I know Matt must be the source of this mess. Kay is willing to put up with Matt's messes – when I know she wasn't willing to put up with mine. *This changes things.*

I reach into the melee for my shoe, and I fish it out, along with something orange and lacy. I pick up the undies that are so out of place with all the tools and files under the bed. It's a…sheer, gauzy (read: cheap) scrap of underwear. I feel sick to my stomach knowing this sliver of lace can't be Kay's because:

A. She's Kay.

B. She's never met a pair of white granny panties she didn't love.

C. I watch enough "20/20" to have learned that no good ever

comes from unclaimed lingerie.

I peel the tacky panties off of my shoe and shove them back under the bed, but my mind is reeling. This is Matt's doing, but I'll never be able to prove it. Unless Kay has met some disreputable new character at church who needed a place to stay, I'm willing to bet Matt's responsible and that this won't make a bit of difference to Kay.

Granted, if I could blame the entire fall of mankind on Matt at the moment, I'd do that, too. So I'm not exactly thinking clearly, but why? Why doesn't Kay know she deserves so much better than Matt Callaway?

"Ashley, everyone's arriving!" Kay calls out from the kitchen.

I panic and shove everything on the floor under the bed. It's nothing, I tell myself. My imagination is working overtime. I'm feeling lonely and rejected and looking for someone to blame.

I breathe in deeply and tell myself to relax. Outside on the quiet neighborhood street, a car door slams and I peek out the window to get my first look at Seth in two years. *Still bald.* Yes, I'm immature, but this brings me a slight elation. *Kevin has hair!* Seth comes around the car, opens the passenger door, and Arin's spindly, stick legs kick to the side as she plants her earthy sandals onto the curb. Seth doesn't help her out, instead, he slides open the back door, reaches in and pulls out a toddler like a sack of potatoes. He sets the kid down on the sidewalk, and the little boy looks up at his mom and smiles.

He's darling. The toddler, not Seth. He has reddish-brown hair, which is gelled into a spiked style, and he's wearing brown plaid shorts and an orange T-shirt with a matching brown plaid animal of some sort on the tummy. A twinge of jealously stabs at my gut as I see how easily everything came together for Seth with his ready-made family, complete with mini-van, while I'm still in flux.

I don't even have a job.

"The guy lives a charmed life."

It makes sense that Seth would have kids first. After all, Arin was pregnant at my wedding—do the math. It's the reason Seth married her—because missionaries who end up pregnant outside of wedlock aren't exactly employable. They rescued one another. Seth wouldn't have been motivated to get married unless someone needed him. Arin *needed* him. It didn't hurt that she was blonde, beautiful and a size two. If Quasimodo needed his help, Seth probably wouldn't have been so anxious to rescue, but it's a love story in its own right.

Arin shouts something at Seth. I can tell by the slumping expression on her face it wasn't sweet nothings. Seth's face darkens into a soulless gaze, and he lobs back some caustic remark. At least, that's what I see. My heart pounds as I note the bliss I imagined for them may not be the case, and now I feel badly.

"Ashley!" Kay shouts again.

"I'm coming!"

I twist around and lean up against the wall. My eyes clasp shut and I see the image of their beautiful child against my eyelids. Just another relentless reminder that at thirty-four, I'm no closer to being pregnant than I was two years ago when I first got married. I thought I was fine with that, but as I spy Seth's son, maybe I only told myself that because I didn't have a choice.

I hate how this beautiful, innocent child makes me feel; covetous and never satisfied, unlike the Christian wife I promised to be when I stood before God at the altar. It was only two years ago that I thought marrying the man of my dreams was all I needed in life to be happy. I open my eyes and capture the trail of the small family stepping onto the path, and my eyes burn with bitter jealousy. Their life has started, and Kevin is so heavily involved in saving other people's families that he has no time for ours. His life is his. And mine is…beige.

Arin carries an oversized bag and she hops a spritely step. She's just as I imagined. Still skinnier than me, with a small bulge poking out of her yoga pants. *Yoga pants when she's pregnant. Shoot me now.* Seth takes the diaper bag from her and heaves it over his bony shoulders. I hide behind the curtain and remember how many nights

I spent in this room wondering if I would ever be somebody's bride. Now I have a husband, and it appears maybe contentment is like chasing a rainbow. I let go of the curtain and hightail it to the kitchen, barefoot before the young family rings the bell.

"She's in yoga pants," I say to Kay, "and with the hips of a twelve-year-old. That's just wrong."

"May I remind you those cute hips of Arin's got her Seth Greenwood, your castoff. He's not exactly Prince Charming." She lowers her tone. "I think they're having troubles, so be kind."

"I was really more his castoff if we're honest. It's not him or her that I'm jealous of, it's that little boy. Their jobs don't get in the way of their starting a family."

Kay smirks. "I thought you were coming here to tell us all you were pregnant."

I shake my head, feeling like a failure. "That would have been awesome. Is that why no one seems happy to see me?"

"Put the chicken nuggets in the oven. I'll answer the door and give you time to compose yourself. We'll tell them you're channeling Raggedy Ann for dinner with that hair." She opens the fridge and puts the salad on the middle shelf. "This needs to chill a bit."

The kitchen smells divine, a mix of fresh cilantro and lime. "I miss the fresh veggies being so readily available." But I'm talking to myself because Kay is gone.

The shrimp are cooked already and a deep pink, but there's no noxious odor, just the tangy rice wine vinegar. I will never understand how Kay can make everything happen like she does and there's no sign of any effort. I look down at the cookie sheet dotted with a few dinosaur nuggets on it and call after her. "You trust me with these nuggets?"

She reappears in the doorway. "Not really, but I'll have to go on faith unless you want to answer the door." Kay's eyes widen. "Yeah, I didn't think so."

I hear the front door open, Kay welcoming them, then the clatter of the small family echoes across the foyer, through the small house.

At the sound of Arin's teenage voice, I want nothing more than to run back to Kevin and forget this idea of trying to go home again, but instead I venture to the foyer. Seth and Arin are obviously livid with each other. They don't even seem like they're together and I find myself angry at them both. Come on, this was the great love affair that broke my heart. Get it together!

This dinner party gives me the sudden urge to run, and I abhor exercise. Seth and Arin and their gorgeous little family is darling – but I could have said so on Facebook and been perfectly at peace. A face-to-face meeting? It's awkward and I search for the proper greeting. *Hey, great job on the procreating! Kevin and I are still mulling that thought!*

I duck back into the kitchen, unable to think of a thing to say, when I see another car pull up outside—Seth's old Saab—and I know it must be Sam, Seth's parasitic friend who never understood the concept of a date. In fact, you might think *The Bachelor* franchise started the two-on-one date idea, but I'm here to tell you that it was Sam. And apparently, he doesn't understand the concept of marriage either, because here he is, alone. Just like old times.

I hear the friendly chatter at the entryway and set the timer for twenty minutes on the chicken nuggets. My time is up. Sucking in a deep breath, I exit the sanctity of the kitchen and meet Seth's brilliant blue eyes for the first time since my wedding. "Seth."

He envelops me in a cold, stiff embrace and then, softens and pulls me closer to him. I break away as Seth has never been one for actual human contact, so I'm caught off-guard by his sudden display of affection. *Affection* is too strong a word. *Humanity* might be better.

Arin is bent over her little one and whispering in his ear. She straightens in all her wispy, blonde glory and smiles broadly. "Ashley!" She comes toward me and side-hugs me so as to avoid her belly, which looks slightly larger close-up. Slightly. As in it's honey-dew versus a cantaloupe.

"Arin, you look young as ever. I can't believe you're old enough to be a mother." And I can't. Kevin's mother's words come back to haunt me and I fear I may never be a mother.

She rubs her belly. "Believe it. Nearly two times over now."

Rub it in. "I know, right?" I say like I'm thirteen.

"Ashley?" She blinks a few times. "Your hair."

I rake my fingers through my style and feign confidence, as if to say, *yes, isn't it great? A new French stylist!*

"Did you do that on purpose?"

"Yep. Always being the proper doctor's wife, I wanted to break free now that I'm back in California. Shake it up a little."

"Well…" She clears her throat. "You've certainly done that." She rubs the top of my arm as she speaks. She always was too touchy-feely for my tastes. "I can't believe it took you this long to come back. Don't you miss California? Your parents? Kay? We sure miss your voice at church."

Seth chimes in, "Yeah, we do. Your replacement is terrible. She sounds like a moaning hound."

"Seth!" Arin slaps his arm. "She's not that bad. She's just—"

"Tone deaf," Kay deadpans.

"So do you miss California?" Arin asks again.

"Intensely, but life keeps rolling forward." *Other people's lives.* Not mine necessarily.

"How's Kevin?" She hoists her son onto her Barbie-doll hip and I half-expect the kid to slide right off, but he clasps his darling meaty thighs around his mother and he's happy as he rests his head on her shoulder.

"Somebody's tired." I reach out to gently touch Arin's son, but he shakes his head 'no' and buries his face deeper into his mother's shoulder. "Busy. Kevin's busy." Thinking that sounds negative, I'm quick to add, "And great. He's doing a lot more surgeries." With Arin holding her son, I'm struck by his russet-colored eyes and how much life they hold. "Who's this little guy?"

Arin untucks her son's chin so I can see his Baby Gap face. "This is Toby. Toby, say hello to Miss Ashley. She's an old friend of your dad's and mine."

"Unh-uh," he says, and shovels his face into Arin's shirt.

"Toby," Seth says.

"Don't worry about it. Maybe you'll be my friend when I tell you I have chicken nuggets shaped like dinosaurs for dinner."

"And Miss Kay made your favorite cookies for dessert!" Kay says.

"Awesome!" Seth says.

"Your *son's* favorite cookies," Kay corrects.

"Oh," Seth says with disappointment.

Toby's face reappears and his eyes are wide. "You are so cute!" I touch his soft cheek and I feel the sting of tears behind my eyes as I look into his beautiful, miraculous healthy face. Kevin's job has made healthy babies feel like an anomaly, and to see one up close is like finding a magenta unicorn in the midst of Palo Alto.

The little boy finally ventures a gaze at me, but he's not won over yet and tucks his face back into his mother's ample, pregnancy-induced chest. Arin hands the boy over to Seth, who raises him up like the cub in Lion King. One would never know the boy wasn't Seth's by birth. It warms my heart to see him with his son. It shows me how God truly knows best and I need to remember this moment the next time my overly analytical mind goes into high gear.

Seth once told me that I didn't need rescuing. I'm sure I didn't, but I never forgot him saying that when he started dating Arin. She did need rescuing and Seth needed to be the hero. Together, they provided something for each other and this loved little boy is proof that it worked.

Seth sets Toby down. "You're too big to be carried around. You have to get ready to be the big brother."

Toby has a train clutched in his chubby fist and he opens his palm to me. "Who's that?" I ask him.

"Toby."

"Like you?"

He nods.

I kneel down and look in his sparkling eyes. "I wish I had a train named after me."

The doorbell rings again, and without waiting for Kay to answer, Sam bursts through the door. "Ashley, missed me, huh?" Sam shouts as he slams the door. "Lord almighty, what did you do to your hair?"

"Good to see you too, Sam."

Sam never developed a volume control, and unfortunately, he doesn't come with a mute button. Sam was never my biggest fan, but he wouldn't let that keep him from a dinner invite. A free meal is a free meal.

"How are you?" I ask him.

"Oh you know, same old stuff, different day."

I currently feel completely caught up on my old life. "Would anyone like something to drink?" I ask, as this used to be my job since Kay rarely let me in the kitchen.

"Sure, you got any Pepsi?" Sam says, as he plops on the couch and kicks his feet onto the coffee table. Kay is used to the boorish behavior, but it hasn't ceased to annoy me.

"I've got Pepsi," Kay says. "Arin, you want something?"

"Ice water with lemon if you have it."

"I do," Kay says. "Seth?"

"Nothing for me thanks," Seth points toward the easy chair across from the sofa. "Sit down Ash, I want to hear all about your not working. What are you doing with all that excess time?"

"No, he doesn't," Arin says. "He wants you to tell me how fabulous it is to stay home and not work."

Seth looks guilty. One thing about Seth, he can't lie and get away with it. "You're working outside the home, Arin?" I ask.

"She wants to. With another kid on the way. Can you believe it? Tell her how satisfied you are being at home." Seth's eyes beg me to do so.

I stutter over something to say, "I—uh…"

"Gainnet is still struggling through, but you don't miss that garbage, do you, Ash? Answering to a boss all the time? Having to dress up for work?"

I try to compose myself. "Gainnet has some key patents, so I always believed they'd make it, or at least sell their technology and—" I don't finish my sentence, and I look for something bright to say. "Gainnet's stock price should have been quite good to you."

Seth grins. "Bought a house with it."

"We need a bigger one," Arin says as she rubs her belly.

There's an awkward silence. Which is actually preferable to the talking.

"I'll just go help Kay in the kitchen," Arin says. "Seth, why don't you and Ashley take Toby out to the backyard and let him get some energy out? Let her get a taste of how fun it is to be home with a toddler."

"Oh, be careful," Kay calls from the doorway. "Matt has a lot of equipment out there. I'm not sure if there are any loose nails or the like."

"He's had his tetanus." Arin grins, and I can't tell if she's joking or not.

Seth and I stare at each other uncomfortably, but like the "reasons" we are, we do as we're told and head to the backyard—even though neither one of us has anything to say to each other. Or so I think. We go to the backyard, which is a little more than a patch of grass amidst a woodpile and countless tools for the pergola.

"I'm not sure this is safe for Toby."

"I'll keep my eye on him. I was hoping I'd get a chance to talk to you."

I stare back at Sam in the house, who is still stretched out on Kay's sofa, with his hands clasped behind his head. "Oh?" I smile at Seth. "So how's everything? It looks like you've adapted well to being a father."

"The marriage isn't good." He doesn't look at me while he says this. He's got his eyes on Toby, who is running along a stack of two-by-fours. "Isn't it obvious?"

"No," I lie. "You probably need a vacation. I forgot how frowned upon a vacation is when you live in Silicon Valley. It's like you're not allowed to take a break or you'll be replaced. Give Arin a respite. Can't be easy staying home with a little one all day."

"That's not what I meant."

I know that, but I don't want to go there. Seth looks older than his years. He's a ghost of himself, and I knew immediately that his marriage was not good, but I don't want to hear confirmation. "Has Toby started in on any sports yet? T-ball? Soccer?" My attempt at changing the subject.

"I made a mistake, Ashley," he blurts.

"Haven't we all?" I say casually as I stare straight ahead at Sam and wonder how he manages to stay in the most expensive real estate market in the country without ever doing a day's work.

"No, I mean I made a mistake marrying Arin."

I turn back to Seth. "No, Seth. This is just a rough time." Just like when we were dating, Seth continues to throw the friend card in my face. Not that I mind now, but I do wonder why he can't ever talk to Arin. What am I supposed to do for them? I have a natural inclination to want to fix things – and granted, I may mess them up more often than I fix them, but I do try. And there is nothing I can do about this, so I fail to see the point of hearing about it.

He shakes his head. "It's more than that."

"Then, fix it." I notice how Seth is always the victim. Nothing is ever his responsibility and how convenient I made myself. Gosh, I'm a dolt. No wonder he kept me around, buzzing like a bee around someone else's honey. Pathetic.

"She never loved me. You all knew that, didn't you? I see the way everyone looks at me when we're here. Like, *Poor Seth, he doesn't know any better.*"

"I have to get your son's chicken nuggets out of the oven."

"Ash?" He gives me his best puppy dog eyes.

Seriously, you are not having this pity party with me, Seth. "No one is doing any such thing. Arin married you. She's having your child. What other proof do you need? Do you want her to have a parade set up every time you enter a room?"

Seth wags his head. "I provide everything for her, and she suddenly wants to go back to work and have some daycare raise our children. Why? When she has a choice? Don't women beg to stay at home?"

"Not all of them." I stick my fingers in my ears like I'm Toby's age. "Seth, I don't think this conversation is appropriate. I have no idea why she wants to go back to work, but have you asked her? Rather than me?. Maybe she's not the stay-at-home type."

"Then why did she get married? She could have been a single mother and worked to her heart's content."

"Seth, didn't you have this conversation before you got married?'"

"Yeah," he says angrily before a pause. "Maybe not."

Seth looks past me with his thoughtful gaze. Seriously, what did he expect he and Arin were going to discuss at night, string theory? Of course they had nothing in common. He went for the package. Surprise, the package doesn't contain a quantum physicist. I mean, Arin's smart. She's educated. She's a believer, but she's not…I don't know…aware that a world exists outside of her?

All of Arin's missionary work, all of her contact with the church, it was all on a shallow level. No one ever really got to know her, but that's who she is. 'That's what you chose, Seth. Take some responsibility and ownership, for crying out loud."

His far-off gaze returns to me. "Ashley." He steps toward me.

Why does every conversation I have with Seth make me want to bang my head against the wall? And why did it take me years and 2,500 miles to see this relatively simple thing?

"Just talk to her, won't you? Tell her how happy you are at home.

How much you love being there when Kevin gets home at night."

I just stare at him, blinking. Seriously? I had a crush on this guy! Like, for a long time, too long to pawn it off as a delusional phase.

"How hard is it to tell her that?" he pushes.

"As your ex or as a casual observer?" I've flustered him. Admittedly, not hard to do, but it stops him in his tracks long enough for me to make my escape toward Toby. Never one to take a hint, Seth follows.

"This book I read said all women want to be treated like princesses."

"Which is great if your wife wants to be treated like a princess, but what if she doesn't? Arin has traveled all over the world by herself. She's quite capable and she doesn't need rescuing."

"But the book said—"

Engineers! "The book is an inanimate object. Seth do you remember that old joke about men having an on and off switch and women being a bevy of buttons and knobs?"

"Yeah—"

I raise my brows. "Yeah. That."

"You're not going to talk to her? Is that what you're saying? I'm not pushing the right buttons?"

"Argh!"

"Ash, now you sound just like Arin."

"Why don't you just ask Arin what she wants? She's not some random chick who will adhere to what some book is telling you. She's Arin; world traveler, missionary, Stanford student and adventurer."

Man, when I say it like that, she sounds a lot better than me. No wonder he married her.

"I'm done. She doesn't listen."

At this point all the rage I once felt for Seth and his lack of forward motion comes bubbling to the surface. "Well, it's a little late for that. You've got another baby on the way. Man-up and quit your whining. Sometimes, life gets hard and you have to deal with it!"

What I say doesn't affect him in the least. "Arin knew I wanted out, that's why she got pregnant."

I can't *un-hear* this. Is it just me, or do men really believe women are capable of getting pregnant by themselves? Same ol' Seth—nothing is his fault. He's just a victim to his circumstances.

"Seth, you're angry at her. You don't mean any of this. This is your way of getting back at her."

"Maybe," he admits. "But I wanted you to know, I get it. Love isn't a flash-in-the-pan infatuation. I didn't know what love was and I suppose I always saw us together. I thought you'd be around and we'd survive the Kevin and Arin effect. Tell me that you don't wonder if we were meant to be together all along."

"I don't," I say flatly. "Here, all this time, I thought I was the drama queen. Are we done here?"

I look to his son and wonder how he can say such things in front of the little boy. Whether Toby understands or not, it isn't right. I clamber to get back into the house to get away from Seth and his momentary delusions. I'm trapped by Seth's words. I can't tell Kevin. He'd want to come out and throttle Seth. I can't tell Kay because it will force her to lie to Arin. I feel like he's saddled me with information that wasn't mine to know and now it weighs on me heavily. Once again, it's so he doesn't have to deal with the consequences of his own actions. So very convenient. Secretly, I wonder if it's ever crossed Kevin's mind that he married the wrong woman.

I head into the house, and I can't even look at Arin. I feel as if I've betrayed her, when I've done no such thing. Her husband has. Sam is still sitting with his feet up on the table, making no effort to participate in any part of the dinner party, other than the eating portion. I sigh aloud.

"Ashley, are you all right?" Kay asks as I enter the kitchen. "You look pale."

I shake my head. "It's just the hair color. It does nothing for my skin tone."

Kay looks straight at me as if she knows I'm hiding something, but I won't give it up. Looking at Arin, and the ways she's been betrayed, makes me want to be sick on her behalf. Then, I notice that Kay's eyes are moist with tears of her own.

"Kay?"

She shakes her head.

"Tell me what's happened."

"No one's coming. Pastor Max and his wife canceled. Everyone's here already, and Arin and Seth are fighting. It's a complete disaster. Why do I do this to myself?"

I used to wonder the same thing after one of Kay's dinner parties. My hands ball up into fists. No one has ever appreciated all that Kay has done for them, and I've never seen a touch of emotion from her, but seeing her now, willing herself not to cry, I want to throttle Pastor Max and "sweet" Kelly—this isn't the first time they've done this, and they have no clue as to how much time or money Kay spends to make this all happen.

"I'm sorry, Kay. They don't deserve you, they really don't, but you know they mean no harm. They just have no idea how much it takes to do this." I march out into the living room, and with one sweeping move, throw Sam's feet off the sofa. "This isn't your mama's house! Show some respect!"

"What did I do?" Sam puts his soda down and looks at me as if I'm starring in a movie from the Lifetime network.

"We should throw a party for Kay." I look directly at Sam. "Don't you think, Sam? Wouldn't that be nice? I mean, she buys fresh ingredients, she throws these great dinner parties—"

"She likes to do that," Sam says.

"I thought we could show her our appreciation for all she does."

"I do appreciate Kay," Sam cries. "I think she's the most generous person I've ever known." He looks at his watch. "But I have a deadline at work. I should go."

As long as I've known Sam, he has never had a regular job. He was always pitching some new gadget to change the world and waiting for his commission check to clear. He slinks out without saying goodbye, and Kay glares at me like I'm the bad guy, because my helpful suggestion only managed to have one less mouth at her failed dinner party.

"What?" I shrug.

Toby saves me. He's in his mother's arms wailing as if he's just lost a limb. His face is beet red.

Arin pipes up, "He's just desperately in need of a good sleep. It's been a long day. Kay, please forgive us, but I think we should go too."

"Dinner is ready," Kay says, panicked. "Let me put it on the table and I'll have you out of here in twenty minutes. You have to eat anyway, and Toby's probably hungry, that's why he's overreacting."

Arin swishes her blonde hair back and forth. "No, really. You're too kind. We don't deserve a friend like you, and I'm afraid if we stay, we'll lose another friend to parenthood." The melancholy in Arin's voice strikes me particularly hard. I want to tell her how much Seth loves her and give him a good slap upside the head – but that wouldn't be Christian.

"Let me put together a plate for you to take home then," Kay begs.

"Sure," Seth agrees.

"No," Arin barks and her answer leaves no room for discussion. "She's already gone through enough work, Seth. I'm sorry, Kay. It hasn't been a good day." Arin glares at me as if to remind me the reason for her very bad day, and honestly, I just want to hug her.

The small family disappears out the front door, and Kay's full wrath turns toward me. If looks could kill, I'd be six feet under.

"Really? You cleared out an entire dinner party before anyone actually ate? Not even random people, but our church group? People who haven't visited a grocery store in probably a good month because their schedules don't allow for it, and they all just suddenly lost their appetites?"

I twist my hands together. "Look at the bright side, we can have an all-you-can-eat shrimp night right here. It will be like old times. Just the two of us."

Kay grunts at me and marches back to the kitchen like a drill sergeant.

Could it possibly be? The "Reasons" actually seem less functional without me. Kay doesn't want to throw dinner parties. Seth doesn't want to be married. Arin doesn't appreciate Seth's love (like this is news) and I am dyed orange like a clown. I definitely over-romanticized my life in California. I was just as dysfunctional here as I am in Philly. Somehow, I feel like the repercussions from this dinner party may be worse than others I've ruined in the past.

I tap my heels together and chant. *There's no place like home. There's no place like home.*

Chapter 7

K AY IS VISIBLY upset by the evening, and of course, what she views as my part in the fiasco. I'm not saying I was completely innocent, but…no wait, I was completely innocent. At least this one time. Maybe I wasn't particularly nice to Sam, but he's Sam, so it will have no effect on him whatsoever.

"Don't be angry with me," I say after our silent dinner. "Why don't you go to bed, Kay? I'll clean up."

"I don't like the way you clean up," she snaps.

"You'll survive. Go sit down. Watch some English Premier League or whatever cheers you up these days."

"I can't. Not until this mess is cleaned up. You'll use the garbage disposal. I don't use the disposal—all of that food goes into composting." She starts to scrape a plate of its leftover food into a large, plastic bowl. "Disposals don't last forever, you know. You have to treat them gently."

"Yours will last forever, doesn't that cheer you up? You never use it. It's like a win-win. The environment…your garbage disposal."

"I can't sit down until this mess is cleaned up."

"No one even ate off all of these plates," I say over the dinner table.

"They were exposed. They've been contaminated."

I can't even respond to that. And I know Kay won't sit down even after she's done cleaning. In order to "allow" herself to watch television, she has to climb onto her elliptical trainer like a hamster on its wheel, as if she's powering the electricity herself. I'm surprised that she doesn't have it rigged that way. I lift the cookie sheet with the chicken dinosaurs on it, and Kay plucks it out of my hand and takes to scrubbing it like she's at war.

"I shouldn't have come, all right? I get it."

She scowls at me and lays the cookie sheet in the sink. She's leaned up against the counter, and it's then, for the first time, I notice how much younger she looks than when I left. She's dressed in normal jeans, and by normal, I mean, not mom jeans that rise up to her chest and compete with her bra for space. She's got a light blue cotton blouse on—where she would normally wear some kind of flannel, plaid number, and she just seems lighter in nature.

"Come on, how long are you going to be mad at me?"

"At least as long as it takes for you to be a brunette again."

"I didn't even notice your new look, Kay. I suppose that makes me a terrible friend, but you look really nice. You bought new clothes. Without me."

"Some of us don't make big changes like Ronald McDonald hair to get attention. You have to look closer to notice."

Kinda rude.

Kay pulls in a breath and shakes her head. "I thought I wanted your help, but now I'm not so sure."

Her words hurt. "I should just go back to Philly. My mom's busy with houseguests. I've upset your dinner party, and Brea's too busy for me. At least at home, Rhett needs me."

"If you must know, I wanted you here to help me with my wedding."

My stomach plummets. "Wedding?" I look around the empty house. "Whose wedding?"

"My wedding."

Oh God, don't let it be Matt. "To who?"

"This is why I didn't want to tell you about Matt. I knew what you'd say about him, that you'd judge him by his one mistake rather than the whole of his life."

"Matt?" It takes every atom of self-control I have to not spurt that there are sleazy orange *chones* under my bed. I want to believe her version of Matt, but he gives me the heebie-jeebies. How does one help that?

"You're too judgmental, Ashley. I take joy in nurturing others through hospitality. It's my gift and I don't think people have to be perfect to have dinner here. You have impossible standards."

"It is your gift," I agree. "It gives me hives, but I wish you'd at least hear my side of things. You're mad at me because you think I judge Matt, is that it?"

"You do judge Matt. He wants to get married," she blurts. "I'm not the girly type. I have no idea how to arrange a wedding and I want your help, but I don't want—"

"My opinion. Are we talking about Matt Callaway?" Oh heavens. *Now I've got to tell her.* I find a chair and lower myself into it. "I thought he was just doing work for you around the house. That you were good friends, as you put it."

"I lied," Kay says.

"You lied? Kay, when have you ever lied?"

"You're wrong about him, Ashley, and I didn't want your lecture. Yes, he's not a believer. We'll be unequally yoked, but it's my life. Seth and Arin are both Christians. Look how well that is working out for them. Then, you've got Brea and John, two fantastic Christians who try to do the right thing, and look what happens to them. They lose their house."

I take a step back. "What?" I struggle to comprehend her words. "Brea and John lost their house?"

She covers her mouth with her fingertips and gasps. "Oh Ashley, I'm sorry. I wasn't supposed to say anything."

"That's why I'm staying here? They lost their house? My best friend lost her house and she didn't tell me? I noticed it looked different on Skype, but I assumed she just moved her desktop."

"Not from anything they did, but yeah. They're living at her mom's house."

"With the boys?"

Kay nods.

I feel sick to my tummy. I may as well be in Timbuktu for how much people share with me over Facebook and Skype. It's like I cease to exist and people seem to like it that way. *Maybe I am too judgmental.* "I thought I was a good friend. I guess I'm mistaken about that."

"Brea didn't want you to worry, Ashley. She knows you, and she swore you'd try to do something about it. She feels adamantly that this trial is from God and they'll get through it. She says their marriage is stronger than ever."

See, that's just it. Brea feels something, and I had no idea.

"But I couldn't do anything about it if I wanted to," I explain. "I'm not working. Kevin barely makes enough to pay for expenses, so that can't be the reason she didn't tell me. I'm a terrible friend. That's why no one has told me a thing since I've been gone."

"Sometimes, people have their reasons for keeping secrets."

"From their best friends? You and Brea probably know me better than anyone and completely kept me out of the loop. That can't be a coincidence."

Kay plants her hands on her hips. "Were you going to tell me that Seth made a pass at you, telling you he wanted out of his marriage?" she asks me, and she may as well have knocked me over with the backside of that cookie sheet. My heart begins to pound, as I hadn't planned on telling anyone what Seth said to me.

"Seth's just angry. He didn't mean a word of that and it wasn't really a pass. Seth couldn't make a pass when he was single and you expect me to believe he's capable of it now and risking Arin? You give him far too much credit."

"I heard him. It was inappropriate. The vent goes right to where you were standing. You may as well have had a baby monitor at your face. I had to keep Arin out of the kitchen so she didn't hear her husband acting like a complete dirtbag."

"Seth is delusional," I tell her. "We never had any such torrid love affair. It was one-sided the entire time. It took him saying that to me for me to realize it. He loves Arin, and he hates that because it makes him weak. Emotions are Seth's Kryptonite."

"I agree. But, were you planning on telling Kevin?" Her brows rise. "What about Brea?"

I pause. "Kevin knows I have no interest in Seth, so what would be the point? To make him worry needlessly?"

"Which is why I think you should tell him, Ashley, but you definitely shouldn't judge Brea for keeping her secrets, or me for keeping mine. We had our reasons."

"I want to go home." I saunter out of the kitchen. "Kevin's at home saving lives. I really doubt that he cares that Seth is going through hallucinations and an early midlife crisis. Seth just can't control Arin, and that has to drive him nuts."

"I'd still tell Kevin."

"I'm going to pack."

"You're not going to help me plan my wedding?"

"I didn't even know you were dating. I'm going home."

"Quit being a drama queen. It's a simple wedding. We'd like to get married in the backyard. What did you think the pergola was for?"

"A picnic! I thought it was for picnics and BBQs."

"Matt says he loves me and he respects my faith, so why can't I respect that he doesn't have a faith?"

Um, because he's got some chick's thong under your guest bed?

"I get it. It seems to make practical sense, but you act like if you don't marry Matt, you'll be alone forever." Which, let's face it, would be an improvement!

"I want to have a child," Kay says, and I'm gobsmacked.

"Since when? You do know that children make messes, right? I mean, like worse-than-me-as-a-roommate messes."

"Is being alone and not having a partner in life something God really wants from me? Is this my reward? The casual, drive-by friendships of 'The Reasons'?"

I laugh. Most inappropriate time ever, but, she caught me unaware. "I've never heard you refer to the group as 'The Reasons.'"

Kay shrugs. "It's taken me this long to see that I don't want to spend the rest of my life like this. I've always admired you, Ashley."

Now I know she's lost it.

"You've admired me? Kay, you've spent the entire duration of our relationship telling me why my life was utter chaos and how to fix it. How is that admiration?"

"Not your organization ability obviously."

"Obviously."

"I mean that you knew you wanted to get married. You believed in Prince Charming, and he came for you. What if my lack of faith in my prince is what is holding me back?"

"You're simplifying things, Kay. Matt Callaway is a—well, he's got a history, for one thing. Did it ever occur to you just because he's here he may not be Prince Charming?"

"So I should judge him for his past? Did you show Kevin your credit card statement before you got married?"

Touché.

"Matt and I may have a different faith, but we have the same values. We believe in treating others the way we'd like to be treated ourselves. When I make him a beautiful dinner, he washes the dishes and fixes something around here for me."

"You let Matt do the dishes?" An uncomfortable twinge settles in my stomach.

"Ashley, focus. Seth and Arin, they don't believe in the same things. Sure, they believe in the same God, but what that means to them individually is completely different. She believes in traveling all over the world to tell people about Jesus, but at the same time, thinks it's okay to marry a man she doesn't love if she 'acts' like she loves him. Something she can't do most of the time, so she's living a lie. How godly is that?"

I shrug. "I don't think it's a comparison. Just because Seth and Arin are working things out—"

"Meanwhile Seth thinks she's going to turn into Albert Einstein suddenly, plus want nothing more than to darn his socks and homeschool their children. Can you imagine? They'd get to simple division and be stalled."

"Kay!"

"I'm sorry. I know Arin is smart, but she's missing something in the practical arena and she married Seth. Why does she have to be so mean to him?"

"In her defense, there were days I was mean to him too. For a reason!" *Let's face it, look up exasperating in the dictionary and there's Seth's picture.*

"No one knows how to have a dinner party because they don't need to. I'm enabling. Pure and simple." She puts her gloved fingers to her eyebrow as if the entire thing has given her a headache. "No one brings so much as a hostess gift. You know, I don't care about a hostess gift, but on what planet is that acceptable, Ashley?"

I stare at her, my mouth dropped open. Since when does Kay care about a hostess gift? All this discontentment is coming from somewhere, and if I don't figure it out, she's bound to think Matt Callaway is the answer to all of her problems. I can pretty much guarantee that he's not an answer. Unless the question is, *Who does Kay not need in her life?*

"I agree, Kay. They should know better," I say absently as my thoughts return to Arin. In actuality, Arin has an Ivy League education. That doesn't mean she's fit for homeschooling, but it's still worth mentioning. She's not nearly as dumb as I'd like her to be, but watching her with Toby, it shows me that she'd be perfectly happy to put her kids in an American school on a foreign mission field.

Kay picks up the soapy sponge. "I don't know. My patience just ran out, I guess."

"I can see that. It's unnerving, but you can't blame God for the way His people act, and you certainly can't marry Matt because there are no great candidates in the Reasons. Why don't you try another church?"

"I love Matt." She tosses the sponge into the sink and glares at me.

Why?

"This may be my last shot to be a mother."

There it is. Her true fear. The driving force that makes Matt Callaway appear as acceptable husband material.

Kay squints. "Walgreens is open late. Go get yourself some hair dye. You're not going home."

"I brought you something," I say sheepishly. "A hostess gift for you—even though I didn't actually think I'd be staying here. I knew you'd have at least one dinner party. It's who you are, and I appreciate it."

She shakes her head. "Not anymore. It's not who I am anymore. When I have Matt's clients here for dinner, it's different. I don't feel like I'm babysitting."

"You're entertaining Matt's clients?" That sick feeling permeates the rest of my body and I wish I could see some glimmer of likeability in him – just for Kay's sake.

"Yes…and don't make that face. Did it ever occur to you that I deserve to be loved, too?"

"It always occurred to me. I just want to be sure Matt's the one. Before you make up your mind, can I show you something?"

"He's the one. I have made up my mind," she answers firmly.

"What if I had evidence that proved he wasn't the one?"

"You don't," she says flatly.

My chin drops. "Let me go get your hostess gift."

I stride into the bedroom, determined that I'm going to pick up the wayward orange undies and ask if they're hers. But when I get there, I pause at the sound of Matt's voice and can't bring myself to grab them. My gift, a bottle of black truffle oil, isn't enough to make her stop thinking of Matt Callaway as husband material – and worse, neither might a pair of orange undies. I quietly shut the guestroom door and start to pray.

Chapter 8

WHEN I WAKE up, the first thing I notice on Kay's pristine white pillow is that my hair is still neon. Truthfully, in Silicon Valley, no one will notice. They're so imbedded in their smart phones, I could dance naked on the streets and no one would raise an eyebrow. When I shower, the tinge of orange puddles in the water around my feet, and I'm reminded of my lacy discovery.

I try to come up with alternative ideas to Matt's being a cheater, but I'm flummoxed. That old saying haunts me, *once a cheater, always a cheater.*

I never expected Kay to make a decision based on emotions – especially emotions I didn't even know she had!

When I enter the kitchen, Matt Callaway's hulking figure is hunched over the breakfast table opposite Kay. It's weird. In front of him sits the remnants of a Cracker Barrel style breakfast: Eggs over easy; toast (of course he doesn't eat the crust, being the child that he is), and from the smell of things, bacon, but I see no sign of that pork goodness.

Kay jumps up from the table at the sight of me. "Good morning, Ashley. Did you have a good sleep?"

I shrug. "Yeah, thanks."

"Do you want some breakfast?"

I glare at Matt, trying to catch a glimmer of the magic Kay sees in him…trying to feel some semblance of their connection, but there's nothing. I know Kay isn't me, so I try to channel her anal-retentive self and see the practical qualities in Matt. *Again. I got nothing.* If there is a special connection with them, it's akin to a dog whistle, on a completely different frequency from what I can hear. I don't ask the obvious question: Was Matt here all night? But I will when he's gone. If he ever has the decency to get lost.

"No thanks, I miss my coffee shop. I thought I'd walk down there this morning." *And hopefully, Matt will be gone by the time I get back.*

"I figured you might. I left a gift card for you on the counter."

"Seriously? You think of everything, Kay." Silently, I'm praying she's forgotten all about the failed dinner party and my ratchet opinion of Matt. But organized people have organized minds, so I'm not hopeful.

"Someone gave the card to me, and I never go there. I can't imagine the sheer number of bacteria in every cup."

"It strengthens the immune system," I say. "I was never sick when I lived here. Thanks for this." I hold up the card, hoping to avoid any conversation related to marriage at such an ungodly hour. You see my point though. She knew exactly where a useless gift card was the moment she needed it. What sorcery is this?

"When you come home," Kay says. "The key is in its normal hiding spot."

"Thanks." I slip my sweater on over my colorful Maxi dress. "I'll see you later." *Not you, Matt.* The sight of him at the breakfast table is enough to bring back up any good meal. I hightail it out of the house to the nearby coffee shop—where once spending $5 a day on a fancy coffee seemed like a reasonable expense. Employment. It was a beautiful thing.

Today, escaping the reality of Kay and Matt seems highly reasonable even without the gift card.

The coffee shop is far dirtier than I remember it—which makes sense, since it was dirty when I left, and no one's cleaned it since. Nowadays, it's mostly Facebook employees, judging by their lanyard tags. I miss being part of the lanyard crowd and officially belonging to something. I order, grab my iced soy latte and sit down at a table in the corner. I start to read the newspaper on my phone when I'm interrupted.

"Is this seat taken?"

I look up and see Seth standing over the table, with his hand possessively on the chair. I stand up. "I was just leaving. Feel free."

"Ashley, I just wanted to finish our conversation."

"You never wanted to finish a conversation when we were dating."

"So you're still mad at me."

"I'm not. I don't even think about you, Seth. You're married. I'm married. This isn't appropriate on any level." Isn't it ironic that the only person who wants to spill secrets with me is Seth Greenwood?

He stands in front of me and blocks my path. "I need your help, Ashley. We're friends. Why would I come to see you at Kay's house last night?"

"Um, the free meal didn't have anything to do with it?" I mean, really, am I supposed to believe that Arin has become a chef all of a sudden? All Arin ever did was prance around in her tiny jeans, and travel on someone else's dime under the guise of being a missionary. But even with those qualifications, she doesn't deserve her husband chasing down his ex, looking for advice. That, no doubt, he won't follow anyway.

"I came to dinner to see you. That's why we were invited. That's why I came."

"Seth, we haven't spoken since my wedding. I would say more aptly that we *were* friends and it's just as well that we keep it that way."

"Why are you here, Ashley? Why did you come home?" His incredible eyes, which are aquamarine, and haven't changed a bit in their intensity, stare me down. "If everything is so wonderful in your marriage, then why are you here all by yourself? In Silicon Valley of all places?"

"I'm asking myself the same question, at the moment. I can assure you, I'm not escaping anything, other than my lack of employment. My mom and dad are here, my best friends are here. There are lots of reasons to be in Silicon Valley."

I wish I could say I'm unfazed by his presence, but I'm not. I see how easily he controlled my feelings, when logically, I knew exactly who he was. Inherently, even back then I understood on some level that he would continue to break my heart. Yet, still I had run back towards him for the leftover scraps I got before he married Arin. *I was as dumb as a brick.*

It still haunts me.

Now I want to shop, and Seth's bald head seems to light up—like the apparent shopping trigger it is for me, a recovering shopaholic. All those times that I agonized over a pair of the perfect shoes, it was avoiding the hard truth, that Seth would never love me. The perfect pair of shoes changed nothing. To him, I was a worn-out pair of Crocs—he'd never see the Christian Louboutin in me.

Hindsight really is 20-20.

"You're telling me everything is perfect with you and the good doctor?"

"Everything is wonderful in my marriage, and even if it wasn't, I'd deal with the issues with my husband. I wouldn't be talking to my ex-boyfriend about it. Excuse me." I try to pass him again and he blocks me once more. When I was dating Seth, I practically had to chase him down and beat him with a stick to get his attention – now I can't shake him.

"That's what you consider me? Your ex-boyfriend. That's all? Ash, we had years of friendship. Years. We were there for each other, and now I need help."

Ah, the guilt. I almost break down – I'm not without a heart.

I sigh, grab my coffee and take a swig. "Actually, it's more accurate to say that I was there for you. You haven't changed a bit, Seth. You want someone else to fix this for you, but you're just going to have to do the work."

"I want your advice, that's all. I want you to talk to Arin and tell her how lucky she is to be at home with Toby."

"I don't know if she's lucky to be home with Toby. I certainly don't feel lucky to be home with Rhett."

"Rhett's a dog." He only remembers that because he bought Rhett for me – showed up at my doorstep with a wild liability who eats me out of house and home. Not that I'm complaining because Rhett is always there for me, but the point is still the same. He doesn't consider others in his decisions.

"I feel underutilized at home without kids. Maybe Arin needs more. I get that you don't like to deal in emotion, but you can't avoid it forever in marriage. You're going to have to deal with it, or someone else will."

His face contorts and I know I've hit some sort of truth center within him.

"Ever dramatizing things. Life is not a soap opera, Ashley. I want Arin to stay home with our children and in your mind, she's cheating on me?"

I ignore his ridiculous accusation. *I will not engage. I will not engage.* "You and Arin have to work it out. There is no shortcut. There is no third party in marriage, other than God. Figure out why your wife's unhappy and help her."

"I wouldn't have married her if I'd known how she felt about me."

Baloney. I shake my head with how easily Seth revisits history. Not only would he have married her, he may have chained her down to make sure it was official.

"I'm thinking of embarking on a second career as a ballerina." I put my coffee cup down and lift my arms above my head and pose in fifth position. If Seth won't listen, I will get his attention.

"Ashley, what are you doing?" Seth looks around him. "Put your arms down."

"Ballet!" I allow my handbag to fall off my shoulder onto the table. "I need more room if I'm going to spin – do you mind?"

"People are staring." He presses my arms down and I reach for my handbag again.

"I just wanted you to remember how you really felt about me. I seem to remember you saying that I didn't need you, but Arin did. Well—" I raise my arms again. "Remember, Arin will never do ballet in public."

"Sometimes, I really wonder what's wrong with you," he says.

"I know, and here's the beauty part. Kevin never does."

I should feel guilty, but Seth knew how I felt about him. He felt no compunction whatsoever to marry me or to let me go completely. He strung me along for years, and when Arin strutted in, he acted as if I were invisible and should simply know to get lost. He dropped me like last year's technology when pregnant Arin needed a husband.

That's not true.

I have compassion for him, though I saw his future—and I'm no psychic. He was just too proud to listen to anyone, and there are consequences to pride. I just pray his children don't pay the price. Is it wrong to feel just the slightest tinge of justice here? It probably is.

"I have to go, Seth." I stand up and drain my coffee with all its bug-fighting bacteria. I smash the cup in my hand and toss it in the overflowing garbage can.

He tugs at my shoulder. "Why didn't you tell me? You knew that she was using me."

"Seth, I'm not having this conversation."

Seth looks at me like I'm speaking a foreign language, and I suppose, speaking in emotional terms, I am speaking a foreign language. "You spoiled me, Ashley. You didn't question my every motive."

Uh, because I was too afraid you'd run. Arin didn't care.

He always did have some way of pulling me in and making his problems, mine. My cell phone trills and I look down to see Kevin's name. I suddenly feel incredibly guilty.

"Kevin," I say in a whispery voice. "I'm at my old coffee shop," I blurt, and turn away from Seth. "I ran into Seth here."

"Seth Greenwood?" Kevin asks me.

I stare at my ex, as if he's the enemy for putting me in this awkward situation. "The very same."

"How are he and Arin doing?"

"They're expecting!"

"I know that. It seems as if the entire world is expecting." I hear the drop in his voice, the reality that our lives are on hold while he finishes his fellowship.

"Did Emily arrive?" I try to keep the villain out of my voice when asking the question, but let's face it, Cruella De Ville has nothing on plotting when it comes to my sister-in-law.

"She did. That's why I'm calling. She wanted to know if it was okay to use some of your make-up. She left hers at home."

How convenient. Let me translate. Emily left her Maybelline at home, and now must sacrifice and borrow my Laura Mercier and Nars that I struggled to pay for. Why am I not surprised? "Sure," I say to my own detriment. "She's free to use anything she likes. I'll pick up some more at Nordstrom while I'm here." Granted, I know this strikes the fear of God into my husband – me going to Nordstrom.

He ignores my veiled threat. "Can I talk to Seth for a minute, Ashley?"

I stare into those familiar aquamarine eyes. "You want to talk to Seth?"

"Yes, please," he says. "I just want to speak to him for a second."

I hesitate, and then hand the phone to my balding ex. "Kevin wants to talk to you."

He reaches for the phone eagerly. There's a bunch of back and forth and I strain to hear the contents, but I can't make out a word Kevin is saying. Seth is nodding, occasionally offering an affirmative reply. "Did you know your wife is taking up ballet? She's doing it here in the coffee shop!"

It seems like an eternity before Seth hands me back my phone.

"Kevin?"

"Call me later. I'm working late again, but don't worry, Emily is home with Rhett. Your baby is fine." He pauses. "Please stop doing ballet in public. I'm sure it has something to do with wanting to ditch Seth, but Ash? You're no dancer."

"Rude."

"Emily promised to take Rhett for a walk."

No doubt, in full make-up.

"All right."

"Ashley?"

"Yeah."

"I may not be reachable for a few days."

"Wait, what?"

Kevin hangs up before he answers me.

Seth stares at me, blinking several times like a lizard in direct sunlight.

"What was that all about?" I ask him.

"It doesn't matter. I have to run." He moves so quickly, he knocks the chair back with a loud clang onto the tile floor. And he leaves. Just like that. I don't know what Kevin said to him, but it's clearly a skill I need to learn. It's clearly more effective than public ballet.

Chapter 9

I CALLED A taxi from the coffee shop. Who knew they had taxis in Silicon Valley? Well, Google apparently, because that's how I figured it out. I was under the assumption that when you moved to Silicon Valley, you inherently purchased a Prius, Leaf or Tesla and that was the end of it. Public transportation is virtually non-existent, although fancy Apple and Google busses are readily available. If you're employed, they're going to make sure you're getting to work—even if you don't have the compulsory hybrid.

The taxi driver is Sikh and he's wearing a turban. He's listening to foreign music that lights up some Pavlovian part of my brain and I suddenly feel as if I'm getting dropped off at some outdoor market-place. He's extremely polite when he plugs the address into his GPS, but after that, he doesn't say a word until we reach my destination, so I'm left to ponder how America misses out on all the great outdoor Bazaars in lieu of malls.

"Thank you," I tell him as we get to Brea's mom's house. I double the fare to make up for the short ride.

He takes the money and hands me a card. "You call if you need a pick-up."

"I will, thank you."

As I stand on the sidewalk and stare at Brea's childhood home, it occurs to me how often I've avoided my best friend's mother. The house is a two-story, blue Colonial with white shutters and birch trees lining the circular drive. In other words, everything is picture-perfect…until you enter and understand how Mrs. Browning's iron-fisted control keeps it that way.

I ring the doorbell and wait. I can hear Brea's boys inside, so I know she's in there, but the quick harsh steps on the marble entry tell me that her mother will answer the door. And I will cower.

Mrs. Browning swings open the door and glares down at me from atop her pointy nose. Seriously? *Why do mean people always have pointy noses?* Which comes first, the nose or the mean? Mrs. Browning always scared me, as she never thought I was a good influence on her daughter.

Let's be honest, we weren't a good influence on *each other.*

It takes Mrs. Browning a minute to comprehend me at her doorstep. "Ashley, is that you? Whatever did you do to your hair? It looks ghastly. You're married to a doctor, looking like that?"

"Uh, thank you?"

"What are you doing here?"

"It's nice to see you, too, Mrs. Browning. I came to see Brea." I avoid adding *duh.* She always kept me waiting out on the front stoop, as if my very presence in her home would pollute its purity and sully her good name.

"It's kind of early for a social call, isn't it?"

A social call? I suppose she wants me to leave my calling card and return when she's accepting visitors. "It's three hours earlier than my time, so I guess I haven't quite adjusted yet. I assume Brea would be up with the boys."

"Well, she is, but—" Somehow, I feel like if Brea were in San Quentin, it might be easier to get in to see her. Mrs. Browning opens the door reluctantly. "Have a seat. I'll fetch her," she says wearily, and I'm actually shocked I've been invited into the great sanctuary, rather than left to ponder my worth on the front porch.

I once asked Mrs. Browning why she didn't like me. She didn't even deny it. She simply told me that she expected Christians to act better than the average population, and she didn't think I met that criteria. *Right back atcha, Mommie Dearest.*

I'm glad Jesus has a better entrance policy than she does. I admire those who have no clue when others don't like them. They live in that ignorant bliss and have normal conversations with people who can't stand them. I have no such luck in my life. When people reject me, I'm well aware of it.

The Browning house, which was always spotless—and not like Kay's house, where it's homey and the cleanliness calls to you like a *Real Simple* magazine—is in that *don't-sit-there, not-there-either* way. It's as if the house has proverbial giant hands, open-faced and ready to shove you out the door as you arrive.

Today, however, the house is chaotic. Toys litter the usually pristine living room with its white carpet and the same ice-blue sofas from when we were children. The 60's lamps, with their bulbous aqua glass bases, are catawampus on the carved end tables, and there are remnants of fishy crackers smashed near the fireplace. I can only imagine how well this living situation is going.

Mrs. Browning is a widow, which surprises no one, I suppose. The fact that Brea's dad made it as long as he did is more of a mystery.

Brea comes down the stairs with her hair, which is usually a mass of springy curls, in a wild pineapple bun exploding off the top of her head. She looks tired and drawn. Unreasonably so for her age, and I want to fix it. Why I think I can fix things, when they usually end in disaster, I will never understand.

"Auntie!" Miles comes at me and nearly takes me out by grabbing my knees. "Did you bring us more presents?"

"No, but I want to take you out for a yummy breakfast. Have you had breakfast yet?"

"No," Jonathan yells. "Can we get pancakes?"

"We can get pancakes. Brea, you up for pancakes?"

"Boys, we can have cereal." She is heavy-lidded and not herself. This is the Brea I remember from childhood, the one who was afraid of her own shadow. *I need to get her out of the house.* "We don't really do restaurants. Have you met my boys? They create their own weather pattern. I mean, look at this place."

"Obviously, I'll have to train my own kids to eat in restaurants. Go get dressed. I'll clean up the house, and the boys will help me. Won't you boys?"

They both shake their heads.

I raise my brows. "Not even for chocolate chip pancakes? Because I would clean for chocolate chip pancakes."

They stare me down with their intense eyes and decide I'm serious, then they do some sort of mind meld, nod in agreement and start to pick up their toys.

"Go get dressed," I say to Brea again.

"Ashley, they can have cereal."

Not unless it comes with a side of Prozac. "We are getting out of the house."

Brea visibly relaxes at the order, but I've only incited Mrs. Browning. "Ashley, you haven't taken two four-year-olds to breakfast, have you?"

"They'll be good. Won't you boys? If they were my kids, they'd already be perfect angels in a restaurant, because I don't like to cook."

Mrs. Browning sniffs. "What is it you like to do besides shop, Ashley?"

"I cook every night for my husband, Mrs. Browning. It doesn't mean that I enjoy it."

"You know they can't sit still. Regardless of what they say."

"This will be good practice for me, and if they mess with me, there will be *no more presents.*" I lower my voice. "Brea, go get dressed. I've got this." I take Jonathan by the hand. "All right, first we're going to pick up all the toys. Do you have a box that you keep them in?"

Jonathan nods, runs to the corner, and drags a big, blue plastic tub to the center of the living room.

Brea slogs back up the stairs in her slippers. Mrs. Browning is still present, with her arms crossed tightly across her chest, her spindly fingers crawling up her arms like two daddy longlegs spiders. "Ashley, these boys are not trained for restaurants. They eat healthy, nutritious meals at home. Chocolate chip pancakes?"

"Moderation, Mrs. Browning. I'll take them to the park afterwards to burn off the excess energy." I want to tell her this is her job, to spoil her grandchildren. I want to tell her she's failing miserably at it, and I must interfere.

"In case you haven't noticed, Brea has no excess energy. She's been quite lethargic lately."

Yeah, that's called depression from living in your lair. I remember it well. "I'll bring Brea back home first. I never get to see my little nephews, and Auntie Ashley needs to spoil them."

She tsks-tsks and I feel it as if I was Miles' size. Both boys look at their grandmother, as if preparing for the great unleashing, but she refrains.

"Why don't you go take a long, hot bubble bath and enjoy the quiet?" I suggest.

"Why don't I sit on the sofa and eat bon-bons?"

The boys are still now—looking back and forth between their grandmother and me. "Why don't you? The world is your oyster. I'm sure you deserve the break. It can't be easy having two little ones under your feet all day."

Mrs. Browning softens ever so slightly, and I go in for the kill.

"Come on, Mrs. B. Don't worry about them. You work so hard every day. Pamper yourself this morning. I promise, I can't do any major damage in one morning." Though, after last night's dinner party, that may not be true. That only took me twenty minutes.

"Boys, let's go in the backyard and clean up the toys out there." I open the patio door and step outside into the bright sunshine. The heady scent of gardenias with freshly cut grass meet me. Across the great expanse of grass is the old swing, hanging from the ancient oak that canopies most of the yard.

"Whose scooter is that by the swing?"

Both boys shrug with their darling, pudgy hands up and I jog back to the scooter littering the lawn. I pick it up and place it on the brick path, and I pump once. Just once, mind you. My maxi skirt is suddenly ripped from my body with the force of the nearby NASA wind tunnel. I plunge toward the lawn and try to decipher what happened, as I suddenly feel a breeze on my backside. I spit out some grass and see Jonathan and Miles standing over me as if I'm Lilliputian. My bare, pasty legs reflect the sun's rays and I take note of my skirt wrapped tightly into the wheels of the scooter.

"You're in your undies." Jonathan points. "Mommy says undies stay in the potty. 'Cept at naked time."

"Naked time?" I try to maintain as much decorum as a woman, clad only in her granny panties can, while I yank at my skirt. It's stuck in the scooter's wheels and it won't give way, no matter how hard I tug.

"Uh-oh," Miles says.

"Miles, can you do me a favor and go get your mommy?" I plead while I struggle with the skirt some more, only to hear a telltale sharp rip of fabric, like a sheet being torn in two.

"Uh-oh," Jonathan repeats.

"Jonathan, your mommy. Can you get her please?"

But it's too late. I look up at the white French doors, and Mrs. Browning is between them with her sneering gaze.

Really, what can I say? I'm in her backyard in my delicates with her grandsons. There is no recovering from this. I accept my fate. But she says nothing. She disappears into the house and returns with a towel. "Cover yourself."

I do. I'm grateful to my mother, subscribing to the old adage recommending clean underwear in case you were in a car accident. *Or, you know, a scooter incident.*

My skirt is in tatters, so when I finally slink back into the house with the towel wrapped around me, Mrs. Browning greets me with a floor-length, emerald-green polyester skirt, that I can only assume is her 1970's attempt at the Maxi-skirt. "Now, can I get the boys some cereal?" she asks.

I reach for the textured, itchy skirt and pull it on gratefully. She avoids all eye contact while I do so. "Thanks for the skirt."

She lifts up the scooter, now strewn with shreds and threads from what used to be my skirt. "I think this is history."

I nod, and she takes a pair of scissors to it and hacks it off the scooter's wheels.

Brea comes down the stairs, fully dressed with her dark hair in its familiar loose waves that frame her beautiful face. "Ready."

"Really? You got ready that fast? You've shortened your routine a bit, haven't you?"

"Survival skills. If I take too long, I pay the price in a mess elsewhere." Brea's eyes narrow. "Were you wearing that before?"

"You're really going to take the boys to breakfast?" Mrs. Browning asks again, as if we're taking them before a firing squad. "They can stay with Grandma!"

"No!" The boys whine in unison.

I know just how they feel. Mrs. Browning always brought out the whiner in me, too.

"The boys won't bother Ashley," Brea says. "She's done worse in restaurants on her own. Besides, she's got the clown hair going on, if we get into trouble, we'll just say it's part of her act." Brea shakes her head at me. "You're totally making me crave a Big Mac."

"You're just jealous." I pat my scarlet locks.

If Kevin worried that I was no longer the Ashley with the sparkle, I wish he could see Brea right now. Maybe we need each other to sparkle. Brea loves me for me: Clown hair, her mother's polyester disco skirt and all. I'm home at last, and I force myself to forget Kevin's mystical disappearing act, Kay's dysfunctional version of romance and my lack of employment.

Chapter 10

"OH MY GOSH, this thing is like a boat!" I say as I steer Brea's minivan toward the restaurant. She's snuggled into the passenger seat with her eyes blissfully closed.

"I love that you can just be with me and not talk at me," she says without opening her eyes.

Translation: Her mother never puts a cork in it.

"Our cafe is gone. Look, new owners—" I point to the loopy, red letters in Korean above the sign. "Now Serving American Breakfast."

"They'll have pancakes, so whatever. Are you going to explain that skirt?"

"I'd rather not."

Brea's personality is normally bubbly to the point of exhaustion. She's the kind of woman who can get knocked into a lake, fully clothed, and emerge with a bright smile and say, "The temperature is just perfect! You should come in with me."

That light has dimmed in her, and how do you tell someone they're fading...or that it's probably from the close proximity to their toxic mother? This may require more tact than I possess.

We walk into the new restaurant and the white plastic menu looms brightly over the Formica counter. The menu is sprinkled with unprofessional food pictures—which hardly look appetizing. One side is pale, runny scrambled eggs alongside bacon and pancakes. The other half is Korean—which appears to be tofu, vegetables and green onion pancakes in various combos.

"Something tells me chocolate chip pancakes are not on the menu anymore," Brea whispers.

"Never mind. They still have the aquarium." Jonathan and Miles make a beeline for the oversized tank, filled with large orange and black koi.

"Mommy, look!" Jonathan says.

"Sit anywhere," the waitress announces.

"We'll sit next to the aquarium if that's okay," Brea says. We take our seats in an old booth that's probably been here since 1950 for all of the restaurant's various forms. The waitress hands us menus then gives the boys kiddie menus with coloring crayons. The waitress slides away the chopsticks and replaces them with traditional American silverware cinched by a paper napkin.

"Can I start you off with some drinks?"

"Can I have a Diet Coke?" Brea asks.

"Anything for the boys?"

"Chocolate milk. Ash, you want a drink yet?"

"Just water, please."

The waitress takes off. The boys rise from the bench seat and drift towards the fish tank as if led by a tractor beam. They palm-plant their hands on the aquarium.

"Boys, don't touch the fish tank," Brea says in a weary tone.

There's a brief recognition of Mom's voice, but their hands remain firmly on the glass.

"I forgive you for not telling me you were living with your mother, by the way."

"That's big of you."

"Brea, you have got to get out of there. Do you want to be like me? Giving up all sense of dignity to live in a house bought my in-laws?"

"Thanks, Captain Obvious. Let's talk about something else. What did Kay want you out here for?"

"Next topic—"

"She's marrying Matt, isn't she? I saw them at Easter service, and I knew. Why else would he make an appearance at church?"

I toss the menu down. "I want to support Kay. She tells me she's tired of being alone. That this might be the last chance she has to be a mother. What if she doesn't meet someone else and she blames me forever?"

"Blames you for what? Not liking Matt Callaway? That has to be an exhaustive list."

"No, I found something." I try to be as delicate as possible, considering I have little more than my suspicions. "Do you think Matt would use Kay's own house to cheat on her?"

"I think the bigger question is, do you think he would do that? And if you do, why wouldn't you share your fears with Kay?"

"Because I'm a wuss." I drop my head and sigh. "I've got nothing tangible. Nothing I can trace back to him, so do I really have something to say to her? Or am I putting off planning the most beautiful wedding shower for a friend I love because I don't like her boyfriend?"

Brea doesn't buy my false bravado for a second. "So you'll hide the truth from her, let her get married, have 2.5 kids and then be there for her when she finds out he's still cheating?"

"But I don't *know* that he's cheating." I fiddle with the napkin, wrapped tightly around the silverware. "I just found personal items in the guest room."

Brea's eyes widen. "I don't want to know. But from all I know of Kay, such 'personal items' as you put it, don't add up."

"Don't worry, I wasn't going to tell you. You think I want to defile someone else with my findings?"

"He's gross. I'm just going to say it." Brea wrinkles her nose. "I know everyone has different tastes and all that, but he gives me the willies. He always has. He's like a dirty used shoe at the secondhand store."

"Thank you for that visual. Though I secretly love it when Pollyanna goes rogue and gives us a dose of her truth."

"Just tell her whatever you found, and again," she puts up her hand and says, "I don't want to know what it was. But tell her you found it, and be done with it."

"Last night is the first time I ever heard Kay sound like me—Kay wants a husband and a family. Who knew?

"She wants marriage on her terms though, and regardless of whether Matt cheats or not, there are consequences to her terms. He's not a believer. He's a patent attorney—"

"Excuse me?"

"So you know his hours are long, I mean." Brea shrugs. "You just have to tell her your suspicions. Period. It's like the Gospel. You're called to go out and tell the Good News. In this case, the bad news, but you're not responsible for the outcome."

"If they break up, she'll never forgive me."

"No, I get it. It's a no-win. Kay likes her world so ordered, and you simply can't control love. You have to tell her she will never be able to control this or anyone."

"She controlled me pretty well, actually."

"No one will ever control you, Ashley Stockingdale Novak." Brea gets out a wet wipe and roughly cleans her sons' hands. "Tell her the truth, then if she still wants to go ahead, you slap a smile on your face and plan Camelot. She probably won't listen anyway. You didn't listen to us about Seth, but it's a moral issue, Ashley. You have to tell her. Most likely, it's your own paranoia, and this is all just created drama because you need a job."

"A moral issue? Way to add pressure." I drop my face into my hands. "Oh Lord, I do need a job. I have no purpose, and I came here to discover one, only to find more ways to avoid a purpose."

Brea shakes her palms at me. "This drama? This is why your housewife shows exist. Those women have nothing better to do with their time. The old Ashley would have said, 'Hey Kay, I think Matt might have a different definition of monogamy than you do. It would be a conversation. It would be over, and you'd go back to work, back to flubbing up your next meal for Kevin."

I groan. I hate it when she's right.

"So when are you going to tell me why you're living with your mother?"

"It's no big deal. It's not that bad actually," Brea says in her typical, sunny tone.

"Andrea Bocelli could have walked into that house and felt the tension."

She opens her mouth to speak, but I cut her off.

"Yes, I know blind people are more perceptive in their other senses. That isn't what I meant, and you know it."

"I didn't want to burden you. It's so hard on John. He's so ashamed. Telling people we lost our house just feels like a betrayal toward him and rubbing salt in the wound. It's not his fault."

Something pops into my head, and I lose track of our conversation. "Where were your dogs? I just realized your dogs weren't at the house."

Brea's cool exterior starts to crumble, until she looks at her boys in front of the tank, seems to find strength in them, and straightens her back as if to say she will not be defeated. "The dogs are staying with Kelly and Pastor Max. My mom wouldn't let us bring them to the house." She lets out a laugh. "I should probably be grateful she let me bring the boys."

Brea always saw the glass not just half-full, but overflowing and brimming with abundance. If fairy godmothers painted a muse, she would look like Brea. Noting her ashen expression, I know the average person would be slitting their wrists by now. "Are you going to tell me how you got there?"

"You realize you're doing it again?" Brea says. "Stirring up my troubles, so you don't have to face your own. Worrying about Kay and her impending engagement. Even having dinner with Seth and Arin. Why are you here, Ashley?"

"I'm not! I'm concerned about my best friend living with her mother. I don't want to come find her corpse in a rocking chair."

"Why aren't you working?" she asks me point-blank. "The real reason."

"I thought of getting a job at Starbucks, or Nordstrom to pass the time, until we move again."

"Ashley, I hate to remind you of this, but you were never great at keeping jobs, even when you had all the right credentials."

"I kept my jobs."

"Barely. Let's be honest."

"Let's not. Pretending is so much better on my ego." I try to defend myself. "The work was never my problem. It was the drama. I was working for a cocaine addict. Then, my ex-boyfriend came to work there, then—"

"What's the common denominator, Ashley? For the drama, I mean? How many people do you know who worked for a cocaine addict?"

"Well, everyone at Gainnet for a time, smarty-pants."

"And how many people have their ex-boyfriends come to work for that company at the same time as they break-up?"

"Are you suggesting that I invite my own drama?"

"If the shoe fits—"

"Buy it," I say, finishing her sentence. But as I consider that Seth did approach me at the coffee shop this morning, maybe there's truth in her assertion. "How does one invite drama? Do I have a calling card?"

"I wouldn't know. As you can see, my life has very little drama unless it involves a toilet and missing Lego blocks."

I raise my eyebrows. "Seriously? You're living with your mother and you have two little monkeys. That's dramatic."

"I not a monkey," Jonathan says.

"It's an expression, Jonathan. Of course, you're not a monkey. You're far cuter than a monkey," I tell him, while thinking I clearly need to work on my parenting skills.

"I like monkeys!" Miles says, slapping his hand against the aquarium. "Auntie, will you take us to the zoo?"

"Before I go back home, yes, I will take you to the zoo."

"Want to go now!" Jonathan sings.

"We're going to have Mickey Mouse pancakes now," I say calmly, as I point to the picture on the Kiddie menu.

"Zoo! Zoo! Zoo!" the boys begin to chant.

"We can't go to the zoo if you don't act nicely in the restaurant." The boys quiet and I stare at their mother as if to show her how it's done.

The waitress brings Brea's Diet Coke, and she shoves a straw in the glass and sips.

Miles stands up on a chair that he's pulled over to the tank. "Fishes!"

"Fish," Brea says. "The plural of fish is fish."

"Fishes!" Jonathan repeats.

"Sit down on your bottoms," Brea says firmly, and they know she's not messing around. He sits down like she pushed him with an invisible hand. *Ah, to wield that kind of power.* "John's got no money trouble at all. It's a certain paternal figure in John's life."

I nod in understanding. John's father always lived life on the edge. Talk about creating drama. If I created my own, John's dad was an entire season of *Downton Abbey*.

"Indian casino," she whispers behind a cupped hand.

My eyes widen. I never took John's father for a gambler, but if I've learned anything in life, it's that no one knows what goes on behind closed doors. He was a deacon at the church.

"He stole some money from the church coffers, so John felt responsible to pay it back. They trusted him."

My heart grieves hearing this. "I'm so sorry. How long do you think you'll be at your mother's? Will you be able to buy another house?"

"Eventually. A smaller one—maybe a townhouse."

"It's too bad you can't buy your mom a townhouse. She doesn't need all that space, and you're in such a good school district there."

"Yeah. Too bad it would never occur to her to sell to us. Okay, let's talk about something else. Don't get involved Ashley. The world has gone on without you here for two years."

"It really hasn't. When I left, I burned Kay's clipboard. I spoke to the singles' group and told them to get a life and send a thank you card to Kay. You know what? She's doing exactly the same thing, enabling their bad, parasitic lifestyle. You and John are living with your mother. The entire reason everyone's life is falling apart is because I'm not here to tell it like it is. That's the problem. That's my calling."

Brea starts cracking up. "You are so freakin' narcissistic. You really think we've all fallen apart without you. I don't think that's it, Ashley. Remember, it's only your truth, it's not like it's Gospel."

"Seriously!" I say to convince her. "Seth even said as much to me this morning."

Brea rocks her head back and forth. "What do you mean what Seth said to you this morning?"

"He showed up at my coffee shop this morning and we ran into each other."

"You ran into each other, or he stalked you?"

"Stalked me? Gosh, that's very exciting to think about, being stalked at my age." I lean in toward her. "Do you think he was stalking me?"

"See what I mean? Drama. No one wants to be stalked but you, Ashley."

"Okay, I don't really want to be stalked. I just think it's cool to be exciting enough to have a stalker."

"Your life really is boring in Philly."

"If you only knew. The people on the infomercials are my best friends. I know the home shopping network hosts by name."

Even saying it out loud I'm stunned to hear what my life has become. "Everyone seems stuck in some way, Brea. When is God going to loosen this grip and let us run free again?"

"He may not think we need to run free. Besides, maybe God wants us all to see that we're not as stuck as we think we are." Brea's lost in thought for a moment. "That we have options and need to make some hard choices—like we had to when selling the house. It was either let the entire church take the fall, or our family."

"That's very noble of you, but honestly, I'd be happy to know I was living with my mom because it had some purpose. I feel like everyone else has this spiritually-profound purpose in life, and I'm just an extra in a red shirt on *Star Trek*."

"You're in Philly because that's where your husband is, and he's your world. Maybe you're bored because God is trying to prepare you for how monotonous motherhood can be." Brea looks at her boys and her entire face lights up. "Dear Father God, they are so beautiful, aren't they, Ashley? But some days, if I have to read 'The Foot Book' one more time? I think I'll go stark raving mad."

I look over at her lack of monotony. "They are beautiful." I pause and gaze at the boys longingly. "And so healthy."

Brea drops her hands onto the table, hard enough for the silverware to clink. "That's it. You're afraid to be a mother."

"What? Kevin and I are waiting for—"

Brea looks at the boys and screams. Miles is *in* the fish tank. He's splashing water as he tries to get to he surface, and before I can blink, Brea is on top of the chair fishing him out. The little boy sputters as Brea pats his back, and I'm still too in shock to do anything but grab Jonathan's hand and pull him away from the tank. I reach into my purse, grab a $20 bill and leave it on the table as we scramble out of the empty restaurant with Brea shouting apologies as she snuggles her dripping son close to her.

My stomach is in knots as I think about seeing Miles' face under water with the glass between us. "Oh my gosh, they move so fast!

What are you feeding them?"

I take off my light, white sweater, and Brea wraps it around Miles. "My baby," she says, as she clutches him tightly to her and cups his head into her body. "My sweet baby."

"Oh my goodness, seriously? That's parenthood? They move so quickly—it's like containing lightning." I look back at the fish tank, and it's at least four feet from the top of the chair. "There is no earthly way he could have gotten in there."

"I'm a terrible mother!" Brea bawls. "God is punishing us. He's punishing John for marrying such a stupid woman."

"Brea, stop it. You're a fantastic mother. What's happened to you? You sound like me, and the world only has room for one of me."

"I just fished my kid out of a fish tank."

"How did he get up there?" I ask her. "It was physically impossible."

We soon fall into giggles as I take the slippery Miles into my arms while Brea unlocks the minivan and gets Jonathan in his carseat.

"In his defense," I say, "he did tell you he wanted to go to the zoo. I'll concede that maybe breakfast out and deep conversation was a bad idea."

"Mommy, I hungry," Miles says.

Brea clicks him into his carseat. "Then you shouldn't have gone fishing before breakfast."

Brea and I ply her boys with Noah's Bagels, then we visit Target for new outfits to erase all signs of koi kissing. We bring them back to Kay's house, bathe them and basically start the day all over again.

As I slip the little T-shirt over Jonathan's head, I tell him, "Reset! We're going to start this day all over again."

Jonathan shakes his head. "No, no."

"You didn't have to buy them both outfits, Ashley."

"Your mother's still going to ask why they're dressed differently. At least this way we can say I needed to shop. That much she'll believe."

Brea pulls a shirt over Miles' head and agrees.

"You can't keep living like this," I tell her, as the boys occupy themselves by jumping up and down on my bed. *Well, Kay's bed.*

"Living like what?" she asks, as if we haven't spent a full morning trying to hide Aquarium-gate from her mother. I know I'm speaking at her about all she needs to change, when I'm just avoiding that I need to change things myself. It's so much easier to see other people's garbage, isn't it? I mean, everyone has a PhD in dealing with other people's issues, but they're in the alternative school when it comes to their own. Rather than reveal my own fears and mistakes, I go after hers with zeal.

"Like you might get caught making a mistake. No one is perfect, and you can't live like this—ever vigilant. It's like being in fight-or-flight mode all the time. The body is only equipped to deal with adrenaline overload for short spurts of time—like when you're running from a tiger."

"Have you met my mother? It's all I know."

I flick on the Nickelodeon station for the boys. She puts little sandals on Miles, which he wants no part of and wriggles as much as possible.

"No sues," he says.

"Yes, shoes." Brea flips the sandals with a faster motion than I've seen from an airport shoeshine guy, and then, the boys are in monkey motion again.

The doorbell rings and the boys stop jumping on the bed momentarily.

"Who could that be in the middle of the day? I hope it isn't Bob the Builder—I mean, Matt Callaway."

"Bob the Builder! Bob the Builder!" the boys squeal while they jump on my bed.

I leave the bedroom and make my way to the front door. It's a man that I don't recognize on the porch. He's wearing a grey suit with a yellow tie, and a baby blue shirt. He looks innocuous enough, but he could be a vacuum cleaner salesman, and they are impossible to get rid of. "Who is it?"

"The name's Thomas Galway." He leans in towards the door. "Ashley? You don't know me, but I'm Matt Callaway's business partner. I'd like to discuss a proposition with you. It's regarding your status as a patent attorney."

I unlatch the door and open it. "I recognize your name," I tell him. "You used to be at Silicon Graphics."

"I did." He nods. Although he's clean-cut and well-groomed, there's something wild about him. He's got the slightest touch of Mick Jagger in him, a lawless look that I can't place, but I imagine makes him very popular with the ladies in Silicon Valley.

I open the door. "If you're looking for Matt, he's not here yet." *And you should tell him to work from his own house because his presence annoys me.*

"No, I'm actually here to see you."

There was a day when that sentence would have had me planning my wedding. Brea and the boys come out of the bedroom. "I'm interrupting," Thomas says.

Imagine that when you show up unannounced? "This is my friend Brea and her boys. Brea, this is Thomas Galway. He works with Matt."

"Nice to meet you." Brea shakes his hand. "We'll just wait in the bedroom."

It was obvious that Brea was ready to go, but upon finding a strange man in the living room, decided to wait out his visit. No doubt her finger is perched on the 9-11 button. She always claimed I was too trusting and I do manage to get myself into a bit of trouble occasionally, but Thomas is probably an engineer and a lawyer. How much damage could he do? Not to mention that I could probably take him.

"So what's this about?"

He stands a little straighter, as if he's preparing for some grand speech. "Matt told me you were staying here, and mentioned your outstanding credentials, but figured you wouldn't believe him about the role we had for you." He lifts up a navy blue paper folder.

It's not that I don't believe Matt. I just dislike him. And I think that my cocaine-dealing boss should always be the worst one I ever had.

"Role?" My eyebrows rise of their own volition. "Why don't you have a seat?"

He wags his head, which shakes the Mick Jagger scruff on his neck.

"I live in Philadelphia now, so I'm not really looking for a role in California." But let's face it, I am looking for a role. I mean, the role of surgical intern's wife is a lonely one. Possibly more lonely than when I was single.

"Just hear me out," Thomas says. "You don't like Matt – which is completely understandable."

"I know, right?" I cover my lips with my fingertips as I realize I said that out loud. "I mean, how did you know that? Do I have a sign on my back or something?"

"Matt told me he wasn't your favorite person and that might influence your wanting to work at the firm. He's not a very likable person, I'll grant you that, but he knows his stuff." He claps his hands together then pulls a folder from his briefcase. "I'll get right to the point. I've seen your background on LinkedIn and I want to make you an offer. You can stay in Philly, but we can work with you from there. You'd have to be here maybe one week every two months, but this is a lucrative business and I'd make it worth your while."

My heart is pounding at the idea of getting back to work and litigating patents stolen from unsuspecting creatives. I can see myself in a Wonder Woman costume, twirling my lasso to attack the aggressors. In a figurative way, of course. No longer would I be beige, but I'd be red, white, and blue and pursuing truth, justice, and the American way.

Brea is behind me with a kid at the end of each arm. "We've got speech therapy."

Translation: *Thomas looks okay. I'm leaving.* She heaves a giant bag over her shoulder, but she stays put.

I look back at Thomas. "I'm not really in a position to accept a job. My husband is home, and we'd need to discuss this together." Saying the words, I realize how much it annoys me that I'm supposed to check-in with my husband who never answers his phone, and isn't actually available to me. But I don't want to think about that, so I focus on Kay's problems with Matt, instead.

Thomas Galway may know more about Matt's dating activities than Kay. He might even have some idea as to where the lawless undies came from.

"Have you ever been at Kay's place before?" I ask him.

His expression contorts, as if I've asked him if he's into threesomes. "Why would I come here before? Matt said you were staying with a friend. I've taken the liberty of putting my offer on paper and explaining rights, rules and our company expectations and payment schedules for successful patents." His face is still pruned up like a dried apricot.

"Matt didn't mention any connection to my friend? No engagement or entanglements of any sort on his side?"

"Matt and I make it a policy not to discuss our personal lives. We don't have time."

"That sounds healthy," I say sarcastically.

"We're on the job at different times, at all hours, you know how it is. We need more patent attorneys, and most of them are making so much at their firms, they're not willing to risk coming over for percentages of start-ups, but you—you haven't had anything going on for over two years now."

"I'm happily married," I tell him, as if this is all I need find fulfillment. If I were cut from the same cloth as Brea, maybe it would be true. At the moment, my lack of fulfillment seems like nothing more than another character flaw.

He ignores this personal data. "I want you on our team, Ashley. It's a highly profitable business with a significant level of satisfaction in saving these smaller companies from those using the laws falsely." He drops a folder on the coffee table. "Look it over, and call me before you leave for Philadelphia. My business card is in there."

"That's it? You don't want to interview my past employers or anything?"

"I've seen your work. If I cared about your personality, I wouldn't be working with Matt, would I?"

As quickly as he appeared, Thomas Galway disappears, and for the first time in months, I have options. Well, an option.

I look at Brea and think about how truly different we are – being married is enough for her. It's always been enough for her. What's wrong with me? If I were living with my parents, I'd move heaven and earth to get out. Brea just accepts what comes her way and floats along like a leaf on a current.

"That was weird," Brea says.

"I know, right?"

"I've got to get the boys to their speech therapy. Do you want a ride to your mother's house?"

"Thanks, not yet. I want to make sure her houseguests are gone. Plus, I need to look for something here."

"If this has to do with Matt, you need to decide what you're going to do. If that's the man Kay wants, it's the man she wants, but you need to tell her the truth. And before you take a job, any job, you need to figure out what you're running from."

"Don't be ridiculous. I'm not running from anything. Friends don't let friends date dirtbags."

"Sometimes, friends have no choice."

I don't even finish the sentence when Matt walks in the door— without knocking. He sizes up Brea in an inappropriate manner, then looks at the kids. "You running a preschool?"

"On that note, we'll be leaving." Brea exits with the boys. "Matt," she says under her breath as she passes him.

Matt and I stand in the foyer staring at each other awkwardly. I try to think about how to ask this question appropriately, but it boils over. "Did you have some chick here in Kay's house? Some tramp who left her underwear behind?"

"What?" His wrinkled forehead suggests I'm in need of a straight-jacket.

"Look," I tell him. "I may have some issues, but I know where my underwear are at all times."

"I'm sure you do, Ashley."

"Normal people don't leave their chones behind at other people's houses, and I know those aren't Kay's."

"I have no idea what you're talking about. Do you know how peaceful it is without you here?"

His words take the breath from me. Is that how Kevin feels too? But I'm on a mission.

"Last night, I found a pair of orange unmentionables underneath my bed. They were gone this morning. I don't need to tell you that Kay isn't the sort to wear orange unmentionables."

"For unmentionables, you sure are mentioning them enough. I have no idea what color underwear Kay wears, they're probably hers. And for your information, I didn't even know you could buy such things in orange. Are we done now? Because, this is beyond awkward. When are you leaving?"

"What if I said I'm not leaving?

"I'd assume that what I said all along is true. You left to be a wife and mother, and it isn't working out, so you're back."

I'm stunned silent—wondering how many others think exactly the same thing but don't have the audacity to say it aloud.

"Did Thomas speak to you?"

"He did."

Matt looks at the coffee table and sees the folder. "Ashley, take the job. It's clear that you've got too much time on your hands and there's no shame in admitting you made a mistake. Make a clean break from Philadelphia. You're a good patent attorney."

"The implication being I'm not a good wife?"

"I never said that. Quit being paranoid." Matt removes his suit jacket. "I'm here to ask you a favor."

"Me?" *Unless it's to help him off the nearest cliff, I think he has the wrong person.*

"You have to keep your mouth shut. Can you do that?"

"Maybe." *Does it involve you leaving and never coming back? Lips are sealed.*

"I've got an engagement ring picked out for Kay. I want you to come look at it before I buy it."

A numbness settles over my limbs as I realize he's completely serious.

"You're into all that fashion stuff, right?"

I nod.

"So, do you think you can help me?"

This is happening. This is really happening and I can't stop it.

"Will you go with me or not?"

"Will I go with you where?" I finally manage.

"Tiffany's. At the mall."

"Tiffany's? You're buying Kay a Tiffany ring?" Blow me over with a feather. Maybe he does value her more than I imagined.

"Of course. No wife of mine is wearing a cheap ring. I have a reputation to uphold."

My hope fades, but I'm more concerned that all my friends believe exactly what Matt Callaway had the gall to say. Maybe Kevin isn't sure. Did he send me here in the hopes that I'd find my old life again and set him free before children saddled him?

"Can you come with me? Don't make me beg," Matt prods, and I'm too caught up in my fears to argue. Maybe this is the sheer pinnacle form of love that Matt is capable of showing. The question is; am I willing to be an accomplice to his pale form of love—even if it does come in a Tiffany blue box?

Chapter 11

MATT CALLAWAY HAS the uncanny ability to unnerve me; catch me off-guard, which ticks me off. But once again, I wasn't able to speak my truth to him, and I'm on the way to the mall. As if I had no natural power of my own. This is the kind of surreal power Matt has over people—and precisely why I'm worried about Kay. She's so innocent to the world. Thinks the best of everyone. Hopefully, it will protect me when I tell her about the underwear – after I go to Tiffany's with Matt.

I tried to call Kevin while in the car, but surprise. He didn't answer.

I follow Matt into the mall, and with a rush of angels, see the blue glass empire of jewels. Tiffany & Co. The Mother Ship. Or, it would be if I were here with Kevin, and not the incredibly overconfident and thoroughly annoying, Matt Callaway. Tiffany & Co. is elegance personified. I'm more into straight-up bling—not above tacky. Definitely, I'm more Jersey Housewife than Tiffany's. But Kay is definitely Tiffany. Simple. Classic. I'd say that she's actually more REI, but one can't wear a tent or a carabiner on their ring finger.

"You're still mad at me for pointing out your marriage is in trouble."

"My marriage *isn't* in trouble," I state with a smile.

"I get it, Ashley. Your husband just isn't ready to start a family yet." He nods as if I've just lost a relative – supposedly to let me know how deceived I am.

I stop in my tracks. "Do you want my help or not, Matt?"

"Suit yourself." He shrugs. "But like I said, the sooner you get back to work, the better. The longer you're out of the game, the less opportunity you'll have to leave when the time comes."

I clench my hands tightly but refuse to give him the pleasure of acknowledging his words. Before, Matt was just an annoyance, like a buzzing fly. Now he's turned into more of a wasp, and his sting wounds.

I turn my attention to happier thoughts. Tiffany's storefront is sleek, understated glass in their signature blue. There's a security guard at the door, in front of golden, leafy wallpaper on the subtle beige floral carpet.

A quiet, library-like hush comes over me as we walk into the open area surrounded by dark wood and glass cabinets. A friendly sales person greets us, and the others step back, as if this is some kind of rehearsed royal etiquette to meet Her Majesty.

"Welcome." The team takes another step backward, as if to let us browse unencumbered by sales pressure. The wedding department is in the back of the store, a step up from the regular jewels. Matt leads me to a young Asian man in a tightly fitted gray suit with a lavender tie.

"Jimmy, this is my girlfriend's former roommate. The one I was telling you about."

Jimmy smiles broadly. "You must be Ashley. I've heard you have excellent taste."

Since you've met Matt, I obviously, have much better taste than my roommate's boyfriend. I feel guilty for a brief second, before realizing how I'm betraying Kay. What if this isn't what she wants? What if I really did see evidence of Matt's lothario ways? Can she give him an honest answer?

I try to be friendly, but I'm checking out Jimmy's left hand, and he appears to be single. I try to decipher how old he is, and if he might be interested in my very fantastic, very organized friend. But he looks to be in his twenties, definitely too young for Kay, and the weight of one of Kay's nylon tents in the garage might crush him, so I cross him off the suitable candidates list.

"Nice to meet you, Jimmy." I reach out my hand towards him, and he grasps it, shakes it once.

"Let me show you the ring that Matt has selected for his lovely bride. It's one of our finest and the diamond quality is exceptional. He's chosen a two-carat center stone."

Two carats? I take in Matt's movie star glamor and wonder if I wasn't too quick to judge. Two carats at Tiffany's is nothing to thumb one's nose at!

Okay, that was shallow.

Jimmy pulls out a pillowed bed with a classic Tiffany's sparkler on the center of it. It dawns on me that these diamonds, ironically the hardest substance on earth, are treated with kid gloves and better than most humans on the planet. The ring is a classic solitaire set in platinum. Elegant and gorgeous, but somehow, not right for Kay.

Meh.

"That's not it."

"No?" Matt asks, astonished. "Did you see it?" He pushes it closer toward me.

I flinch and bat it away instinctively. "I saw it, Matt. It's two carats, not exactly something my eyes are going to miss. But, it's too attention-hungry for Kay." I look at Jimmy. "It's beautiful. Absolutely iconic, but I don't think it's my friend's taste."

"What's wrong with it?" Matt asks me through his clenched jaw.

"Nothing's wrong with it, Matt. It's stunning. If you don't like my opinion, feel free to not take it." I stare around the room at the other salespeople. "I should just go get a pretzel. Do they still have pretzels in the food court?" I ask Jimmy.

He shakes his head. "It's on the other side of the mall now. They have a Chicken Wow."

"Chicken what?"

"Ashley, focus. The ring isn't for you," Matt reminds me.

"I know, Matt. It's way too tasteful for me." I stare past the ring at Jimmy. "I just don't think it's tasteful enough for Kay. It screams for attention, and I think Kay's ring would whisper." It dawns on me that if Matt really loved Kay, he'd know this.

"Rings don't talk," Matt snaps.

"I think the solitaire sticking up would bother her. Like it would get stuck on things, and be in the way while she cooks. She's very hospitable," I share with Jimmy. "The ring has to work with her, not be the center of attention."

"I can tell you from experience that most women wouldn't mind having that problem." Jimmy laughs.

"Kay's not most women. Listen, I agree with you. I figured out how to do laundry around my giant rock, but Kay's not like that. She's much more practical. Can we see that one?" I point to a round solitaire in a smooth, modern bezel setting. The diamond is protected by the simplicity of the platinum, as if it's hugging the diamond in a maternal way.

"An excellent choice," Jimmy says, as he looks to Matt. "It's less expensive than the one you've selected, but it's very sleek. Very modern."

"I don't like it," Matt barks. "You can't see the whole diamond. I'm buying a perfect diamond, and I want Kay to see that. I don't need to cover up the stone," Matt snaps. "People will think I've got something to hide."

Do you?

"It's an exquisite ring," Jimmy inserts. "Why don't you try it on, Ashley, so that Matt can see what it looks like on your hand?"

I extend my right hand toward Jimmy and he slides the ring on my finger. I wiggle it appropriately and watch it sparkle under the intense lights—as anyone who slips on a two-carat ring would do, to see the glint and glimmer under the brilliant bulbs.

From the corner of my eye, I see a Tiffany blue package drop to the floral carpeting, and instinctively, I reach for it. Everything unfurls in slow motion after this.

"Ashley, no!" Matt yells out, but my hand is on the package when I'm tackled from behind. The package flies into the air as if it had wings, and I'm thrust toward the exit. The security guard's uniform is a blur as he comes toward me, and my body is jarred like a sacked quarterback from behind. Whirls of colors, lights and textures fly by me as I glide across the air before landing face-first on the cold, hard tiles in the mall. I struggle to push myself off the ground when the heavy attacker strikes again and crushes me against the floor.

The world passes and tumbles around me in a mass of colors and sensations. A high-pitched alarm peels through the air, piercing the tranquility of the upscale mall with its warbling and threats of chaos. I moan in agony as my senses return to me.

"Stay down!" Matt's voice snipes at me, and I realize it's him on top of me, pressing me to the cold, flat surface. The feet of the security guard are in front of me, the cuffs of his official uniform mere inches from my head as Matt shelters me from the storm.

"Matt, move! You're hurting me." I writhe and struggle against his weight. I realize the mall cop must be after the ring, and yank it off my finger and throw it towards him, with a tinkling sound—but the fake officer makes no attempt to grasp the jewel, and it halts a few feet away from us, unclaimed like a gumball machine trinket.

Finally, the lanky, uniformed guard bends to grab the ring when another abrupt explosion shatters the delicate, blue glass from the shop's storefront. Tiny sprinkles of glinting gravel rain down over us in a destructive hail. Matt's arms surround me, and he covers me with his body.

After the explosion, I can hear people running and screaming through the cavernous, upscale mall, but Matt's burly arms cover my eyes. I struggle to get free of his grip, but he only tightens it.

"Ashley, be still," Matt whispers loudly in my ear, over the alarm.

After what feels like an eternity, the commotion stops. Everything stops but the alarm, which continues to squeal its annoyance. The police finally announce their presence, and Matt sets me free. I push off the floor, but my wrist gives way and I pummel back into the ground, nose first. I groan – of all the ways to see the mall, I never thought my face plastered on the tile would be one of them.

"Ashley?" Matt looms over me, his hand outstretched. "Are you all right?"

Instinctively, I grasp my left arm. "I think something's wrong with my wrist." My hand hangs limply and it throbs with pain. *Seriously, I'm jewelry shopping. How does this stuff happen to me?*

Tiffany's looks like the center of Beirut in the 90's. The storefront has virtually disappeared. The neat, pristine glass and wood cases are in crumbles and salespeople stand shell-shocked inside the skeleton of the shop. I roll onto my knees and rise without the use of my arms, thinking at this inopportune moment that I need to exercise more and build my core muscles.

Armed police officers and a swat team have infiltrated the mall—and it's like something on the ID network. It's not a scene I belong in—let's be real, I'd be on Bravo.

"What happened?" I ask Matt—since he clearly had a better view on top of me.

"The store was robbed. That package you reached for—"

"The pretty one wrapped like a Tiffany's gift?"

Matt nods. "It was an explosive."

"How'd you know?"

He shook his head. "I don't know. It was not there one minute then suddenly appeared, and instinct took over. It didn't seem right."

I choke over my next words, "Thank you."

Two policemen approach us. They're not in SWAT gear like the others, but regular police uniforms. "You found something of mine in the guest room," he says ominously.

"What?" I try to register what he's telling me.

"You found something I believe. I made a mistake, not the one you think I did, but I swear, never again. I got tired of waiting for Kay, and then I realized she was all I wanted. I think we should keep your discovery between the two of us."

My mouth is open, but words won't form. *What is he telling me? Are we talking about the same discovery?*

"We have some questions," an officer interrupts my spinning head and separates me from Matt.

I bury my face in my good elbow as I realize if I tell Kay, I'll break her heart. If I don't, I'm stuck with this terrible secret forever, wondering when he'll make another "mistake." At the same time, I don't know if he's actually admitted to anything? But if not, where did they go? Kay wouldn't have left that mess under the bed to carefully extract a pair of wayward undies.

"Can you stand there against the wall? We'll need a statement," my officer says. He's polite, but asks me about Matt. Seriously, if I knew more about Matt, I wouldn't be here. He eventually decides I've got nothing to say about Matt.

"Your full name?"

"Ashley Wilkes Stockingdale Novak."

He glares at me. "Really?"

"Really."

"That's a mouthful."

"On television, they give you a chair when you're being interrogated."

"You feel interrogated?" His brows raise and he gives a slight shrug. "What were you doing in the store?"

Forget what we were doing at the store. Why don't you ask him what he's been doing in his fiancée's house while he pretends to be a faithful boyfriend? They're missing jewelry, but Kay could be missing her calling.

It becomes clear after questioning that Matt and I are suspects—seriously, if I'm going the theft route—I'm not doing tasteful elegance. Rather than worry about the implications of being suspect, I wonder how I'm going to explain my situation to Kevin. A reporter, who I recognize from television, is setting up with a camera—he's got a sport coat and a tie on with a pair of faded jeans. The timing of the reporters in comparison to the police officers really makes me question public safety.

As the cameraman hoists the camera onto his shoulder, I want to melt into the wall and disappear—which isn't likely to happen with my clown hair. *What was I thinking? Why can't I just go through life like a normal person and find my next job?*

I wonder if you can claim posttraumatic stress disorder from a bad anniversary gift? Probably not. The airplane ticket would need to be one-way, most likely. Kevin did provide me a way home, but after today, I'm not sure he's going to claim me at the airport.

As I see the camera's red light go on, my heart pounds as I try to speed up the cop. "Am I going to be here long?"

"Just a few more questions. I have another officer on his way to take you to Valley Med and get your arm checked out."

"I'm fine. Totally fine," I tell him. "Was anyone hurt?"

He stares at me, but doesn't answer my question. My heart thumps in my throat, as the news camera, in all its official capacity, is aimed in my direction. I pray that none of my old coworkers will recognize me with the Ronald McDonald hair and Maxi dress. *I'm incognito as a fashion "don't."*

"So you had not seen the package prior to it landing on the carpet in the store this morning?" The policeman asks again. He's a short, squat little thing—built like a fireplug. He's bald, good-looking and official in every way, but he's really short, and for some reason, I can't get past it, because it seems like I could take him down. Maybe I'm just feeling tougher after playing *Survivor* in the mall.

"There are no height requirements for officers anymore?" I meant to just think it, but my mouth does not always comply with my brain.

If looks could kill, *shortstuff* would not need the gun perched on his hip.

I shrink a little against the wall. "No, sir. I never saw the package.

I thought someone behind the counter must have dropped it, so I went to reach for it. I'd forgotten I had the ring on. I guess that's why the security guard jumped on us."

"You've been arrested before," he says, scanning his computer. "Resisting arrest with violence? Violence against an officer?"

"That was a long time ago, and it was a big misunderstanding. I wasn't thinking straight and—"

"Mrs. Novak, you hit an officer with your handbag."

"It was a Prada," I tell him, and I can see he's not impressed. "I was really, really tired from jetlag. At the time, I worked for Gainnet, and my boss turned out to be dealing in cocaine. I think I'd just come back from Korea." It dawns on me that there's a reason there's a fifth amendment. "I'll shut up now, but seriously, the Prada store is right across the way. Go see how much they cost; the leather's like butter. I didn't hurt him. I realize you can't wield handbags at police officers now. Trust me, you're safe."

"This is not a joke, Mrs. Novak. The bomb squad will discover the origin of that package, so if you have anything to tell me about your friend's involvement, or your own, it would be best to tell me now. If you're holding back any information at all, you need to come forward."

"We were there to buy my friend Kay an engagement ring. There's nothing more to tell. He picked a gaudy ring. I fixed it, and then, this happened."

"You saw the package before your friend did?"

"I think we saw it at the same time. He thought it might be dangerous, I guess. It never dawned on me that it could be."

"Why would he think it was suspicious?"

"You'd have to ask him. When I reached for the package on the floor, he jumped me and threw me on the ground outside the store." Sudden recognition hits me like a delivery truck. "Matt Callaway..." I sputter. "Matt saved my life."

"It appears that may be the case. He saved a lot of people by acting the way he did."

"Then why are you suspicious of him? That makes no sense."

"The way he reacted was not conventional. That's why we need to know if you'd seen that package before with your friend."

"Matt saved my life. Matt hates me."

"Hate is a strong word."

"I know. That's why I used it. Matt dislikes me greatly. He only asked me to the jewelry store because he doesn't want to blow it with Kay. And he was totally going to blow it. You should have seen the giant ring he picked for her. My friend Kay, she's really conservative and she would have—"

The cop's expression warns me to stop talking. And I do.

"Does Matt hate a lot of people?"

"What?" I stammer to correct myself rather than commit slander. "No, no. I don't know. He's just a jerk. You know, a fellow lawyer. We both like to be right."

"Can we confirm that you're staying with this Kay individual and that you haven't been with Matt for the entire day?"

"You can confirm it with my best friend Brea. I was with her this morning. Oh, and with Matt's business partner. He offered me a job." I give him Brea's information. "I'll have to send you Thomas's information. I don't remember his last name."

Another officer appears, and short stuff introduces him. "This is Officer Gray. He's going to take you to Valley Med and get that wrist checked out. If we have further questions, we'll be in touch."

Officer Gray gives me a half-smile—not knowing if I'm victim or perp.

"He really doesn't need to take me to the hospital."

"Procedure, Mrs. Novak."

Procedure. Forget procedure! I'm on vacation!

Chapter 12

HOURS PASS IN the turbulent emergency room—if hospitals billed by the hour as lawyers do, triage would happen in a much timelier fashion. Officer Gray allowed me to make my "one" phone call—as I'm not under arrest, this annoys me, but after the Prada incident on my record, I simply call my mother without complaint. Kay was out of the question, since I'd have to explain why I was at Tiffany's, Kevin's in surgery, and Brea is probably still trying to explain to her mother why her boys came home in different outfits. That left Mom—my only friend, because she obviously has no choice. She gave birth to me.

The local news blares out over the waiting room, hoping to divert attention from patients' long wait. I see myself on the screen. *Strike that.* I see my hair. A little boy at his mother's knee points at me. "Look Mommy, it's that clown lady on the TV."

I try to hide behind my hand. I am making a hair appointment before the day is over.

A voice booms from the news, and it's the man in jeans with the sport coat. "Channel 14 has learned that one of the women shopping in the store at the time of the break-in was also involved in an unrelated altercation in a local Korean restaurant earlier in the day. The owners recognized the woman from our earlier broadcast, and called the studio to offer this footage.

"Really?" I say to Officer Gray.

My eyes slide shut briefly, as I silently pray there's another person involved in the mall explosion and a Korean restaurant. *It could happen.* I open my eyes and see the grainy, black-and-white surveillance video of Brea and me fishing Miles out of the aquarium. I should mention, it's not grainy enough. The footage is followed by blown-out shots of the jewelry store and my flaming hair in full, obnoxious color against the remnants of the pale, Tiffany-blue glass wall.

How symbolic.

When I was single, I thought I was unlucky in love. Now I know better. I'm just unlucky. I'm basically God's sitcom.

My mother walks in through the emergency room's automatic doors. "It's my mother," I say to Officer Gray. He nods and snaps his newspaper.

"Mom!" I grab her and hug her as if she's been gone for years.

"Ashley!" She swallows me in a hug, and I just start to sob.

"Mom, I'm so glad you're here."

She stiffens for a minute. "Just a minute, Ashley." She marches over to Officer Gray. "Is my daughter under arrest?"

"No, ma'am."

"Then, I can handle things from here. You're excused."

"Ashley Novak!" A nurse calls my name.

"Mom, wait for me, will you? Here's my purse." I hand her my things and follow the nurse into the hospital's inner sanctum. *Maybe my unemployment was more about keeping the world safe from me.*

I EMERGE FROM the ER with my wrist in a splint and my arm in a sling. My mother is waiting with my handbag on her lap. She's wearing a baby blue butterfly shirt, and once again, I contemplate how we can be related. Mom is always dressed like a grown-up toddler in matching, soft Garanimals-type wear.

"It's not broken?" she asks.

"It is," I tell her. "Hairline fracture. But they have to wait until the swelling goes down to put a cast on." I look around the still-chaotic waiting room. "Where's Officer Gray?" *AKA, my stalker.*

"He had other duties to attend to," my mom announces. Just the way she says it, I know she summarily dismissed the officer. The law is no match for my mother. She's easy-going and as flexible as Gumby, until someone messes with her kids. My mom's gentle spirit has a way of getting her whatever she wants—especially if you mess with her children. I often wonder why I didn't inherit that trait, rather than my steamroller version of speaking. If you catch more flies with honey...

"Did Officer Gray say anything? Did they figure out who did this?"

"They don't seem to know anything. At least nothing they're sharing. He did ask that you not leave the state until the investigation is over." My mom smiles subtlety.

"Mom!"

"Well, pardon me if I enjoy having my daughter back home where she belongs. There are some items apparently missing from the jewelry store. I think it had to be an inside job."

"Do you?" I grin.

"That officer wanted to go through your handbag, but knowing how your last police run-in involved a handbag, I knew you wouldn't be comfortable with that, so I told him he'd need a search warrant. I watch 20/20."

"Well, how long do they expect me to stay?" I ask. "I don't live in this state. Did you explain it to him?" I'm already feeling homeless here.

"Oh honey, he's just reading off a script. You'll cross that bridge when you come to it. Let's get you home. I have to start the roast."

I let Mom envelop me in a hug, and wish I'd gone straight to my mom's house and stayed alongside her houseguests. If I never have to see Matt Callaway again, it will be too soon.

"Clearly, I got my disdain for authority from someone."

"Now Ashley, I believe in following the law—but that's just stupid. You were shopping and the place got robbed. That makes you a witness, not a suspect, and I didn't care for them treating you as such. You're a lawyer for crying out loud." My mom cinches her fanny pack tighter around her waist. "Imagine bringing you here to the hospital in a patrol car. No wonder this state is broke. Such a waste— why didn't they allow you to call me from the mall? I'm going to write them a letter and give them a piece of my mind."

"Let me get home first, will you? I don't want Kevin to disown me." She hands my purse back to me. "You haven't said anything about my hair."

"If you don't have anything nice to say…what on earth were you doing with that Matt character? I thought you didn't care for him."

Is it wrong to admit that I had hope in him? It makes me remember I had hope in Seth, and that my hope is woefully misplaced. "Can we talk about something else?" Then, I defy my own words and go right back to the subject at hand. "What if I know for a fact he's bad news? He's proposing to Kay, and I went with him to pick out the ring. It's like my stamp of approval."

"Well." Mom shrugs. "Kay never did think much of your stamp of approval, anyway."

"Mom, I know something about him. Do I tell her?"

"Tell Kay, your old roommate? Well, I'll be a monkey's uncle." My mom's eyebrows rise. "Hmm."

"Hmm, what?" I want to hear her say that this is an impossible couple, and I must do whatever I can to separate the two of them.

"I never really thought Kay was interested in men. She always seemed above the simple things like falling in love. She was too serious for it."

"Mother!"

"Well, I didn't. She always had her nose in that itinerary of hers. If anything…well—" My mother halts. "Kay just never struck me as the kind of woman who could make compromises. Maybe I had the wrong impression of her all along if she's wanting to get married now—after all these years."

Or she might be making one too many compromises.

"Well, you may as well tell me, what on earth did you do to your hair this time?" My mom runs her fingers through my locks. "Ashley, God gave you a beautiful crown, why must you always mess with it? It looks like you let a kindergartner finger paint on your head."

"I get bored. Do you mind stopping at a salon on the way home? You don't have to wait with me, I can take a taxi home. I just need to think—and obviously, fix my hair."

"I'll take you, but dinner will be late if we stop. You'll have to explain things to your father."

My father would starve if dinner weren't served to him at exactly 5:30 p.m. on a warmed plate. Dad assumes this is stand-ard/mandatory wifely behavior. I used to expect my mother to say, "Ward, I'm worried about the Beaver."

"I'll explain things to Dad. Can I also explain that as a grown man, he should be able to feed himself?"

"You may not, Missy." She grasps her saggy purse with both hands and leads me out of the hospital. "If they get home from the rod and gun show early, he'll probably be attached to the news."

My stomach plunges, and then I remember we're talking about my father. "I doubt he'd notice it was me. My hair's different."

"You don't think he'd notice his daughter and her best friend yanking a little boy out of a fish tank?"

I cringe. "Honestly? No. He's known Brea since preschool and he still can't remember her name."

"Well, it is an unusual name."

"Mom, it would be an unusual name if you hadn't heard it for nearly thirty years."

"You can hardly blame the restaurant owner for making the most of her fifteen minutes when she saw you on the telly. I mean, all publicity is good, right? That's a nice fish tank. People will like seeing that—it will probably bring them a lot of business."

"Mom!"

"Well, I'm only saying you need to see it from their point of view." I stand in the sun and relish my freedom. "The owner of the restaurant did mention that you left $20 without getting your meal."

"Only you would see the bright spot in my day, Mom."

"That was very generous of you, dear. You could have snuck out. It reminds me that I raised you right."

I feel the need to defend Brea and myself. "Mom, there is no way Miles could have physically gotten into that tank. It's like he temporary flew or something. I cannot explain it. Does the video show how he got into the aquarium?"

"Welcome to little boy motherhood. Do you remember that kid who climbed into the claw game? That was physically impossible, too. Never underestimate the sheer determination of a boy who thinks he must try something new." My mom leads me to her car and presses the button with a chirp to unlock the doors. "Once, your brother Dave climbed out of the second-floor window onto the roof to catch a helium balloon. He jumped off the roof, and praise the Lord, he landed in a tree. I found him dangling by his belt ten feet in the air."

"You never told me that story!"

"That's why you have to pray without ceasing. Without divine intervention, I don't know how any typical boy makes it to adult-hood. It's one of God's mysteries—to this mother at least."

I just laugh thinking about my brother. He's a bus driver with a wife and a small son. He loves his job. He knows his place in the world, driving college students around their campus. Maybe I just think too big. "Mom, you were happy being at home your whole life?"

She smiles as she sits in the driver's seat. "I never wanted anything more. From the time you graced us with your presence, you want-ed...you just wanted more."

I used to take that as a compliment. Did I go past my allotment of lifetime joy and received my gifts in full because I asked for too much? Maybe I was never meant to be married at all, and I forced it on Kevin and this is my punishment. "Do you think since I made my choice for marriage, I should lean into it fully? Maybe if I take some cooking classes and learn to do more things like you do, I won't feel so restless."

My mom laughs. She actually laughs at my tender moment.

"Oh," my mom says, pressing her hand to her chest. "You were serious."

I blink back the moisture pooling in my eyes and my mom's expression softens, so that the lines near her eyes crinkle with genuine concern.

My mom's CRX is pristine, with leather so waxed one glides into the bucket seat as if there's silicone on your bum. That's the impossible secret about my mother. I never see her clean a thing, and yet everything around her sparkles. She has some kind of gift, like King Midas. Instead of turning everything to gold, she leaves everything in sparkling, spotless order. This is a genetic gift that was not handed down to me.

Mom stops at a stoplight and glares at me. I know that disappointed look. It's the same one she gave me right before she told me old boyfriends got married, and she'd hand me the paper with a photo of the virginal bride, who was not me, alongside an old beau.

"Mom, I know, all right? I know. I could have been killed, but everything's fine now. If I take some culinary classes, maybe I won't be so disappointed with staying home all day. You and Brea did it. How bad could it be?"

"It's not why I'm concerned. Your phone started buzzing, and I thought Kevin might have been texting."

I shake my head. "Kevin hates to text. He'll always call, unless he's trying to keep quiet in a meeting and wants to snark on a superior."

"Kevin will do that?" My mom's face scrunches up in disbelief.

"He's not as innocent as he looks. Trust me."

"Speaking of innocence, when I read the texts. Three of them," she says, looking over her glasses pointedly. "They were from Seth Greenwood."

My throat catches. My mom is not a fan of Seth's, but seriously, does she know me at all? "What? I'm suddenly the wanton woman because I have no job? Slap an *A* on my shirt, why don't you?"

"Never mind. I simply wrote him back and reminded him that my daughter was married, but then he texted again. He said your old boss, Purvi, is back in town and would it be okay to give her your number? I told him that would be fine and no more communication was necessary."

I laugh. "Of course you did." I try to explain further, lest my mother think I'm starring on an episode of *Scandal*. "Seth wants me to help him with Arin," I say truthfully. "I guess things are tough with them, and I thought—I don't know what I thought." *Maybe I was slightly flattered.* "I tried to avoid him, Mom, I swear, but maybe there's some part of me that felt superior to Arin, which made me feel some part of *Successful Ashley* rather than *Failure Ashley*. And right now, all I feel is *Failure Ashley*."

"You make it sound as if you're two Barbie dolls. I'm curious, what would *Failure Ashley* wear?"

I hold up my wrist as far as it will reach. "Black. She wears a lot of black and migrates to Starbucks, hoping to find someone who can speak technology to her and make her feel like less of an alien."

"You realize that's all in your head. The old Ashley who left here would have taken the bar exam. She would have risked it, even though she was only planning to stay in Philly temporarily. It would have been a notch in her lipstick case."

"Uh, I think that's a sex reference, Mom."

"Well, you know what I mean."

"I thought I could help Seth and Arin, and maybe that's why God allowed me back home for a time. I was misguided. Then, I thought I could help support Brea, and her son ended up in the drink. Again, I was misguided. Finally, I tried to put my personal feelings aside and help Matt propose. That led to personal injury, so I don't know. I have no better idea about my life's purpose here than I did in Philadelphia. It's not the setting, Mom. It's me."

"Well, in Matt's defense, Ashley, everything seems to lead to personal injury with you. Remember that time you tried to get attention from that boy and wore floaties into the pool when you were thirteen?"

"Can we not bring that up?"

Mom starts to laugh, and soon she's in full-fledged giggles. "The look on your face when you got stuck in the filter with that big orange blob on your arm. The whole pool emptied out when you started screaming."

"It was traumatic. If I'd been a toddler in floaties, I would have gotten proper sympathy and been pulled out by my parents."

"We were trying to figure out why you were screaming. Besides, no one could lift you. They were all laughing too hard—oh Ashley, the way you tried to get attention. I thought some of your outfits were wild, but you really did give us some great times."

"Good times at my expense!" I remind her why the joke is lost on me.

"The other mothers asked me why you'd put them on—I had to defend myself, explain that I'd taught you to swim. I had no idea why you'd put them on."

"You always had my back, Mom."

"Now, you know I did, but my point is, you did some crazy things. Maybe God wants you to worry about what's next for you, and not busy yourself with other people's issues."

"Why can't I move forward, Mom? I'm a terrible housewife, and now, truthfully, I'm not sure Kevin even wants to have kids. I've wasted two years when I should have taken the bar right away."

"Because you're always afraid to make a mistake—don't you get it

Ashley? Trying to be perfect doesn't save you from any of life's humiliations, so you need to be willing to make them. If Pennsylvania's bar is a waste of time, it's really just another something to put on your resume."

I can't get past the wasting of two years. That I've been in a holding pattern for two years—as if I never left.

"I'm more concerned that we haven't seen Kevin out here. Is everything all right with you two?"

My wrist pain suddenly gives way to my real fears. Is there a reason Kevin sent me out here alone? Are all men like Matt, only less honest about it?

"Oh look." My mom swerves the car as she sees a *Hair & Nails* sign. "I'll bet they can fix your hair without an appointment."

"Here?" I ask. "It's dingy. Looks like the kind of place that doesn't have real beauty accreditation."

"May I remind you that you didn't have any kind of accreditation either, and they can't muck it up worse than Ronald McDonald Red."

"I suppose you're right." It's pretty bad that everyone has equated this hair color with the McDonald's clown, separately.

"Ashley, if you go home looking like that, your father will think you've lost all sense of well-being, and since you haven't been working, he will be convinced you're going to hell in a handbag. Besides, my friends might recognize you from the news with the red."

"Ah, so that's it. I've only been with you for two hours and already you want to distance yourself."

As my mom opens the door, there is much chattering in a foreign language—followed by giggling, the universal language. "How we help you?"

"My daughter needs her hair dyed."

More giggling. "She do herself?"

"Yes, she did it herself. Can you fix it?"

"We do it. You want pedicure while you wait? What color you

like?" The gal leads my mom to the display of nail colors. My mom, who has probably never had a pedicure in her life, gets hustled back to a massage chair, and before she can answer, they've got the water running and the vibrating chair fired up.

"You want manicure, too?"

"What?" My mom tries to decipher the woman's English.

"She wants to know if you want a manicure, too," I translate, after years of mani/pedis.

"Oh, no," my mom says. "I think the pedicure will be quite enough."

She has picked a clear polish off the rack, and I chastise her. "Mom, that's topcoat. Pick a color. Live a little."

"I'm not taking color advice from the likes of you, thank you."

The salon is cluttered with hair products and ancestor shrines, but I focus on none of that. I close my eyes, and when I open them again, I'm a brunette. A brunette with a lot of unfinished business, but a brunette nonetheless. Sometimes, you have to be grateful for the small things. A good hair day is nothing to sneeze at.

Chapter 13

AS I ENTER my mother's house, and all its old, familiar smells, it occurs to me that maybe I never wanted the big career that I worked so hard for. Maybe all I wanted was to feel important—and I've found out that doesn't come from being a star attorney. It certainly doesn't come from having obnoxious hair or being someone's wife.

"Ashley, your father will be home soon. Can you put your stuff in your old room? Fish and Clara are staying in your brother's room."

I nod. My mom has an agenda of course. She's the hospitality queen and they have friends staying—this takes priority over their long-lost daughter coming back into town—especially without my husband. The roots of my discontent are suddenly starting to show like ugly growth before a touch-up.

I drop my handbag in my old bedroom and plop myself on the family futon. My room, the den now—my dad's man cave—though he was too lazy to paint, so it's a pale pink man cave, which takes some of the testosterone out of it. It does have a red and gold San Francisco 49ers' poster, clashing over the top of it, a wooden case of empty beer bottles, and a deer head plastered above them. Poor deer. It's disturbing to think of an animal missing its head, and to have it summarily attached to a bubblegum pink wall is the height of indignity. My dad's flat screen is too big for the room, and so it feels like you're in the first row of an IMAX theater while you try to watch.

I text Kay that I won't be there for dinner—that's enough explanation for now.

My mom appears in the doorway and smiles, "It's good to see you back where you belong. I'm going to get dinner started—your dad is late, so it must have been a good boat show." As she disappears, I wonder at her ability to enjoy the simple things in life—making dinner, my dad coming home from the boat show.

Being here makes me miss my own home—which I normally regard with disdain. Kevin's parents bought it for us as a wedding gift. It's a dumpy, little rancher with a sagging roofline and more mold than ten-year old cheese in an abandoned mousetrap. But it was free.

All you can really say when someone gifts you with a mortgage-free home is *thank you*. With a big grin. Even if you're thinking, *I hope this place comes equipped with copious amounts of bleach, because it is disgusting and bears a striking resemblance to a house I saw once on "Hoarders."*

Life, and ugly encounters, has taught me that you can't say everything you think. Even if you think people might really need to hear the truth. It's not my place to tell them that truth. Granted, it should be, but it isn't. As in the case of Kay's engagement to Matt Callaway.

So, my house... Philadelphia is a real estate paradise with an enormous amount of history and style behind its architecture. There are converted fire stations, brick walk-ups, historical Victorians, former carriage houses, Cape Cods, incredible bungalows and stunning, new condos.

From what I can tell, the Novaks went out of their way to pick out the most mundane, soulless house available in the entire city. It's like a part of me dies every time I enter it, and yet, here I am in the pink death room, lamenting my house. From its mossy brown carpet with baby blue walls, to its summery-yellow kitchen, complete with ochre appliances and earthy-green cabinetry, our house is a "before" shot in every room.

I feel as if the Novaks placed me into the house to test my meddle. Like some kind of Philadelphia poverty experiment a la *Survivor.* At one point, I'd started to decorate it, but I abandoned the project when paint and curtains fixed nothing and only made everything else appear more depressed. It was all just lipstick on a pig, and I wanted to scream out, "Why do you hate your son this much?"

Of course, Kevin said this was ridiculous—that maybe I was a little paranoid. "My parents struggled when my dad went through his residencies," he'd told me. "They didn't want us to have to endure that, to suffer like they did. This is their way of saying they want us to have it easier."

Since my own generous salary had evaporated, it seemed like a sweet offering. Until I walked into the house and my soul started to be sucked away.

"Ashley?" My mom sticks her head in the room and smiles. "It's so good to see you dreamily staring up at that ceiling. I miss that. You spent many hours in here, staring at that ceiling and listening to your dreadful music."

I sit up on my elbows. "I miss that, too. It's peaceful in here—well, except for the decapitated deer, I suppose."

"I just wanted to tell you, I unplugged the DVR. It will take your father long enough to figure out why the television won't come on—maybe he'll miss the news."

"Thanks, Mom." I nod. "Do you think a house can suck the life out of you?"

She exhales deeply. "No, Ashley. How can a building, an inanimate object, suck the life out of anything?"

I didn't know the answer to that question. I only knew that the house in Philadelphia affected me in ways that made no earthly sense. "Just pondering."

"Well, dinner will be ready in an hour and I need you to be on your best behavior for our guests."

"I'm not thirteen, Mother. I'm a lawyer. You don't have to tell me to act appropriately. Besides, it's Fish and Clara, right? They've known me since I was a child."

"Exactly. You are rather opinionated, and that doesn't always make for polite dinner conversation, and I shouldn't have to remind you that you've been on the news for two separate incidents on your first full day in California."

"Yeah, yeah. I'll concede that." I flop my legs on the futon.

"Did you get a hold of Kevin?"

I shake my head. "I texted Kay I wouldn't be there for dinner. Maybe I can crash here on the futon until I think of what to say to her."

My mom's lips flatten, and I sense her disapproval, but she comes in, lifts my feet and sits beside me. "You and Kevin will be moving on soon. Wherever you end up, take the bar. The worst thing for you is sitting around. This is just a time of waiting, Ashley. You're not used to it, and maybe it's what you need to learn. Patience. Lord knows you're going to need it as a mother."

"I've been patient, Mom."

"You've gone after what you wanted your whole life, and right now, your goals are on hold. It's all right to be bored once and while and take the time to figure out what's next—the only other alternative is studying for the bar exam as a hobby. Even if you don't stay."

"Do you think Kevin and I should have kids by now? I mean, at least a bun in the oven?"

"Ashley, Kevin's too busy to have children right now."

"He's too busy to have a wife right now," I mumble.

"Don't start pouting and feeling sorry for yourself. It won't feel that way when you have your own goals again, Ashley."

If I have my own goals again. After my hair and retail fiascos, I'm beginning to wonder if I'm safe in the world.

"This too shall pass." She pats my leg. "Get ready for dinner."

Why do I feel like everyone is proverbially patting me on the head? I'm jobless, and if I return to Philly, will anyone notice except for Rhett?

She stands in the doorway as if she's about to say something profound and I wait for it. "Philadelphia isn't good for you. You've lost your sparkle. If you're trying to be Mrs. Novak the first, it's never going to happen. You're simply not that shallow." My mom stops and catches herself. "I don't mean shallow, I mean—"

"It's all right, Mom. I know what you mean."

"Ashley, you'd last one day in the Junior League crowd without telling the women something you'd regret. I know you."

For some reason, I'm offended. "I'm totally that shallow. I could do the Junior League."

"Do you even know what the Junior League does?"

"No, but I've seen them put on fashion shows. Are you trying to tell me I couldn't organize a fashion show?"

"There are people out there Ashley, who like the norm. Who do everything to uphold the norm and the typical ways of society and proper etiquette. You are not that person."

I grimace.

"You're a fighter. If there's a wrong in the world around you, you want to correct it and make things right. It's why you can't let Kay marry Matt without her knowing the truth. It's why you tried to help Seth and Arin. You need a battle. Find one before that sparkle disappears altogether. That's your calling, darling. You're not a shrinking violet. You're not the kind of woman who can hold her tongue and do as she's told."

"That really sucks. The Bible says I should be that kind of woman. Submissive."

My mom laughs. "Ashley, when you were younger and just starting to go to church in high school, you told me the story of Queen Vashti and Esther, do you remember?"

I shake my head.

"Esther's obedience was praised—she won the first beauty contest of her day to wed the king after Vashti was banished."

"I remember the story, Mom."

"Vashti, on the other hand, had told her drunken husband that she wouldn't be leered at by his friends. Vashti stood up for right-eousness, too, and demanded respect because the King dishonored her."

"It would be so much easier if I just had a gentle soul like you do, Mom."

"Ashley, don't you see? From that early age, you didn't admire Esther the same way you did Vashti, even though the whole point of the story is to admire Esther. Those women were called to different paths. Maybe Kay is called to the path of Esther, and Matt's learned from his mistakes. You don't have to assume the worst."

I don't, but I totally do.

The doorbell rings and interrupts us. My mom hustles out to get the door and I call after her, "Let's not forget, Vashti was banished from the King's presence. That's hardly a love story for the ages."

There's a rush of voices, and Kevin's voice rises above the fray. *Kevin?*

Shoot. Now I'm hearing voices! Just bring me the strappy white coat already.

Chapter 14

AT THE SOUND of my husband's voice, I migrate toward my purse and yank out lipstick and apply—as if I'm some kind of Stepford wife. It scares me when my mom's voice in my head is reflexive. I drag a hairbrush through my tresses—which thankfully is back to its normal color, and therefore, offers less of a visual pointing to my temporary insanity. The color-fix took an hour in the salon, where I understood next to nothing. Language barriers did not stop my stylist from trying to upsell me other products. Eventually, I gave into the cheapest option: Eyelash extensions. They make me feel like a flirtatious gorilla flirting with a Silverback from across the jungle with my coquettish gaze.

"Ashley! Ashley!" my mother shouts, and I snap back into reality. *Kevin is really here.* His voice is not just a figment of my imagination. My husband. The man who rarely makes it home for dinner—the man who I haven't been able to reach by telephone, has flown across the country without so much as a word? A sick feeling permeates my stomach, and all Matt's words come back to haunt me. *Is your marriage in trouble? You say he's not ready to start a family? Is he not ready to start a family with you because this marriage was a mistake?*

"I'm being ridiculous! He's taken a vacation after all!" I say aloud and open the bedroom door and step into the living room. "Kevin?"

My raging joy is quickly extinguished by the sight of my sister-in-law Emily standing beside him. Yes, *that* sister-in-law—the one I left Philadelphia to avoid. She, and her tiny belly, are wrapped in a red skirt with a tight, navy-striped shirt and strappy, yellow sandals. I can't help but admire her fashion prowess in the midst of pregnancy—even if her appearance does upset me greatly.

"What are you doing here?" My voice comes out shaky. I don't make a move toward my husband. "I thought you were swamped with the study and surgeries. I haven't heard from you since Monday night." It comes out naggy. I hadn't meant it that way, but the shrew rises up in my voice regardless.

"An emergency came up." He takes a few long strides across my parents' living room and engulfs me in a hug. To my surprise, I stiffen. "Aren't you glad to see me?" He gazes at me with soft eyes, and I melt into his chest.

"She's not glad to see *me*," Emily quips, while she rocks back and forth on her sandals, gripping her belly.

"Of course I am," I lie. "It's simply out of context. I'd be surprised if Kevin was at our own house in time for dinner—much less dinner here on the West Coast."

As Kevin tightens his arms around me, I'm finding my bearings. His appearance makes no sense at all. Kevin is not like me. He's not impulsive. Every decision takes painstaking analysis, and that's why his sudden presence rocks me to the core. But I realize as I wrap my arms around his waist and inhale his scent, how much Tiffany's experience shook me, and I haven't processed the event yet. My body involuntarily shakes at the realization of what I could have lost.

He tugs at my arm. "Ashley, what happened to your wrist?"

"It's a long story. I fell. You know how klutzy I can be. I missed you," I say with my grip clenched around Kevin.

"It's only been two days, sweetheart."

"Did you hear about Tiffany's?" I ask him. "Is that why you're here? Were you worried about me?"

"Did you buy yourself some jewelry?" he asks with a smirk.

"No." I shake my head. "No jewelry." I show him my sparkling wedding ring. "This is the only jewelry I have need of." I clasp him again with a pathetic desperation.

"Oh brother. Are you two for real?" Emily asks. "Get a room. Seriously."

Really? The pregnant wonder is going to tell me to get a room?

My mom hugs Emily. Read: Shuts her up. With Mom's hand on the tiny belly that contains my future niece or nephew, she changes the subject. "Look at this little tummy. I know you're not supposed to touch, but I can't help myself," Mom says. "We're going to have a baby in the family!" She looks toward me as if to register it's my turn to have a baby, but I stare up at the popcorn ceiling until the moment passes.

Emily smiles awkwardly. Her figure is still as statuesque and just as glorious as if she stepped off a Paris runway. Her crown of blonde hair is decidedly darker—a fact that I can't miss. *Emily's not dyeing her hair.* Is it possible my spoiled sister-in-law has a maternal instinct after all?

"Ashley," my mother trills. "Look at Emily's bump." Mom frames it with her hands. "She doesn't even look pregnant! Oh I don't know how you girls do it today. In my day, we were all as big as a house and the maternity clothes were like circus tents with bows."

I sigh. *Story of my life. Being around skinny, wispy women who carry babies as easily as if they're opening a can of soup. I should have been born during my mother's era, when it was okay to be plumped up like a microwaved hot dog when one was pregnant.*

Mom yanks her hands away. "Oh, you'll be staying for dinner. I'd better set two more places."

"No, Mom," Kevin says. "Don't worry about us. We can eat at a restaurant. We don't want to put you out." He gives me that look where I know he needs to talk. I'm glad that for once, the drama in Kevin's life has nothing to do with me.

"How offensive to tell your mother-in-law you'll eat at a restaurant. You'll eat here with your family. Come in and make yourself at home. Ashley, offer them something to drink." Mom trails off to the kitchen, mumbling reminders to herself, just as my father opens the door from the garage.

Dad is with his hunting friends, Fish and Clara Bowman. All three of them are wearing camouflage shirts, as if they've stepped out of a *Duck Dynasty* episode.

"Ashley," my dad says, as if he saw me yesterday. "You remember Fish and his wife, Clara."

"Good to see you both." I raise my hand in a wave, but I don't step away from my husband. I'm still too fearful over why he's here and I don't want to let him go. I certainly don't want to remain back in California and let him leave me again. Which is probably codependent and a whole list of Dr. Phil subjects wrapped into one small feeling.

My dad stares at Kevin and then Emily. "Well, the whole gang is here. We're having a party?" He sticks his hand out to shake Kevin's. "Kevin, good to see you, son." He pumps Kevin's hand harder than necessary. "You're not bringing her back for good, are you?" He nods his chin toward me. "I gave her away fair and square. You knew the deal when you married her. No Ind—."

"Don't say it, Dad. It's politically-incorrect."

He chuckles. "She always was too quick for her old dad."

"Not giving her back on your life," Kevin says, and I'll admit, I'm relieved to hear it. His sister's presence has me unnerved and I keep waiting for the other shoe to drop.

"Fish, Clara." I feel ridiculous calling a grown man Fish, but it's clear my dad doesn't remember Emily's name. "This is my husband Kevin and my sister-in-law, Emily."

"How was the gun show?" my mom asks from the kitchen's doorway. "Isn't this delightful that Ashley, Kevin and Emily are here!" my mom trills, trying to give my dad subtle reminders as to everyone's name.

"The gun show was terrible. You won't let me buy what I want, so I just wandered around like the poor boy outside the movie theater without a dime."

"You don't need another gun," my mom says. "Does he, Fish?"

"I wouldn't touch that question with a ten-foot pole."

"You could have let me buy a new scope."

"You need a hearing aid before you get a new scope."

"What?" my dad yells, missing the irony.

"What can I do to help?" Clara asks my mother, and I just wish all this normalcy and friendship would go away so I could ask Kevin why he's here. More importantly, why the woman I try to avoid is here.

"Nothing at all, Clara," my mom tells her longtime friend. "Just sit down and make yourself at home. You've been trudging around that rod and tackle show all day. You're such a trooper to do that."

"I have to talk to you," Kevin whispers into my ear, and the sounds of the gun show talk fade. His warm gaze meets mine and it's as though I've never left Philadelphia. I can hear only his deep voice, see only what he's trying to tell me about Emily with his eyes. "Privately."

I grip his hand tightly. "Why didn't you call? I've been trying to reach you at the hospital and you never returned one of my calls.

"It's a long story." He looks at his sister. "Emily, will you be all right for a while?"

"I'm fine," she says, while she stares at Fish and Clara as if they've been set free from an Atlanta trailer park. Something tells me Emily hasn't spent a lot of time around people who wear camouflage. In truth, Fish and Clara could buy and sell the Novaks. They live in Napa on a giant estate overlooking acres of vineyards. Vines they only have because that's how Fish wanted his hills landscaped. Fish just sells off the grapes to local vintners for the view he always wanted.

"Ash, you coming?" Kevin asks me, and I follow him into my old bedroom.

"Are you staying tonight? I miss sleeping beside you—I can't sleep without knowing you're there."

He shakes his head. "I have surgery in the morning. I'm catching the red-eye back tonight. I got Emily a room at the Four Seasons in Palo Alto." Kevin faces me, my hands in his, and my heart is in my throat.

I snuggle up against him. "Mmm. You smell like hospital soap still."

"You realize you're the only one that scent turns on,"

I grin. "Don't forget it. I've missed you so much. I didn't realize how just being next to you invigorated me. I'm so glad to see you." Admittedly, I'm avoiding the reason he's here. I'm not that interested in why Emily is here. I simply know it's going to involve me in ways that my body will physically reject.

He steps backward. "But you're suspicious."

"Maybe a little. You never come home from work early and now you fly across the country at a moment's notice? It's not like you. You must admit that." I run my hand across the stubble on his chin. "You didn't shave before you left."

He starts to pace the small bedroom, his eyes falling momentarily on the ill-fated deer. "Rhett's fine. The neighbor has him."

"Kevin, it can't be as bad as all that."

"It's not that I think it's as bad as all that. But it is bad. The point is, I'm not sure my sister is ever going to be able to manage life for herself. It dawned on me as I was flying here that once again, I was pushing off my responsibility to her onto you. I don't want to do that, but I obviously have no idea what to do with her at this point."

"When I married you, I married your family. You've got to put up with Elmer Fudd out there hunting wabbits, I've got to put up with your sister."

Kevin laughs and the green in his eyes sparkle with joy. "And my mother, but let's not keep score. I'll lose." Then comes the glare of severity where I know I'm about to be hit with the truth. "I'm leaving Emily here with you. She doesn't like to fly by herself and she needed to get out of Philadelphia. I couldn't think of anywhere to send her where I could trust that she'd take care of herself. I promise, this is the last time I'm going to push her off on you."

"No, it isn't," I tell him. "Truthfully, I'm happy for the diversion. At the moment, I couldn't feel more useless. That's what this trip was all about, to find out what's next for me, and I've got nothing."

"You think you need a job to be valuable to me?" Kevin comes closer and wraps me in his arms. "Ash, you just don't seem to understand how much I love you. How I'd be lost without you and your light in my life. I trust you implicitly." He winks at me. "Even with a credit card."

"That *is* serious."

"You've put your life on hold for my career and I know what it's cost you, Ashley."

I nod. *I know my husband and he's about as wonderful as they come—except when explaining family drama.* "You're avoiding the real subject. Spill it."

He laughs. "No, this is related. You agreed to marry me under false pretenses. I haven't told you something, and I'm worried about how you'll react."

I slide down on the futon.

"Remember when you found out I'd been engaged before?"

"In fairness, you did tell me when we were registering at Bed, Bath & Beyond for our wedding. There were some chick's plates under your name. We should have stayed at Bloomingdale's."

"Well, compared to that. This is nothing!" He gives me that sideways glance, where his green eyes are at their gorgeous best. Kevin's ideas of secrets are that he ate a cupcake and not really a muffin like he told me he did. I can't say I'm afraid there's a great, dark family curse in his history, but I am concerned what Emily's problem means to our future. Emily is here. Kevin told me implicitly that he didn't have time for this vacation. So, I'm a smart girl. I do the math. And the calculations aren't pretty.

"I knew there was a reason you sent me here alone. It wasn't just the study at work. I have that sixth sense."

"You do. And it scares me sometimes."

I lift one brow in that way that lets him know he's in trouble.

"It turns out that my sister came to Philadelphia to see you. She was none too happy when she found me alone in the house. I'd explained to her that you wouldn't be here, but I guess she didn't believe me."

"Emily came to see me? For what purpose? She didn't have anyone's life she might interfere with in Atlanta?"

Kevin doesn't even comment. He's not listening. My angry eyebrow has absolutely no effect on him. I'm totally losing my touch, and by the looks of things, perhaps even my connection where I understand him without his speaking.

"Kevin—"

He's staring out the window. His laser-like focus is elsewhere, and it dawns on me what he has to say is serious.

"How did you know I was here and not at Kay's or Brea's?"

"I went there first. Kay is ticked at you, by the way. She had dinner planned and said you didn't show up and you didn't call."

I shrug. "Par for the course. Just wait until she finds out what she really has to be angry about. I texted her, she just never gets her texts."

My cell phone beeps. "Oh, on the subject of texts." Kevin crosses his arms in front of him. "I just wanted you to know Seth's texts to you are coming to my phone, too."

"What?"

"The cloud, Ashley. I wasn't spying on you. His texts came through to me."

"I didn't answer him," I say guiltily.

"I know that, too, but I thought I should mention that I texted him back that even though I have taken the Hippocratic oath, that if he texted my wife again, he'd put my 'do no harm' promise to the test."

I smile. "Really? You told him that?" A giggle escapes. "That's kind of hot." I sidle up beside him. "Very John Wayne of you."

Kevin grimaces as he stares down at me. "You would find that sexy. It's Seth. It's not like I'm taking on Dwayne 'The Rock' Johnson for you or anything."

I kiss him anyway.

"Are you going to let me finish telling you why I'm here?"

"Not if I can convince you to stay longer," I purr.

"Ashley." He gently puts his hands on my shoulders and looks me straight in the eye.

"Come on!" I stamp my foot. Really, I do. I'm not proud of it, but I stamped my foot. "You sent me away on my anniversary on someone else's frequent flier miles. Now you've got the nerve to play hard to get?"

"I'm here on a mission," he says with all the emotion of a typical engineer. He draws in a deep breath and his chest expands brusquely. "I don't even know where to start." He rakes his hand through his hair and once again skirts the topic at hand. "Did you learn anything while you were out here? You know, any idea what you might want to do in the future? Will you go back to being a patent attorney? Maybe you could start your own consulting business."

"Kevin, you didn't come out here to talk about my career aspirations. What is bothering you? Why is Emily here?"

"You know how you're always telling me how perfect I am, and I tell you that it's too much to live up to?"

"You are perfect for me, Kevin. You're fun to be around, you don't have great taste buds, so it doesn't matter that I don't cook very well, and you like to see me dressed well. It brings you joy to see me happy. What could be better as a husband?"

"Ashley, don't—" He makes a guttural sound. Now he has my attention. "I found out who the father of Emily's baby is."

"Oh."

"He followed her to Philadelphia." Kevin doesn't look pleased with this announcement. Something tells me there's no romantic wedding in Emily's future. She has not found the love of her life—her *Kehvin*. "Emily needs legal advice, and I know you can help her. You can find her the right lawyer in California, maybe get her a room at Kay's house until the baby comes so she can establish residency. My parents will pay the rent, but Emily says she must go. She can't stay in Atlanta. I know I said that I wouldn't stick you with her problems, but she refuses to go home and—"

"Kay's house? Residency for what? Oh Kevin, that's not a good idea. Kay is—"

"I'll make it up to her, Ashley. I swear I will. You must think I'm the worst kind of husband, leaving you with this, but that study is at a crucial stage, and I didn't know what to do. She claims she can't stay with my mom."

Of course she does. That wouldn't be enough drama for Emily.

"Forget that. You're the best kind of husband, and you know it." I wave my hand. "But I don't understand. Did Emily invite her baby daddy to Philadelphia?"

"Don't call him that," Kevin says through clenched teeth. "Do you know what I go through to save wanted babies every day? This man doesn't deserve a gold fish!"

His quiet rage stops me in my tracks. I draw back a little, as it's completely out of his character. I watch his jaw twitch and understand that his anger roils beneath the surface. Instinctively, I understand that Emily has gotten herself into a 'fix' as she likes to call it.

"She ran from Atlanta. She wants to tell you the rest herself, but I felt I had to come so you knew I wasn't just pawning off my responsibilities onto you. Emily wants you on this, not me."

"She's in some kind of trouble?"

"She wants to explain the rest. But will you help her get settled here, find a place to stay? Maybe that room with Kay? I'd feel better knowing she was being looked after."

"Emily's an adult, Kevin. She's about to be a mother. It's time she looked after herself, don't you think?"

"You act like that means anything that she's an adult. She's a spoiled princess who has never been responsible for anything in her life. She has no idea how to do the simplest task for herself. Honestly, when we got here and needed a rental car, you would have thought I was asking her to explain quantum physics. She can plan social events and create beautiful flower bouquets. That's it. The sum total of my sister's life skills."

He forgot Emily's best skill, that she can manipulate with ease to get her way.

"Emily can't stay with Kay. She's dating Matt Callaway. I mean, really dating Matt Callaway, and that would be awkward to have Emily running about pregnant. Besides, I'm staying with Kay, there isn't extra room."

"Oh," Kevin says. "What about Brea?"

"Brea is living with her mother. They had some kind of financial setback."

Kevin sits on the bed with his fists pressed against his forehead. I knew Emily would become my problem. I had these dreams of grandeur, boundaries and all that, but she's pregnant. And alone. I just need to get a job quickly—before my permanent position becomes Emily's keeper.

Chapter 15

IF I THOUGHT dinner with my ex and the "Reasons" at Kay's house was awkward, I had yet to experience family dining with my father, and a man named Fish and his wife, Clara. A fraction of the guests belong at an Atlanta all-white Country Club (granted, they don't call it that, but they may as well) while the remainder belong in a duck blind throwing back a few brewskis.

Kehvin, as Emily likes to call him, and I belong in neither place. We're from the alien planet called normalcy. And when I'm the normal one at the table? This is cause for worry.

My mom has set the dining room table with her everyday dishes. I haven't figured out my mom's equation for what constitutes a "china" dinner. When one's friends own a vineyard the size of four football fields, and your daughter is home from Philly, I would think that would warrant the good dishes. But I'd be wrong.

The table looks like we're having a regular family dinner, but with more people. There are paper napkins, Mom's ancient scratched silverware, plastic tumblers and mismatched bowls for the side dishes. In the center is a silver platter where the roast takes the position of honor. It dawns on me that I could have learned quite a bit about being a housewife from my mother. She never seemed bored.

"Everyone take a seat," Mom announces, and we all gather around the table. My father sits at one end of the table. Kevin takes the other end, and my mom will sit by me in the spot closest to the kitchen.

Fish and Clara flank Emily, and God bless them, try to engage her in conversation. "So, Emily, when's the big event?" Fish asks, as my mom carries the roast around the table so everyone can help themselves partake. It's like a medieval setting, and we should be gnawing on a turkey bone with complete ease. I'm suddenly feeling all Braveheart.

Emily blinks her salon-assisted lashes (like my own—I'm not judging) and shakes her head. "Event? I'm not getting married or anything."

"The baby," Clara clarifies. "When's the baby due?"

"Oh," Emily says, helping herself to two slices of roast beef. "In October. October 11'th."

"Do you know if it's a boy or a girl?"

"Yes." She takes a dramatic pause. "It's a boy or a girl."

Fish laughs. "Well, we didn't think you were giving birth to a trout, did we, Clara?"

"Trout lay eggs," Clara says.

"I know they lay eggs, Clara. It was just the first animal on my mind after today. We didn't think you were giving birth to a platypus," Fish says, and looks to his wife. "Better?"

"At least it's a mammal, but I would have gone with something indigenous to the south."

Fish rolls his eyes.

"Emily, would you like some mashed potatoes?" My mom puts the bowl alongside my sister-in-law. Emily nods, scoops up a giant spoonful of spuds and plops them on her plate. I've never seen her attempt to eat that much in the entirety of our relationship.

"Is there gravy?" Emily asks.

My dad has started the side dishes around the table, in the opposite direction of my mother. "Of course there's gravy. Who serves roast without gravy?"

"Kevin, could you pass your sister the gravy?" My mom points to the gravy boat with her free hand.

Emily floods her plate until there are a few wayward peas floating to the top. Then, she takes the salt and pepper and douses it heavily. My mother looks horrified—not at Emily's lumberjack appetite, but that possibly, she hasn't made enough gravy.

"Emily, can I get you anything else?" my mom asks.

"Uh-uh," Emily says with a mouthful of food.

"Emily," I say. "I've never seen you eat so much. Did you have anything to eat today?"

Emily stops her fork mid-bite and my mom snaps at me, "Ashley, don't be rude."

"I didn't mean it rudely, Emily. I've just never seen you eat like that. That's all." I don't want to say I'm worried that she's going to head straight to the bathroom and purge everything from her system. Wouldn't that be ruder? I thought I showed great restraint by not mentioning the propensity toward projectile vomiting.

Kevin intervenes. "I think what Ashley is trying to say is that my sister isn't much of an eater."

"Do you know, I never get a homemade meal. I mean, when we were younger, we had the cook, and she made nice meals and all. But fancy meals, you know? Like duck a l'orange, and stuffed quail. Weird food for a kid. I just wanted some mac 'n cheese. Maybe a hot dog, you know?"

"It must have been nice to have such meals prepared for you," my mom, politically correct and optimistic to the point of annoyance, says.

And really, is anyone buying this? The poor little princess had to have duck whatever? I look around the table, and clearly I'm the only one without a heart.

Sometimes, when people continually look on the bright side of slop? It gets annoying. Let the girl whine. Her mother was too busy with the country club to microwave her a hot dog. That's the stuff of a Dr. Phil episode—sometimes, you only want validation. In this case, I'll let the rest of them give it to her – my heartfelt thoughts for

Emily are stretched.

"If I lived in your house, Mrs. Stockingdale, I'd be like four *hunddered* pounds. No wonder Ashley is bigger. I suppose I never gave you *propah* credit, Ashley…that you don't weigh more than you do," she says in her southern drawl, which is always more pronounced when she's issuing an insult. And there it is. My *real* sister-in-law. The one I'd been waiting to show up.

Kevin exhales. "Emily."

"It's a compliment! She knows I meant it as a compliment. Don't you, Ashley?"

I smile. "Of course I do." *One of your backhanded niceties that sting for a while.*

"It was impossible to gain weight eating my mother's food. I was merely pointing out that Mrs. Stockingdale can cook well, and such glorious meals provide temptations that I did not ha-ive. That's all, dear brothah. Is thay-it a crime?"

"Not in my book," Fish says. "I wouldn't waste a second look on a woman who couldn't cook. Helps if she can clean and skin a deer, too. I wouldn't want a twig either. Real men want women with curves."

"Well," Emily says. "That's terribly honest, isn't it?"

The phone rings. "Don't answer it," my mother says. "It's dinner-time. They'll call back."

But my father can't help himself. He rises and picks the living room phone off the side table. "Hello." He pauses. "Yeah, she's here. You want to talk to her?" More silence and my dad grabs the TV remote. "Channel 4?"

The living room TV, in all its sixty-inch glory, looms large, and soon I, with my flaming red hair appear on the screen. In HD. If I thought my hair was heinous in clown orange, I had yet to see the fullness of it's ugly glory on high definition.

"Well, I'll be. Yeah," my dad continues. "She's sitting right here, Dave. She's fine."

My brother, Dave. I should have known he'd rat me out.

So far, my dad has yet to recognize me in living color. There I am diving for my life, then instantaneously, I'm underneath Matt Callaway. It all happens so suddenly—just like the first time. Our Medieval soiree has just gone digital. Everyone is watching the screen, their mouths dangling like melting icicles.

"That's your sister? She's sitting right here," my dad says again. "With her normal colored hair. At least I think that's her normal-colored hair, she's been messing with it for so long, I suppose I don't know what her real color is...No, I have no idea who that guy is," I hear my dad say into the phone. "You're sure that's your sister? The one with the clown hair? Well, I'll be. She's wearing the same clothes. Yeah, I'll call you back." My dad hangs up the phone, but continues to stare at the TV.

Just when I think it can't get any worse, the black-and-white footage of Brea and me fishing Miles out of the aquarium follows the mall footage. Incidentally, the clip doesn't show how Miles got up there, and it's still a mystery to me. Everyone has ceased eating, and is staring at me.

"Really? There's no bigger news story? It's my luck that I have to screw up royally on a slow news day."

"I think it's that the story is visual, dear," my mom says in her upbeat tone. "People love to be shown a story. It brings it to life for them."

Thank you, Barbara Walters.

Kevin's mouth is still open. I start to tell him that I can explain, but really, can I? Or is it just better to let him imagine the rest for himself. This is me we're talking about. He knows if something can happen to me, it will. I am clearly God's sitcom—the lighthearted part of His day.

I look at him as if to say, *Seriously? You want me to fix your sister's life? You trust me with this? I am unemployed and that's the least of my issues.*

"Ashley, it appears you've had quite a traumatic day," Clara finally says. "What on earth happened? I'm shocked to see you sitting here so calmly. Why didn't you say something?" Clara gets up and comes to rub my back. "You poor dear."

"The jewelry store got robbed." I gaze directly at Kevin and feel my eyes swimming in tears. "Matt asked me to help him pick Kay an engagement ring. Everything happened so fast after that. I reached for a package. It was an explosive. Matt threw me out of the way."

Kevin doesn't miss a beat. "Matt Callaway saved your life? You didn't think to mention that to me?"

"You're after me? Kevin, I haven't been able to reach you since I left, and now you're simply here unannounced!"

"You didn't think it would interest me that you made the evening news and I might have lost my wife?" He pulls me into a hug and grasps me tightly before pulling away and looking straight into my eyes. "That's how you fell on your wrist? You left a pertinent part out."

I nod. Now I feel badly for snapping at him. *Bad Ashley.*

"Matt's getting married?" Emily asks, as she drops her fork for the first time since she sat down. "To Kay?" The fork clinks on the plate, and all eyes are still on me.

As I stare at my husband, I see the light in his eyes. The sparkle, and I know what he's conveying. That he's thrilled I'm alive and that even though I may be God's sitcom, he's relieved that God keeps me safe in the midst of His cosmic entertainment. I feel the warm embrace that I know he wants to give me right now.

"I think Ashley would rather talk about something else," Clara interjects. "What's Davey doing these days?"

My dad grunts. "Dave lives in Merced now. He's driving the campus bus at UC Merced. Good job. Less stress. They've got a house down there."

Merced is about three hours away, and Mei Ling, my brother's wife, appreciates that she can be at home with their son. It's much cheaper to live there than in the Bay Area without a Masters' Degree, but obviously, my brother still has plenty of time on his hands to remind my father why he will always be the chosen child. Davey's room is still put together like a shrine—while mine has become the den, complete with a deer that met its untimely death, hanging on a Pepto Pink wall of shame.

Emily's eyes fill with liquid, which dries mine up like a Merced Riverbed. She has legitimate, watery tears, and suddenly, talking about my fiasco at Tiffany's seems like the proper channel to reroute her emotions. It dawns on me that Matt getting married must bother her on some level. She is running from the supposed baby daddy, and when Matt Callaway appears to be the "one that got away" you know you're tackling deep, emotional issues.

"Emily?" Clara's voice is gentle. She places her hand on my sister-in-law's wrist. "What is it, Sweetheart?"

"It's not a big deal, really. I'm just emotional," Emily says, patting her tummy. "Hearing what Ashley endured today has me choked up."

No. What was it really? Did the attention veer off of her for a second?

My dad sets the phone down and sits at the head of the table. He looks at me and shakes his head. "Forty-something years I been watching the evening news. Never did I see anything like that, and my own daughter has to be in the middle of it."

I swallow hard. "Dad, I—"

"Ashley, your brother lives his life. He goes to work and he comes home and has dinner. Why is that simple life something that eludes you? You always had to be different."

"If only I had the answer to that question, Dad…the clouds would part and heaven would open."

Kevin gazes at me intensely and the outside world disappears between us. "If she had the answer to that question, she wouldn't be my Ashley." He offers a slight smile, and I lap it up like a quenched dog.

"Nor mine," my mom says.

I see a flash of something cross Emily's brow, and it's clear to me that I have everything a girl could ever want. So why does my life feel so empty?

"Well, I've seen enough of that." Clara rises and takes the remote control from my father. "I assume if your daughter wanted us to know about her day, she would have told us. Besides, she probably can't talk about it." She looks straight at me. "Isn't that right, Ashley?"

I smile back at her. "It's probably best until the investigation is over."

Kevin's eyes embrace me. *I feel his love. But he looks away just as quickly and I wonder where my husband is – how could he find the time to traipse across the country for Emily, but he can't return a simple phone call for the woman he promised to love, honor and cherish?*

"So Emily," Fish says to break the silence. "Did Clara tell you that we have another pregnant lady staying with us? She's due in November, so that's why my wife feels as if she knows you already. Isn't that right, hon?"

Emily puts down her fork. "Is this woman related to you? Is her husband staying with you, too?"

Clara purses her lips. There's no judgment in the action, but it's clear she doesn't want to give away anyone's secrets. Clara sees something in Emily that she clearly wants to capture and rescue. Clara has that way about her. She rescues things. They lost a son when he was a teenager to drunk driving. He was their only child, and after he died, they took in his best friend. I've never known their house to be empty since. She picks up strays like a highway worker in orange picks up trash.

"Where'd you pick up this one?" my dad quips.

My dad. Ever the compassionate one.

"You know Clara," Fish answers. "I think she met this one in downtown Sonoma. Outside The Cheesecake Factory. Isn't that right, Babe?"

"This one, Fish, her name is Maggie. She's not a dog for crying out loud. She's a lovely young lady who has been sent a lot of hard blows in her short life."

"No, if she were a dog, I'd remember her name," Fish jokes.

"Are you charging her rent?" Emily asks.

Clara hones in on Emily. "Are you looking for a place to stay, Emily? You are welcome with us."

"I, uh—" Emily shoves a forkful of potatoes in her mouth and stares at her plate.

"Emily, can I talk to you for a minute?" I ask her.

We excuse ourselves and go into my room. "I'm sorry about my room. I know it's like Playskool's Vlad the Impaler castle."

Emily doesn't crack a smile. "Did you tell Clara about me?"

"I don't even know about you, Emily. Clara is extra perceptive. She lost a son, and I think she just sees a need in people."

"What did Kehvin tell you?"

"That he knows who the baby's father is, and that you came to Philadelphia to see me."

She pauses, and then meets my gaze with her wide, green eyes. With her beauty and connections, Emily could really have anything she wanted—at least that's how I've always pictured it for girls like her. The world is their oyster, but somehow, everything Emily reaches for, slips through her fingers.

"You think I'm a loose woman," she accuses.

And no, I really don't, but she is pregnant and there's a great secret about who the father is, so let's not be too condemning. "Kevin says you need my legal help. I'm here for you, Emily."

"But you don't want to be. I know you left when you found out I was coming to Philadelphia."

That's truer than I'd like it to be.

"Your brother bought me the ticket for our anniversary. I went when the ticket said it was time to go. I know we've had a rough start, but you love Kevin. I love Kevin. Because I love Kevin I will do anything you need me to, so spill it."

"My first boyfriend…" She walks across the room and drops on the futon. "My only boyfriend, really."

My eyebrows shoot up subconsciously.

"Yes, I've dated. But this is the only man I've evah loved. Do you see how you judge me?"

"So what's the problem? Isn't he a southern gentleman?"

"Oh Ashley." She falls backwards on the sofa. "He can't marry me. He's a football player."

Silence, while I try to figure that one out. Which annoys me, because haven't I learned by now that it's not going to make sense? *Consider the source, Ashley.*

"I'm sorry. I fail to see the connection. Football players can't be married?"

"He's famous. In our little town, he's famous."

"He's not married, is he?" I'm exasperated. I fail to see how this drama fits into my vacation plans. *I mean, is it me?*

"No!" she squeals. "Honestly, what you must think of me—"

"Emily, I'm assuming that you want this baby. You're going through a lot of trouble to keep it, and I'm thrilled for you. I know how hard it had to be to tell your mother about the baby."

"We made a mistake, Ashley, but he's just graduated from a big Christian college. He's been recruited for a NFL team. He's got endorsements for every kind of product." She looks me deeply in the eyes. "Because of his squeaky clean image, I'm his dirty little secret." She rubs her stomach. "We're his dirty little secret. I just need to hide out here until the baby comes, and I need some paperwork prepared. Adoption papers. Do you think you can help me with that?"

"First off, you're no one's dirty little secret, do you hear me? Are you giving the baby up for adoption?" I'm confused. "You need to establish residency in California if—"

"No, no. When the baby comes, Josh can marry me. You know, he'll rescue a single mother and be the best dad ever and his fans will embrace me."

"That is the stupidest thing I've ever heard." I gaze at Emily's wide eyes and realize I've just said this aloud, so I try to backpedal. "Emily, any real man would take consequences for his actions. You're not someone's dirty little secret. You're the mother of his child— mistake or not. God doesn't make mistakes."

"I simply need time, Ashley. When the baby comes, everything will be fine."

Prickles of horror run down the back of my neck. That's exactly the way Kevin deals with issues – he'll think about them tomorrow. Is everyone from the Atlanta region nursing a Scarlett O' Hara complex? Is it my calling to be in a lifelong waiting pattern?

I'm almost afraid to ask, but I bite the bullet. "Where will you stay until then?"

"I was hoping I could stay here. Clara's offer sounds incredible. Do they live in a place big enough where she means what she says?"

The fact that Emily is willing to stay with people, virtual strangers, who she probably thinks live in a doublewide trailer, is incredible to me. She is far too desperate for me to believe any aspect of her story. Emily's truth is usually like an iceberg. The majority of it is just under the surface, and it's the part that does all the damage.

Chapter 16

I FELT AS if I've lived a week in this one day. And in reality, I suppose I have, because it's more than I've done with the last six months of my life.

"You'll be all right?" Kevin asks me, as he gets ready to leave me on Kay's front porch. I can see the guilt emanating from his every pore, but what choice does he have, really? He has lives to save. I glance at Emily sitting straight-backed in the rental car. I wonder what would happen if she just had to sink or swim—like a normal person.

I stare at him as if he's a stranger. I never thought he'd break my heart, but understanding the truth of the fact that he had time to come across the country for Emily, but not take a vacation with his wife, speaks volumes. How can the man I love be so gullible?

"You're sure she's telling the truth?"

He checks over his shoulder., "I'm not sure of anything. That's why I thought it was better to do what she asked and bring her to you. I don't understand my sister."

"You don't understand me either."

His face tightens. "What is that supposed to mean?"

"It means we have different priorities, Kevin. I can't explain it to you any more than that."

"It's ironic, isn't it?" Kevin asks. "I spend my days saving the lives of babies who are struggling for breath, and in my own family, I can't do a thing for my own niece or nephew."

"Yeah. It's ironic."

"What if she can't parent that baby, Ash? She barely takes care of herself."

"She takes fine care of herself, Kevin. She knows exactly what she's doing. She runs, and everyone chases her."

Kevin bends and kisses me on the forehead. "I don't deserve you."

"I don't deserve your sister."

He laughs, and against my better judgment, the sound brings me joy in my soul. Love makes no sense at all.

Kevin's face is troubled, and he inherently understands that I'm hurt, but I can also tell he has no understanding of why. He's doing what he must. He's focused, and my feelings will have to wait.

"Isn't this romantic, being on this front porch?" I ask him. "It's like when we were dating. Remember how we were on fire for each other, and had to go to our separate spaces until we were official?" I sigh. "Good memories."

"Yeah, I'm a guy so I don't remember it quite as romantically as you do. Because if I had my way, my sister would wait in the car and I'd take my wife to her old room with wild abandon."

"Mmm. Wild abandon, huh?" I wrap my arms around his neck, and he unclenches them by grasping my good wrist.

"Don't start something you can't finish, you little Minx."

I giggle, but my laughter dies abruptly. "I'm ready to come home. Next time you send me away as a gift, maybe you could make the return trip sooner?"

"Trust me. There won't be a next time. I've had more chicken potpies than I care to admit to in the last two days, and the Bible is right. It's not good for man to be alone."

"You're not saying you miss me for my cooking."

He laughs. "Trust me, no one is ever going to say that to you, Ashley."

I pout. "Go. You're going to miss your plane."

He jumps off the porch and stares back at me. "You don't think it's too weird that my sister is going to live with Fish and Clara?"

I give him all the reassurance I can muster. "Weird is the new black. In this family, it's probably the only color."

He hops back onto the porch and kisses me ravenously. I can feel his energy, and desire courses through my veins—everything behind the small moment—the promise of more to come. The regret of what isn't. There is a beauty in knowing someone so intimately that their very presence brings peace and puts your soul at ease. I squeeze his hands.

"I've learned my lesson," he says, as he cradles my chin in his hands. "Sending you away to find your goals sounded so sacrificial and heroic." He trails his finger along my jaw. "Now I realize it was me, avoiding that I've screwed up your career."

"I needed the push. I could have humbled myself and taken the bar a long time ago. Or I could have found contract work. It's not you. It's not Philadelphia."

"Tell the cops they can't have you longer than your return flight home, no matter who ripped off Tiffany's."

"I will."

"You're the best thing that ever happened to me. And if you see Seth," he shouts over the car at the street, "remind him, I'm the worst thing that will ever happen to him if he texts my wife again."

"Got it," I say through my grin. "You're hot when you're jealous."

I run towards him at his driver's door and reach my arms around his neck. He kisses me intensely, and my body melts into his. "Don't leave, Kevin."

"I have to," he whispers into my ear. "Come home to me, Ashley."

The passenger door opens, and Emily stands up and glares at us under the streetlight. "Look, you two. Either get a room, and get on with it, or let's go already."

"Goodbye, Emily." I let go of my husband. "I'll pick you up

tomorrow morning about ten."

She grumbles at me and I run to the porch and wait until I watch their headlights turn off the street. My heart is broken, and I can't even explain why. It might be that my so-called vacation just turned into an extended babysitting job from *Clueless*.

✦   ✦   ✦

FACING KAY'S FRONT door, I'm tentative. Only the foyer light is on, so most likely she's in bed, but the last thing I want to do is face her. Now I not only have to tell her about the rogue find under my bed, but I should probably give her some hint about Tiffany's. I unlatch the door as quietly as possible, and slip my shoes off where the "landing spot" used to be. Landing Spot = Kay's euphemism for where I could stash my stuff when I got home, so she didn't have to be reminded of my presence in her pristine existence. A small cabinet for my shoes, for my handbag, which back then were like art, so I never understood the point of hiding them. Regardless, the small white space is gone now, testimony that my presence no longer intrudes upon her bliss and serenity.

"Ashley!" Kay charges out of the dark hallway and nearly gives me a coronary. I reach for my chest.

"Kay, what on earth!"

"Where have you been?" she asks like a parole officer.

"I thought you'd be in bed by now." Read: Go there now. I start to rub my eyes in over-exaggerated motion. "What a tiring day. I'm so tired! Aren't you tired? And you've got to get up for work tomorrow."

She says nothing. Just stands with her fist to her hip like Brea's mother did every time I spoke as a child.

"I suppose you heard Kevin was in town."

"Kevin your husband? How would I hear that?"

"Yeah, that's why I went to my mom's house for dinner –"

"What happened to your wrist?"

I raise it slightly. "Oh you know me, so klutzy. I'm sorry I didn't call rather than text. I was icing my wrist." *Well, the ER nurse was doing it.*

"Actually, I saw Kevin on the front porch. Was that Emily sitting in the car?" She flicks on the lights, like she's preparing to give me the third-degree.

Oh my gosh, make it so, Kay. What do you want from me? "Yeah. Emily's here. Kevin is off to the airport to drop off the rental car." My thoughts drift to the reality of that situation. "Oh, I suppose I should have kept the rental car. I need to drive my sister-in-law to Napa."

"Ashley, what is wrong with you? You're nervous as a cat in the shower?"

She's right, and my body is trembling as I contemplate how I'll get around her to my bedroom. I can't look her in the eyes. I exhale raggedly. "I'm really tired. Do you mind if I crash?"

"Look at me."

I look into her prying gaze and straight back down at my bare feet.

"Where were you today?" she prods. "Never mind. I know exactly where you were."

"Kay, can't we talk about this in the morning?'"

"First, I want some answers."

"I was going to tell you about Tiffany's, but I—"

"Tiffany's?" She steps back. "The jewelry store?"

I shrug. "Well, what's left of it, I suppose."

"What on earth are you rambling about?"

"You didn't know I was at Tiffany's today?"

Worst fears confirmed. I slap my forehead. "Why do I always volunteer information? How many Proverbs are there about just keeping your mouth shut? Why don't I ever get it?"

She just keeps glaring at me the way she used to over that scary clipboard of hers – like if I didn't volunteer to be the next victim at open mic night, I was destined to live a life filled with pajama jeans and pleather handbags. I make a last-ditch effort at diversion. "You got rid of the landing spot—that little cabinet where I could put my stuff away when I got home. I never understood that."

"I wanted guests to avoid tripping over the myriad of shoes you left in the doorway. You were like living with a sloppy kindergartener." She raises her eyes to the ceiling and crosses her arms. "How quickly you forget."

"Look, he asked me to go with him—"

"Who asked you to go with him?" Kay holds up a plastic baggy filled with the orange unmentionables that have now been mentioned more times than I care to admit. *I'm going to be sick.*

"What are you doing with those?"

"Are they yours?"

I stammer and search for words, anything to avoid the truth that my gut knows. "They're not mine. When I found them the other day—"

"You've seen these before?"

Kay has a better guilt-inducing expression than even my own mother. Heck, a better one than Brea's mother. Pantygate is on.

"Ashley, please tell me they're yours."

No, Kay. Don't go soft on me now. Please.

And here it is. I must tell her the truth now – that Matt admitted – admitted what? Maybe he didn't admit anything. Maybe his mistake had nothing to do with my "find." My head is about to explode. If he did mean these garish things, and nothing happened and he has repented – which I realize is a lot of "ifs" and Kay wants to marry him, is it my duty to tell her a truth that will only harm her? When I don't even know what the truth is? But then again, what if he's just the lying, cheating dog I always thought he was? What then?

The burden is too much.

"What if they are Matt's?" I ask her. "What if he did bring a woman into this house? Could you forgive such a blatant lack of respect? It's your house, Kay!" I say this only because I think she must have respect for the house – herself and dating Matt, I'm just not so sure.

"It's obvious you know more than you're saying. You're the worst liar on the planet, Ashley. You can't even open a gift without your true feelings pouring out of you. I know what you think of Matt."

If she only knew how good my poker face was—because at this moment, I want to spill my guts and tell her to run. Then, I remember her telling me that I didn't understand what it's like for her. *I wasn't alone.* And Matt did save my life today…

"I thought they were yours." Kay straightens the already-straight picture frame. "I was so embarrassed when I saw the mess Matt left under the guest bed. How could I have missed that?"

Kay knows the awful truth. I can see it in her eyes, and she just wants confirmation. I try to lighten the mood.

"I'm offended you thought I'd wear those. That lace was for the tackiest Quinceanera on the lowest budget." I keep trying to redirect this conversation, so I can think about what to tell her. *How to tell her.* I don't want the responsibility of telling her this truth because she knows I've never liked Matt. She knows that I don't want her to marry him, and everything she hears about Matt comes through that filter of *Ashley doesn't want me to marry Matt.*

"He doesn't know I've seen them. I wanted to ask you first if they were yours, but I knew…" her voice trails off.

"Did you have a guest stay? Maybe you don't remember?" I want to smack myself. I know full-well where those came from, and I've just entered into collusion." I drop my head in my hands and then lead her to the sofa. Everything in her eyes pleads with me to lie to her, but I can't do it.

"Don't insult my intelligence, Ashley. I know who stayed with me in 1994."

"They're Matt's," I blurt. "Well, I mean, they're from someone who was with Matt. I don't suppose he's wearing women's underwear at the moment, but you know—"

"Ashley, stop. When I found them the other day –"

"You didn't ask him right then? Honestly, I don't know how that kind of stuff just doesn't fall out of your mouth? How do you keep suspicions like that to yourself? I would have tracked him down at work and—"

"Stuff like that doesn't fall out of most people's mouths. It falls out of yours." Kay walks across the room, tosses the baggy on the coffee table, and drops to the couch. "Who were you at Tiffany's with?"

"Matt," I say sheepishly. "So much for the surprise."

"Are you telling me Matt is planning to propose?" She sits up straight on the sofa. The grin on her face seems to negate every suspicion she's just shared and ignore my tale.

"Did you hear me, Kay? He admitted to me they were his. That he'd made a terrible mistake and wanted to marry you."

"You went to pick out an engagement ring to make me happy when you knew Matt cheated on me?"

"No." Finally I can tell the truth. "No, he told me while we were at the jewelry store."

"But you knew they existed. You asked him about them."

"Kay, stop. I did it all wrong, okay? I admit it. You told me you wanted to be married and I didn't want to hurt you based on my assumptions. Then, when they were more than assumptions, it was too late. Matt said he'd made a mistake and wanted nothing more than to marry you. What options did that give me?"

"The point is, it wasn't your option, don't you get it? You betrayed me by going to him first. You're my friend, Ashley. Or you were supposed to be."

The accusation backhands me. "What can I say? You're right."

"I don't even know who you are anymore, Ashley Wilkes Stockingdale Novak. I'm not like you. I would survive without a boyfriend."

"That's low, Kay. I've survived most of my life without a boy-friend or husband. You're the one who told me I didn't understand, that you didn't want to be alone forever. I was only—"

"You were going to allow Matt to propose to me when you knew he'd cheated."

"May have cheated. And no, I was going to tell you—"

"When?"

I sit up straighter. "When I knew for sure he'd cheated – I mean he claims nothing really happened, but yes, he apparently had someone here. I think. I found out only today, at Tiffany's, and you and I hadn't talked since then."

"But you had your suspicions, and you never shared them with me," she accuses. "I can't believe I never checked under that bed before I had a houseguest. You see how I'm slipping?"

"Um, I beg to differ. I think you knew very well how I felt about Matt, and you shut me down every time I tried to bring it up."

"You knew that mess wasn't mine though. You had to know I wouldn't be caught dead in anything orange, much less unmentiona-bles."

"I was going to tell you before he proposed, but I had to find out for sure first." *I think.* "Kay, I don't know what you want! Do you want to marry him? I mean, if he didn't cheat – and this is assuming he's telling me the truth now and we were talking about the same thing– but he almost cheated and brought someone here for that purpose, does it change anything for you?"

For me, it might change my view on the death penalty, but that's another story.

"I don't know if I want to marry him. I thought I did until I found out he brought someone here to my house. What you did to me made a fool out of me. It seems so cruel. Heartless. Not like you at all."

What I did? What about what Matt did?

"You have to look at my motive. I found a pair of undies under the bed, but I had proof of nothing. I was trying to do what was best, but I didn't know what that was – and I never had time to pray on it, so it was just Ashley being Ashley. No good ever comes out of that."

"Usually, you say whatever you think. What stopped you this time?"

"Your speech on being alone forever."

Kay is silent for a long time, and rather than fill the space as I normally do, I listen for what she isn't saying. Utterly foreign to the Kay I know, I watch as tears run down her cheek. I reach toward her, but reflexively she presses herself further into the corner of the sofa.

"The terrible part of this is that I don't know who betrayed me more. You, or Matt and I have nowhere to go now."

Call me crazy, but I'm going to have to go with Matt on this one.

"Maybe not working has made my brain go all mushy. I didn't think things through and I just wanted you to be happy, Kay."

Kay's expression turns cold, and if looks could kill, Kevin would find me in a shallow grave in the backyard, covered by a newly erected pergola.

I react to her icy stare with more words. "I didn't mean to hurt you. I wanted more time to decide if Matt really had reformed. He told me that he had. That he wanted to marry you, and I didn't know how to dash your hopes and kill all trust in him if he had reformed. What would have been the point?"

"You don't get it. You really don't get it, Ashley. It was never your job to decide if Matt was honest or not. It was your job as my friend to tell me the truth, and I honestly can't believe you, of all people, would let me blindly go into an engagement without relaying that kind of information."

"I was going to! I promise I was going to tell you, but only after Matt confessed!"

"What if it was too late? What if I'd already committed to him? Then, would you have told me?"

I wish I'd never met Matt Callaway. I definitely wish Kay had never met him.

"What a girl wants, and what a girl needs are sometimes, two very different things. That's what friends are for, to be the scale – to provide balance when you're too blinded by love to see the truth."

I nod. "You're right. You're absolutely spot-on correct. I didn't do my job as a friend. I'm not doing my job as a wife. I'm not doing my job as a lawyer. I failed, Kay. At everything, all right?"

Kay softens. "You know that isn't true. I'm not the marrying type. You and Brea, you're the marrying types. If I get married I have to answer to someone else. I have to make decisions with someone else. I have to—"

"You have to be vulnerable, yes. That's what love is. It's allowing someone in—it's giving away the power you have to be in control of everything. It's being vulnerable enough to let someone hurt you. I saw that for the first time when you and Matt were in the kitchen together." *Granted, it made me sick, but…* "You're always in control, Kay. Be here at this time, table set by this time, appetizers served at this time, dishes cleaned up by 9:04, people out by—"

"I get it. You cannot imagine that someone would find my organization attractive, and you noticed that Matt appreciated it."

"On the contrary." I shake my head vehemently. "I never thought that. It's the difference I saw in you, Kay. You let your guard down. You don't have the Fourth of July decorations up yet. You were just a girl with him, and you seemed so happy. Subconsciously, I don't think I wanted to be responsible for killing that part of you."

"Is the ring pretty?" she asks me in a small voice.

"Well, there is no ring. There's an open police case, and there's a broken wrist." I hold my hand up like Simba being presented. "But there's no ring, so no worries."

"Is Matt okay? Was he hurt?"

"He's fine. So was I, by the way."

"I knew you were fine. You always bounce back. You're ever buoyant. Life knocks you down, and you just rise to the occasion and come back better than before. You're not like me. For you, if Kevin went away, another ship would be along to pick you up soon. Some of us don't have all those options."

"Did I miss something? All of a sudden I'm Angelina Jolie and men can't resist me? Revisionist history, Kay. I loved a short, balding software engineer who did not love me back. Could you have told me that Seth wasn't for me, when he clearly wasn't?"

Kay grasps my wrist—the good one. "You have to be here tomorrow, so Matt can't ask me. I have to think. He's going to be angry I led him on."

"Let him be angry. Just hold up the lace."

"I'll never see him again. Once I tell him 'no'." Kay is at odds with herself and I feel her turmoil as if it were roiling in my own stomach.

"I'm taking Emily to Napa. Why don't you come with us? I can stay there for a few days until my mom's guest room is open – Lord forbid my father let me back in my pastel pink man cave."

Kay's agenda self reemerges. "Why is Emily going to Napa anyway? What's she doing here?"

"It's a long story. I'm renting a car and she'll be staying with some friends of my parents."

I know Kay's still not herself because she doesn't even question the ridiculous of this scenario.

"I'll drive you both up there."

Except the reason I'm taking her there is because she can't stay here with you.

"My mom was married three times by the time I was fourteen. I'm cursed."

"You're not cursed. You're just making a decision based on fear. What does your heart tell you? What is God whispering in your ear? Love makes you turn off logic. Until you can feel the decision, you can't make the right one."

"I'm going to bed. Brea was here today?"

"Yeah," I pause. "How'd you know?"

"There was a full roll of toilet paper in the guest bathroom. I didn't think you'd done it."

"Well, thank you for that."

The world has gone stark-raving mad, and maybe having friends is overrated. Chaos is a dust cloud that follows me everywhere. I'm craving my sorry, little lonely life in Philly where I talk to the gal who walks her dog at the same time as I do. Maybe I should look into becoming a hermit.

Chapter 17

I T'S NEARLY NOON when we arrive at Emily's hotel. I texted her our
ETA and she's waiting out front in a sea of trunks and suitcases.
"Seriously, how much did that cost her to get here?" Kay asks.

"She looks like she's leaving on an International voyage, rather
than going across the Bay to wine country. Maybe you and I don't
expect enough from life, Kay. Emily dreams something and it's like
God snaps His fingers."

Emily is wearing a chic, bohemian-style top with a leather belt
that hangs vicariously below her tiny belly and navy leggings. Her
hair is tied back with a yellow scarf as she twirls a tendril around her
forefinger while talking to a uniformed bellmen.

"How do some women get away with flirting while pregnant?"
Kay asks me while maneuvering her Prius in the hotel's driveway.

"Right?" Looking at Kay's fragile state, this seems like the worst
idea possible. "Why don't you let me drop you back home?"

"It's not really your place to decide." Kay cuts the silent engine,
and gets out of the car.

"I meant—"

"I know what you meant, Ashley." Kay shuts the door and walks
toward my sister-in-law. "Emily, good to see you." Kay pumps
Emily's hand in a most unsouthern fashion.

"I can't thank you enough for doing this, Kay. Ashley texted me
that we wouldn't have to rent a car, and I was so grateful, I nearly
burst into tears. I've got so much on my mind, as it is." She presses

the back of her hand to her forehead.

Seriously? If she breaks into the 'never be hungry again' speech, I give up.

"Nah, it's nothing. I'm glad to have the diversion, to be honest. Not to mention they've been nagging me to take vacation days. You should have heard my boss stammer this morning when I told him I was going to wine country. *But you don't drink, Kay,* he said."

I'm just gonna say it. Kay's a bigger person than I am. The lovefest between these two is enough to make me vomit.

The bellmen helps load Emily's suitcases into the trunk. He has to resort to piling the rest in the backseat. Emily, oblivious as always, slides into the backseat, straightens her back, crosses her legs at the ankles and sets her hands on her lap as the bellmen does as she expects and closes the door.

Kay, noticing the bellman's empty palm, pulls a few bucks out of her back pocket and hands him a tip. I make a mental note to add that to my growing debt to her, along with gas, and a heaping helping of humility that I clearly do not possess.

Emily's posture remains erect, as if she's waiting to be served afternoon tea, rather than being banished to the country to wait out the arrival of her baby. If she's self-conscious at all, it does not show in her wide, bright eyes—it seems as if she's off to tour the Continent, and if I've learned anything in my years of knowing her, it's probably true. Life will work out for Emily. Consequences will be thwarted, or dashed off to other, more plebian members of society. Like me for example.

"I've never been to wine country," Emily drawls. "It's ironic that I should go to the wine country when I'm unable to drink, is it not?"

I turn in the front seat to face her. "Are you sure this is necessary?"

"It's not safe at your house, Ashley. We've already established that fact. Your parents' friends don't seem to think I'll be burden. Once you help me get my legal affairs in order, you needn't worry about me any longer." She brushes her palms together. "You can wipe your hands of me."

I'd just as soon give my baby to a pack of wolves over Emily, so I'm concerned that she's got the opportunity to be a mother.

"I imagine Fish and Clara won't even notice my presence."

Oh they'll notice.

Kay, skipping all social graces, goes right for the jugular. "I have to admit, Emily. I didn't think you southern girls ended up pregnant out of wedlock. This guy doesn't even want the child? If I thought anyone would jam a ring on it, you're the first person to come to mind."

"It's not exactly as uncouth as all that," Emily says with her drawl intact. "His family is against the relationship. He's their meal ticket, and as such, he has a responsibility to his family. I told my family he didn't want a child so they'd let us figure it out."

"So he's a Mama's boy," Kay says.

"His upright position in the community is very important to him. I'm sure you understand about appearances in the South."

"But that's not honest, is it?" Kay says. "Knocking someone up and not taking responsibility is the worst kind of dirt ball move. As far as appearances go, what do you tell people about your bulging appearance? I mean, even if he wants the kid, your family is right to be concerned about the guy."

Emily's eyes flash ever so slightly and she speaks her next words through a clenched jaw. "I wouldn't say that it's bad form. Certainly, it's inconvenient, and ill timed, but it is my current situation and I do deal in reality—" Emily glares at me. "I know many people may think I live in a fantasy world, but I assure you, I am very aware of my present circumstances and how they appear."

I can't turn around, nor take my eyes off my sister-in-law. The way she speaks it's as if we should all take her route, and if only we'd thought of it first, we might have. Something isn't right. I know in my bones that Emily's act is for our benefit. The question is, why?

"I want to know why you had Kevin bring you here. You acted as if you were in some kind of danger," I blurt, emphasis on *acted*.

"Oh, I was! But we'll talk about that later. This is a ride for us girls to do some chatting."

"I know football is a religion down there," Kay says. "No one I know here actually follows it, but I imagine this guy is like the Second Coming in the South. That doesn't let him free of his responsibility, and I'm shocked you'd let him, Emily."

I watch Emily's hands curl up into small, tight fists, the outside of her fingers laced by her white hot anger, but it isn't long before she unclasps her hands, and that genteel grin crosses her face once again.

"How long will it take to get there, do you think?" Emily asks. "I think it's best we not discuss my circumstances at present. Suffice it to say, Josh is a good man. He'll prove himself worthy. His family? Well, that remains to be seen."

"He should have married you." Kay shrugs, and pulls out of the hotel's circular driveway.

It's going to be a long ride.

"It's his family. They don't like me."

"Why not? You know you marry the whole family, right?"

Advice I myself might have heeded.

"Once the baby comes, they'll see how much their son loves me. It's his brother mostly. He wants to control every aspect of his life. His brother is who came to Philly – who I ran from."

"So why didn't you tell your brother that, rather than have him worry?"

"Can we talk about something else, do you think?"

Something about Emily's story doesn't add up. I can't put my finger on it, but she makes no sense, and the story keeps changing. First, she's in danger, then she's just worried about his reputation.

"What's his name?" Kay asks. "I can't pray for his profound wispiness if I don't know his name."

I groan. "Kay!" I raise my brows, "Wispiness?"

"I thought it was a southern way to say wimpy. Genteel, if you will."

"It's all right, Ashley. I know what it looks like," Emily says. "If I didn't know him as well as I do—"

"In the Biblical sense," Kay says with a chuckle. Kay can be utterly crass at times, but pitting her against Emily is like bringing Victorian society to a biker BBQ.

Emily's mouth flattens. "If I didn't know him as well as I do, then I might think the same of him. Speaking of babies, Ashley, when are you going to give my brothah a newborn that he can take home with him?"

"I suppose it isn't the same as it used to be. Lots of people having babies first, marrying later," Kay says as a peace offering. "No judgment, Emily. It's just you don't seem the type, that's all."

I'm so grateful for Kay and her bulldozing ways. I can't imagine saying these same things to Emily, even if I was thinking them. I see no reason that she should be forced to leave town, her parents and the life she's known and bear her "shame" alone while this yahoo dances on television like some clean-cut sports hero everyone in the south will want their daughters to marry. It's despicable, and I can't imagine what it's like for Kevin being forced to keep Emily's secret. If there even is a secret.

"Oh, not in the South. Not when your mother is in the right social circles."

"Well, my mother is definitely not in the right social circles," Kay says. "Unless you count your local AA chapter. They know her name there, unfortunately."

"I don't," Emily says with a more pronounced drawl as she pats her stomach. "So Ashley? A little cousin playmate for us?"

"Not yet," is all I say.

"You're quiet about my shunning, Ashley. Don't you have an opinion on my sequestering?"

"Emily, I'm worried for you. You're really willing to have a baby, all by yourself, with complete strangers by your side? I mean, I'll come back when the baby comes, but why would you want to go through this alone? I don't understand it."

"I don't know what choice I have."

"You have a million choices, Emily. It's not like your parents are poor. They can protect you by arming that mansion of theirs, but from what I understand, it's his brother who is dangerous? Or him?"

Emily's eyes dart about as she searches for the right answer.

"You're clearly not too ashamed to have the baby, so why hide?" I persist. "Go home where you can be with family."

"I'm hiding from the scoffing, of course. I don't care what that old country club set thinks of me. I'm beyond help as far as they're concerned, anyway. But that's my mother's whole life and I can't make my shame, hers."

"I'm sure she wouldn't see it that way," I say to encourage her. "She seems genuinely excited about becoming a grandmother. It's clearly more than I can do for her."

"No, she told me that she saw it that way. That if I was determined to have this baby, then I needed to do it away from Atlanta, so I ran and I made up the story about being in danger. It was just easier than explaining I wanted away from my mother and her control. She was micromanaging every aspect of my life!"

"But your parents are Christians. Surely, they only wanted what's best for you." Kay says.

She guffaws. "All southern parents are Christians until their single daughters come home pregnant. Then, they start negotiating with God. My brother won't leave you, Ashley. Not even if you're barren."

What is the appropriate southern response to that statement?

The ride to Napa is annoying and riddled with traffic—each driver doing something more stupid than the next one. "I do not miss California traffic. Everyone here got their license from a Cracker Jack box."

"That's not true. They waited in a six hour line at their local

DMV." Kay laughs.

By the time we reach the vineyard, we have OD'd on Christian music and Red Vines and my heart is pounding as I gaze up at the house, which looks like an old French castle.

Emily sighs. "Seriously, Fish and Clara live here? They warned me it was big, but seriously?"

"Money is everywhere in Silicon Valley, Emily. If you learn nothing else while you're here. Never judge a book by its cover. Some ghetto-rich yahoo can be driving a $100,000 Mercedes without a cent to his name, and someone who answers to the name of Fish and dresses like a hobo, can be worth millions."

Emily shakes her head. "Everything is backwards here."

"That's the truth. No wonder I can't adjust to life outside this cosmic, geeky bubble."

The Chateau at the top of the knoll rises from the golden hills like a French castle that has been restored to its original 17'th Century glory. All of us draw silent as the Prius winds up the snaking driveway, which is caressed on each side by walls of majestic vineyards.

"I need a job," I mumble.

"A job and a trust fund the size of a Kennedy's," Kay says.

My conscience kicks in as I realize Emily deserves grace. God embraces His prodigals, and we're all prodigals. If we're not, we're the sniveling brother who stayed home, and thinks he's better—so he's guilty of pride.

All right, God. I get it. It's Emily's turn. She deserves to be coddled. I have Kevin and my own life. It's hardly Emily's fault I haven't done anything with it since I moved.

We are again silenced in awe. The castle's beautiful spires reach elegantly into the bright blue sky, alongside several brick fireplaces. The drive leads us to an enormous porte cochere cut with dramatic, cathedral archways to appear like a classic abbey.

"Does anyone else feel as if we're going to get arrested for trespassing?" Kay asks. "My little Prius has Maserati envy."

"Oh my," Emily murmurs. "I cannot stay here. Ashley, why didn't you tell me they lived in a castle?"

"I didn't know. They lived in a regular house when I was a kid. I mean, their stuff was always nicer, but nothing like this."

"Let's leave," Emily says.

"Where else are you going to stay?" I ask her. "It's either here, or you're coming home with me to Philly."

She is so not coming home with me.

"Those rough-looking people from your parents' house actually live here."

"They were dressed for a rod and gun show," I say incensed. "Clara is actually quite a beautiful woman. I imagine she'll be dressed more in her usual style today."

Emily stares at me. "No offense, of course."

"None taken. Fish owns the patents on a bunch of different inventions. He's a genius, and unlike many brilliant men, he knows how to make it work for him. I'd say he hasn't done too badly for himself."

The massive walls, which are a combination of brick and limestone, are interrupted by several turrets and topped by a sloped slate roof. Kay sits numbly and opens her window. We are greeted by the tinkling bell sound of running water on an entrance fountain and the deep, heavy barks of what can only be giant dogs. After staring at each other for a time, we finally step out of the car.

"It's like being in a gothic novel," I say. "Heeeeth-cliff!" I shout.

"Mr. Rochester!" Kay laughs. "Do you think they're keeping an ex-wife in the basement?"

"Or maybe in the south wing!"

"What are you two rambling on about?" Emily asks.

"Never mind," Kay answers. "Nerd humor."

The front doors, laden heavily with beveled glass shaped into the same cathedral style peaks of the porte cochere, swing open. Clara appears. "You made it!"

"Clara, seriously," I tell her. "This place is unreal. I have to ask you, why on earth would you ever leave the premises? Much less to go to a rod and gun show?"

She laughs. "The architects and Fish got carried away. You know how they always want to challenge themselves—which translates into the budget being nothing more than wishful thinking and not reality."

"How cool that he was able to do that—"

"A man like Fish doesn't know when to stop. He's always reworking something, so it's a work in progress."

"Kevin challenges himself with new surgeries. Our house is a complete dump," I tell her. "I never knew people really lived like this."

"Me neither!" Emily says, which surprises me. I would have thought her mother's friends might have had at least one acquaintance who lived like this.

Behind Clara, inside the house, there's an enormous mahogany staircase that splits in two directions toward the top. It must be twelve feet across. I lived in Silicon Valley long enough to know this is bad feng shui—that luck will run right out the door and down the hill. But clearly, it hasn't hurt their luck one iota, so I guess they don't believe in feng shui—or they have a plant in the right position.

"This place was a dump, too. That's why we rebuilt it. The land was too precious to harbor our old barn of a house. None of this would have been possible without Fish's ancestors working this land. Well, and I suppose, Fish's inventions so we could build the house. It all worked."

"Does it have a name?" Emily asks. "In the south, they'd name a great house like this."

Clara shakes her head. "Just home." Clara is so tiny and birdlike in appearance that her delicate features make you forget how inwardly stout she is.

"Have my parents been here?" I ask her.

"Many times," Clara says.

I mean, seriously! You think they might have mentioned that Fish and Clara were scions of wine country. You'd think in a decade or two, the subject might have come up. *I knew they were wealthy, but honestly…I would have worn my good Maxi dress.*

"How big is the house?" Kay's mechanical engineering side takes over.

"I'm almost embarrassed to say, but Fish had his plans and he is so hard-headed. I think it's about 18,000 square feet." Clara presses her hand lightly against Emily's belly. "Welcome. Maggie is so excited to meet you. She's been setting up your room so you'll feel right at home and I imagine she will be anxious to not have just us old goats here to talk to."

If this house isn't proof positive that everything Emily touches (except me) turns to gold, I don't know what is.

Emily stammers. I've never seen her so nervous, but she looks as though the house is alive and might attack at any moment. She presses her lips together. "I can't—I'm not…there's no way I can ever repay this debt. I think I should go back home with Ashley."

"Nonsense," Clara says. "God gave us this home for a purpose. Do you think He wants us holed up here alone? Or do you think He wants us to use it for a higher purpose?"

"What will I do here? You'll give me chores?"

"Yes," Clara says. "We'll have you on your knees scrubbing the floors, just like Cinderella. Maybe the mice will talk with you."

Emily's eyes are wide like fine china.

Clara presses a hand on her shoulder. "Emily, I'm kidding of course. You're already working, you're creating life."

"I'd feel better if I had something to do. I'm quite talented with floral arrangements."

"Well, if you like, we sometimes host weddings here for our church. Maggie likes to help the wedding coordinators with where to set things up. I'm certain we could find a similar job for you. I don't expect you to just sit back and be idle. That's not good for anyone."

Emily's forefinger is in her mouth. It seems the reality of being with strangers while she awaits my future niece or nephew, is starting to take root.

"Come inside. You'll see, it's just a regular house underneath its commanding presence. It's just a home like what you came from—with a TV, two unruly dogs and a longer hike than usual to get to the kitchen for a beverage."

Emily makes no move for her luggage, so Kay reaches for it in the open trunk. I yank the rest out of the backseat, but as Emily looks at me, I can see she isn't feeling safe, and for crying out loud, I can't leave her here if she's afraid. I could never answer to Kevin.

I take her hand and squeeze it. "Let's take a tour of the house. When would we ever get an opportunity to tour a house like this again?"

"Never!" Kay answers while she's packed down with Emily's suitcases. She looks far more anxious to be rid of Emily than I am. "Come on, man-up! You're going to be a mother soon."

Kay crosses the threshold first after Clara and I take Emily's hand. "This is weird," I whisper to her. "If it's too weird, we'll leave. Just tell me and I'll handle it if you want to leave." *That, in poker, is what they call a bluff.*

"We drove all this way."

"You've come from Atlanta. A two-hour drive to Sonoma is nothing. I promised Kevin I'd look after you, and I will." And darn it, I will. Guilt is a strangely powerful force.

Emily's eyes well up and she nods in comprehension. We walk into the house and it almost seems like we should kneel or make the sign of the cross. The house is so formal and church-like, I want to drop to my knees. My eyes follow the steps up to the ceiling, which is all wood, but so chamber-like, I almost expect to hear a choir. It's not dark, even with this much mahogany. There are so many windows, that shards of light infiltrate every corner. Tiny rainbows dance across the steps from the sun against the beveled glass.

"This place is ridiculous," Kay whispers in my ear.

My attention is arrested by a young, pregnant woman in a mini T-shirt descending the magnificent stairs, her belly protrudes over leggings. She's also wearing a bandana around her short, cropped hair. She scampers down the steps.

"Take it easy, Maggie!" Clara chastises.

"You're Emily?"

Emily nods. My sister-in-law is clearly not happy to be in the same position as Maggie.

"Maggie," the young girl says. Then, she sticks her hand toward me. "Ashley?"

"Ashley's not pregnant," Emily says to Maggie, then she shakes her head sorrowfully as if to relay my emptiness. I feel an immediate need to defend myself.

"We're not ready to start a family."

Maggie furrows her brows. "How old are you?" As if I'm Methuselah.

"Let's go have some iced tea, shall we, Ashley?" Clara pulls me toward the kitchen with her spritely steps. "Maggie, take Emily and get her settled in her room. Fish will bring up the bags later."

"I can take them," Kay says.

"No, no. You come with us."

I nod. "Nice to meet you, Maggie," I call after the lithe figure. "This is my former roommate, Kay."

"Come on." Maggie grabs Emily by the wrist in a childish fashion. "You can see the rest of the place later." She drags Emily up the stairs, and my sister-in-law stares back at me as if to say, *save me!*

"Now that we've lost the pregnant women, let's get some caffeine, shall we?" Clara leads us toward the back of the great house, and we enter the kitchen, which has a granite island so large, it has stools for eight at its counter.

Clara takes out an old, white Mr. Coffee machine, stained with traces of pots once made, and scoops coffee into the machine, pours some water in, and starts it. "Does anyone want tea? I have passion tea iced, and any kind you'd like, hot."

"Coffee's fine," Kay says.

"Kay, you're probably interested in the rest of the house. I know you were eyeing the way everything was put together. Why don't you wander while Ashley and I make the coffee. Just remember the pool out back is directly behind the kitchen, so wherever you are in the house, you can navigate your way back that way."

"Thanks!" Kay says, and she takes off before Clara rescinds the offer.

Clara, with her short blonde pixie cut, and aged skin looks more like a field hand from the vineyards than she does mistress of the house. The fact that a house has a mistress in this day and age, says it all. Clara's still beautiful for her age, her bright blue eyes, nearly turquoise in color, almost glisten with life.

"We got a strange call last night," Clara says. "Emily's boyfriend knows she'll be here. It seems he called here looking for her."

I shake my head. "He couldn't possibly. I didn't even have your number until last night."

Clara shrugs. "I've seen this before, Ashley. Your sister-in-law is not in danger from the sounds of it."

"No." I shrink a little. "I know she's not. She talked about this guy in the car like he was the second coming."

"So any idea why she might lie to you and her family?"

"Um, she was speaking?" I feel guilty immediately. "I don't know, Clara. I can't figure out what drives Emily. At first, I thought she just wanted to be a married southern belle and have life handed to her on a silver platter with highballs in the afternoon. But now? I have no idea what she wants. If you told me she'd end up pregnant without a husband, I would have laughed in your face."

"This beau of hers knew she was coming because he called here. Emily had to give him our number. We're not listed anywhere. He called here last night and we recognized his name immediately. He's a big name in college football."

"So now what?"

"She's not in any danger. Fish wanted to prove he can't be outplayed. He called the boy on his personal cell phone and told him if he shows up here, it better be with a ring and a marriage license. He said the young man was very polite and just wanted to bring his Emily home where she belonged."

My stomach is swirling. "She's not right in the head. I'm sorry I involved you in any of this. I have no idea what the truth is – what she wants a lawyer for, why she can't stay at her mom's house, nothing—"

"For now, we want to find out what she wants."

"I was thinking a lobotomy," I snark.

Clara pats me on the shoulder and grins. "You're so much like your father, Ashley."

There's the compliment of the day.

"Do you feel comfortable with her here? I mean, I told Kevin I wouldn't be responsible for her, but really, I'm responsible for her. I'll gladly take her back with me. Maybe gladly is overstating it. But she's my responsibility."

"I don't think that's a good idea. She'll be fine here, and we'll work out her issues. We've had a lot tougher cases than her. I promise you."

"Why would you do this?"

Clara pulls a coffee mug out of the cabinet, and I hop onto a barstool. "Because my son drove into that tree on purpose, Ashley. And now, when I see a young person in crisis, I feel like it's my purpose on earth to try and save them. What if some stranger saw something in Jackson that I didn't? What if they kept on walking when they might have taken his keys? I have this innate need to keep other parents from that knock on the door by CHP officers."

"I'm sorry, Clara. I didn't know."

"The only people who know it wasn't really an accident are your mother and father. They've never told a soul." Her face brightens. "Emily will be fine. We'll get to the bottom of this, but don't let her manipulate you. She's staying with us."

By the time Emily and Maggie make their way to the kitchen, I'm oblivious to the extravagance around me. The granite and the French enameled stove disappear, and suddenly, I'm on set in *Girl Interrupted* and Emily is playing a proverbial board game by herself.

Chapter 18

F ROM MY VANTAGE point on the kitchen stool, I spy Emily outside, lounging in the sun by the enormous, sparkling pool. Maggie is lying beside her, and the two of them don't seem to have a care in the world. *The very sight annoys me. Doesn't she know how worried everyone else has been?*

I put my cup down on the counter. "Excuse me, Clara, I think I need to talk to Emily for a minute."

As I cross the travertine floor, through the dramatic arches and cross the oversized family room, I keep my eyes fixed on Emily, so I don't notice when Fish comes by my side near the arched doorways. "Ashley, you made it."

I nod. "I did. I'm just going to speak with Emily for a moment." I point to the pregnant, lounging princesses.

"Before you do, would you mind if I have a word?"

My muscles tighten. "I shouldn't have brought her here. This is Clara's doing, not yours. Let me go talk to her and we'll be out of your hair."

Fish shakes his greying head, his eyes are smiling. Every time I've ever met Fish, he garnered that smile, as if he held some magical secret to the world that the rest of us were not privy to. He is eternally, unnaturally happy, and like a soaring hummingbird, I want to reach out and take hold of some of its magic.

"Sit down a minute, Ashley. Ever since you were a child you were full of that energy and you never stopped." He sits on the couch and raises his arms. "Look where you are. You're on vacation, you're in Sonoma, the heart of wine country, and you're so focused on fixing everything, you're missing the moment."

"At the moment, I want to harm my sister-in-law."

"I imagine that happens a lot with Emily. She's quite a storyteller."

"That's one way to look at it. I'd be more apt to use the term, *deceiver*." Lioness of Satan?

He chuckles. "I'm sure you would, but for today, let's say she's a storyteller and she is queen of her own magnificent kingdom."

I plop on the plush, white sofa and stretch out my legs.

"Isn't that better to take a load off?"

"Fish, leave her alone!" Clara calls from the kitchen.

"We're just having a conversation. No need to butt in here."

"I promised her mother we'd take care of things, so don't go worrying her about Emily."

"Am I worrying you?" he asks me before raising his voice again. "I know, Clara. We're just having a discussion, don't go getting all excited. Why don't you make me a sandwich?" Fish winks at me. "That will get her going. You watch."

Clara appears in the doorway. "What did you say to me?"

"I said, why don't you make yourself useful and slap me together a sandwich."

"That's what I thought you said." Clara disappears for a moment, we hear her rifling through a drawer, and Fish wiggles his brows. Clara appears again with a rolling pin in her hand.

"Do you want to ask me that question again?"

"Not on your life." Fish chuckles. "I'm just talking to Ashley about the job. Give us a minute." He turns back to me. "I have a patent I'd like you to look at it. Your dad tells me you haven't been working much in Philly."

"I know my dad did *not* say that."

"You're right. He said you were turning into a bum and after all that expensive education they mortgaged the house for."

I nod. "That sounds more like my father."

"I've got the new patent written and it's on my computer, but I'm too old to follow through with it. I thought that part of life was over, and I don't know if all the T's are crossed, the I's dotted. You know the drill. The red tape drives me crazy anymore."

I smile. "Red tape makes me a living. What's the patent for?"

"It's a software program for managing a winery and making it profitable. So many wine lovers come up here to retire, buy a vineyard and have no idea what to do with it. Some vintner comes along, offers them money for the grapes and that's where it ends. The business aspect of running a winery is not complicated, but there is a business model. I figure if I can teach them that business model, they can fulfill their dreams of having their own winery and making a profit in retirement. Very simple if you follow the business model."

"The trouble is, no one knows that simple business model," I tell him.

"Precisely." Fish sits back on the sofa and crosses his arms across his chest. "It won't be a huge seller, but that's why we can ask more for it. People can put $1,000 or so into the software and make a living and fund their retirement much more effectively. It will be their decision if they want to just sit on their grapes and wait for surrounding wineries to pull in the profits."

"And if they want to sit on the grapes?"

He shrugs. "By all means, sell the grapes. But I fail to see why successful businessmen retire here and let money fly out the door by allowing the grapes to be mere landscaping. It makes no sense to me."

"I'm happy to look at the patent, but you realize I'll have to research competing software and you may have to make changes depending on anyone else's process. And that this is nepotism, and I'm perfectly capable of getting a job without your help."

"You think way too highly of me. I want you to file it. Do all the research, change the wording as necessary and get it working. I'm not going to pay you; I'm going to give you 50% of the profit. You'll have to make the patent work internationally. I suppose there are idiot retirees in France and other wine regions, too."

I laugh. "I'm certain we do not have a corner on the market of village idiots. But if you have to be the village idiot, this isn't a bad place to be one."

"Agreed."

I watch as Emily flips herself over on the chaise in the sun, and moves the cushions to cradle her tiny belly. "Really, Fish. I appreciate what you and Clara are trying to do, but I need to take her back home with me."

He shakes his head. "You act like Clara hasn't brought home some doozies. I'd say 90% of what they tell us isn't true in the beginning. Sure, there are some honest ones who are really in trouble and appreciate the help right from the start, but the rest of them? Oy! Fahgettaboutit." Fish waves his hand. "They're always the victims, but I guarantee you, most of them have done something to contribute to their situation. Oh we've had some girls that were harmed, I'm not talking about them, of course. But we've had quite a few who set a trap for marriage, and the man-child they were toying with didn't come through in the end."

"I don't even know what her story is."

"Emily hasn't told you truth yet, and she won't until she's ready—or, until she's forced to. That's my experience. Take it for what it's worth. If you back her into a corner, she'll feel as if she's fighting for her survival and the results may be worse."

"She's going to be fighting for her survival if she lies to me again."

Fish laughs. "You wouldn't hurt a fly. You're all talk."

"Maybe, but why would anyone lie for no reason?"

"You don't know that she's lying for no reason."

"She just does the strangest things. She makes no rhyme or reason."

Clara comes from the kitchen. "She probably didn't get enough attention at home."

"No, I don't think that's it."

Clara sits beside me on the couch. "It doesn't matter. Quit worrying yourself over this."

"I feel as if I'm shirking my duties."

"Your duties are to get that patent written," Fish says. "Let me give you a USB drive with the patent before you go."

"Fish, don't hustle her out. I'm sure she wants to stay for an early dinner."

"I couldn't intrude any more than I already have."

Kay jogs into the family room. "Oh my gosh, this place is incredible! Every room has its own bathroom, and there's a place for everything. And it's all laaaa-bled!" she sings in operatic voice. "There are his and her closets, all organized by type, color and season. Can you handle it?"

"You were in their closet?"

Kay's eyes widen. "Was I not supposed to go in their closet?"

"Well, it's generally nice to ask before you walk into someone's closet. It's personal."

"Does that mean I can't look in the kitchen cabinets? Is that personal?"

"Kay!"

Clara laughs. "You can look anywhere you'd like, Kay. We have nothing to hide, and I do appreciate a connoisseur of organization. It's not everyone who would notice the seasonal aspect."

"Kay notices everything. I'll bet she's dying to look in your pantry."

Kay nods eagerly. "I am!"

"Come on, we'll let those two work and we'll check out the pantry and see what's for dinner," Clara says. "You'll let me know if you have any tips?"

From here on out, I will refer to my mother's friend as Santa Clara. A true saint.

Kay claps her hands together. She's actually giddy. Let me mention that I saw none of this excitement when she thought Matt might be asking her to marry him...or that she might be getting a Tiffany ring on that left hand of hers. She saved all that dizzying enthusiasm for a closet of groceries.

Fish leads me across the house, through the enormous foyer, underneath the majestic staircase to his office, which overlooks the sun-kissed hills etched evenly by vines. His office is all wood, but not the dark mahogany of the entryway, but a lighter, airier color. Double glass doors lay open to a patio, and his large desk has nothing on it. "I can't believe I've known you practically my whole life and never heard you built this house."

"It's just a house, Ashley. Clara hates it. She won't say so, but she hates it."

"Only someone who owned a mansion like this would say it's just a house," I laugh. "How could anyone hate this place? This is what I imagine heaven looks like. Only there are pretty, fluffy clouds beneath me rather than gravevines."

He laughs. "Only, in heaven, someone else will do all the work that it takes to keep it up." He sits down at his desk, and opens it, to reveal a pop-up desktop computer. "The house embarrasses her, so she never really invites her friends here. I got carried away. It's a bad habit I have."

"I never thought of that." *And let's face it, I never would think to be embarrassed by my own castle.* "Did you ever think of moving?"

"Oh yeah, and we will someday. When the property gets to be too much. For now, Clara will fill it up with people who need to find their path."

"Someday," I sigh wistfully. "Someday I'll be out of our miserable little house and someday, I'll work again and—"

"Here's the thing about someday, Ashley, it never comes. Don't wait for life to happen or you'll miss it."

"If I make a mistake, I have to fix it, unlike Emily. Everyone just takes care of her. She never has to grow up and take responsibility for herself."

Fish looks up from his computer. "This bothers you?"

"It doesn't bother me so much as it isn't fair."

"I know Someone else Who was nailed to a cross. It wasn't fair either. Did you ever think that maybe Emily has that much faith to trust that life will work out for the best?"

Not Fish too. Emily lives a touched existence. Everything around her turns to gold. And someone else is always paying its price.

Chapter 19

AFTER A LOVELY dinner of curried chicken salad on fresh croissants outside by the infinity pool, all is quiet…peaceful. Emily is on her best behavior. Kay has seen about as much organization that her heart can handle, and Maggie is clearly excited to have someone her own age at the Mansion for Wayward Girls.

"I guess we'll be leaving," I say, as I scoot my chair out from the table. "Clara, this was—" The back right leg of my chair edges off the flagstone patio. I feel it go down into the pool, and struggle to maintain my balance, but it's too late. I'm tangled in the skirt of my maxi-dress. I yank the edge of the table to keep from falling, but instead I grab the tablecloth and see only sky as I fall backwards. The water hits me like an icy breeze and I struggle in my summer dress as it wraps around my legs like a mummy's dressing encasing me. I can see a few glasses and bits of silverware float around me in this surreal Salvador Dali imagery and some part of me just wants to stay underwater, but a need for oxygen makes this dream impossible and I press off the floor of the pool and propel myself upwards.

This is how I'm going to go one day. Some humiliating venture in front of people who matter to me, and they will struggle not to laugh at my funeral. "Bahaha, it was so Ashley!"

"But it's so sad she's gone," someone will say in a hushed voice.

"Yes," Brea will say as she straightens her posture, and tries to maintain her composure before bursting into laughter again. "But really, didn't we expect as much?"

I reach the surface, gasp for air, and lift my elbows over the edge to see everyone's astonished expressions gazing at me. Let's face it, there's really no way to maintain any dignity at this point. Everyone is dressed in their lovely summer fare, staring down at my alien self with wet hair plastered to the side of my face.

Fish bends over the pool, trying to hide his smile, and takes my hand. With one force-filled yank, he pulls my entire body out of the water with ease.

Emily and Maggie are in tears laughing and make no attempt to hide it—Kay is simply mortified and somehow knew I'd ruin the day. It's not like I haven't mangled her parties before, but now, I've taken away her day of organizational perfection—the perfect antidote to her broken heart. I go to jump back in the pool as I see the iron chair and the tablecloth at the bottom, but Fish holds me back.

"I'll take care of that. Go find some dry clothes." Then, he stares at me intensely. "Ashley, you need to slow down. Enjoy life. Don't take it so seriously. Laugh."

He's right. Somewhere along the line, I turned so serious. I'm like Kay on steroids. I keep blinking at him with the revelation, but I can't find words. Clara envelops me in a towel. "Let's go to Emily's room. I've got some extra yoga gear and shoes that will fit you in her closet."

I take one look at birdlike Clara, and I think the only yoga gear of hers that's fitting me is if she plans to roll me up in her mat.

As I'm taken off like a petulant child on a house tour, I gaze back at Emily. Nothing affects her. She's onto the next thing.

"I'm the problem," I mutter through shivering lips to Clara as we cross the museum-sized iving room. "Emily doesn't have a problem at all, does she?"

Clara tightens her hands around my shoulders as she leads me up the grand staircase into Emily's new digs. The bedroom, which is basically the size of Kevin and my whole house, is fit for a princess. I drip onto plush, white carpeting that feels like pillows under my feet as I sink deeply into it. A four-post bed in the same light wood from Fish's office and an incredible view of the entire Napa Valley to the tops of the evergreen mountains at the other side.

This is how Emily is rewarded for her game of lies. I'm on vacation, essentially looking for a job, and my sister-in-law rolls into town for one day and is set up in a spa-like estate for the duration of her pregnancy with no one calling her on her web of intrigue.

"I'm doing something wrong."

"The bathroom is just in there. You'll find towels and a fluffy robe to warm up. I'll gather up some clothes and leave them by the door when you're finished."

Clara's act of kindness makes me want to burst into sobs. I want to sink into it and relish the moment, but my mind is filled with Kay waiting for me. Ready to leave, ready to make a decision about Matt, and again, I'm in her way.

The bathroom is bright and large, filled with shards of sunlight, streaming in crystalline beams through the giant oak tree outside. There's a terrace, and I walk carefully along the slippery tile and open the door to the sun's warmth.

My eyes are drawn back inside to the freestanding bathtub that holds court in the center of the travertine tile, and while it's gorgeous, there is no way I'm getting into another water element that is freestanding on hard Italian tile. I'll be tasting travertine.

"Ashley, do you need anything?" Clara calls from outside the door.

"Nope." Just a fresh start. I step gingerly toward the shower and as the hot water streams over me, my emotions overflow. What is it about the shower that acts as a virtual judgment seat?

No word from Kevin. Again.

Brea's content in her misery.

Kay is waffling back and forth over a con artist good enough to trick me too. (I helped him pick out an engagement ring!)

Seth believes I hold some kind of magical key to his marriage.

And Emily is happily sailing away on life's fun ship cruise.

Everything is all wrong, and somehow, I'm the only one who seems to notice.

I come out of the bathroom in a spa-like robe, a massive, fluffy towel wrapped around my hair. When I emerge, Emily is lying on an overstuffed chair, staring at the ceiling dreamily. She sits up on her elbows suddenly and blinks her wide eyes at me in that faux innocent way of hers.

"I wonder if they have a maid." She flips her golden-brown strands airily. "Do you think someone comes in weekly? Or more often?"

"If I know Clara, she cleans her own house, so I think the appropriate thing to do would be to clean up after yourself." I release my hair from the towel.

"Hmm," she groans. "That's most unfortunate. I suppose I should get unpacked. There's an empty dresser!" Her eyebrows rise briefly. "Just like in a fancy hotel. Isn't that awesome?"

"Everything is awesome," I sing, quoting the Lego Movie. Emily doesn't pick up on the reference.

"Do you want to help me unpack? You're so good with clothes."

With all my heart. "Emily, we have to talk about the truth of your baby daddy."

"My baby daddy? Did you just say my baby daddy?" Only with her accent, it comes out *baa-bee-ah daddeh*. "You make me sound like some cheap floozy. Would you say that in front of my brothah?"

"I didn't mean to make it sound like that. I'm sorry." I cinch the belt of my robe. "I know this stalker business is a pile of rubbish, and that your beau wants to be married, regardless of what his contract states. I need the truth. Not the half-truths you tell us to keep your secrets, but the whole truth. Your brother thinks the world of you, and I really want to, Emily—but I've never met anyone who keeps more secrets than you. It's like you're playing some game in your head that none of us are privy to—so naturally, you're always winning. I don't want to win. I want to help you, but you have to let me inside."

She stares at me with thinned eyes, but says nothing.

"I know he wants to get married. But I want to know why you led your brother to believe you were in danger. Kevin risked losing his position to bring you out here, and I just don't think you get what your antics cost other people. He had to make all that time up, and I can't even get a phone call into my own husband. You sail through life as if your consequences should be everyone else's, and then you flutter those big, beautiful eyes of yours and everything is forgiven."

"My brothah knows family is numbah one." The southern accent is back in full with her righteous indignation. "When a cawwled him, he was only too happy to come home from work. If he doesn't come to you when you cawl, it's because you're not truly his family yet and that is not my fault."

I don't let her get me off course. "I'm not talking about Kevin and me. Emily, tell me why you lied." I know I told Fish I'd let it go, but I see her prancing about like she owns the place, I'm incapable. It's the lawyer in me, ready for a fight and in need of justice, I suppose.

To my surprise, she tosses her legs over the side of the bed, finds a Queen Anne sitting chair, positions herself in it, and looks directly at me. "It was an accident, my getting pregnant. I need you to know that."

That much I believe. Emily is not sacrificing her figure on purpose. I sit down across from her and relax my expression. I try to lose all judgment because I know that's how she sees me—as her judge and jury. I hate that there is probably truth in this. "I know we've had a rough go of it, but I want what's best for you, Emily. So why are you here with people you never met before yesterday?"

She sinks into the cushions, and relaxes her arms alongside the chair. "I'm tired, Ashley. Can we talk about this later?"

"Tell me about this man you love. Can we start there?"

She sighs wistfully. "Oh Ashley, I've loved him since the day I first saw him back in high school. He's tall and sweeter than a pecan pie. He's smart and such a gentleman. He never ever makes me feel stupid. He was raised on the other side of town, but that doesn't matter much. His grandmother raised him with proper manners, and when he looks at me, I feel utterly and unconditionally loved. Is it really so much to ask that I wait to marry him?"

Uh, yes?

"You're not going to get it, even if I explain it to you," Emily continues. "You're one of those modern women, Ashley. You don't believe you need a man and that's why you and my brother can't get along. You're trying to be a good housewife, only you aren't a housewife. You don't know who you are."

"I am a housewife! I consider it an honor to be a housewife. I'm the definition of a stinkin' housewife!"

"Your friend, Brea. She's a housewife. You are far too high maintenance to be a housewife. Your mind moves too fast. Nothing wrong with that, of course. Except you don't own it."

I'm completely insulted. "I can do anything I set my mind to."

She scoffs. "Ashley, you may think me a complete idiot, who does nothing but find trouble and create a whirlwind, but I know who I am. I'm high maintenance. I'm not particularly good at anything, other than arranging beautiful bouquets and maybe incubating a child." She runs her hand on her belly. "I suppose that remains to be seen—I just hope the child doesn't come out looking like a troll. I think I'd have a hard time mothering an ugly baby."

I laugh out loud. "Emily, that's a terrible thing to say!"

"But it's honest. You tell me I'm telling stories, and maybe I am—but inside, I know my truth. Do you?" She gets up and lies on the bed. "I need to rest now, Ashley."

She needs to rest. She needs a lobotomy.

Chapter 20

WE SPEND THE night at Fish and Clara's. I was soggy. Kay wasn't ready to face Matt, and let's face it, leaving paradise for the rat race of Silicon Valley is hardly a priority. After a morning of lounging by the pool, sipping mineral water spritzers, Kay and I get into the same clothes we came in the day before and say our good-byes.

The ride home is silent, and when we pull up into Kay's drive-way, she hasn't said a word about Matt or what her decision might be. I've been silently praying the whole way home that she didn't interpret my trip to Tiffany's as I'm a supporter of Matt Callaway. There's a tall man standing on Kay's front porch in the afternoon sunlight.

"Who is *that*?" Kay's mouth dangles.

"Kay?"

"That man. Have you ever seen a more gorgeous specimen?"

"Gorgeous specimen? Kay, what's gotten into you?" I look at the porch and see Matt's business partner. "It's just Thomas Galway. That's Matt's partner. He must be here about the prospective he dropped off."

"Who?" she asks again, and it's clear she's not processing a word I'm saying.

"Matt's business partner. I take it you haven't met him before." Another red flag, for Matt, the other keeper of secrets.

Kay looks in the rearview mirror, and knock me over with a

feather, she looks at her reflection and presses her lips together. Like an idol-struck teenage girl!

"N-never saw him before," she stammers. And with that one half-thought, I understand instinctively, she was settling for Matt. For all her bravado about loneliness, and a life of cats, Kay is not in love with Matt Callaway. That much is obvious, and my entire body relaxes. "He's been here before?" She looks straight at me. "Ashley, was the house clean?"

"It was pristine, Kay. What's the deal?" I can't break her gaze. "Don't you find it odd that you haven't met your potential fiancé's business partner?"

"Is he nice? Outdoorsy? Metrosexual, what? Is he a Christian?" She giggles then sobers. "I suppose I should have asked that last question first."

"He's a guy who is standing on your porch. He's not a hologram." I open the door and call over the car, "Hi Thomas!"

"Ashley!" He waves and tugs at his yellow bow tie. My eyes are drawn to Kay, who stands between us, and has not taken her eyes off of Thomas since we pulled into the driveway—she is utterly spellbound. He leaps off the porch and comes toward me, but stops at Kay.

"You must be Kay." He grasps her hand, stares into her eyes and then brings his other hand around hers. They stand in the driveway, holding each other's hand, and I suddenly am a third wheel in a romantic comedy. *I'm the awkward friend!* Well, I'm always the awkward friend, but this time it's more obvious.

"You're Matt's partner? How is it I haven't met you before? Until Ashley came?" She asks this breathily. Her voice has taken on this husky tone and she suddenly reminds me of a young Lauren Bacall and I'm waiting for her to offer tips on how to whistle.

"Maybe Matt was trying to keep you to himself. I can't say I'd blame him."

She giggles. *Kay!* Kay giggles. Watch your bacon. Pigs are about to fly.

"Have you eaten?" Kay asks her new friend.

He shakes his head, but never takes his eyes from Kay's.

"I have this tri-tip I'm going to grill," Kay purrs. "Do you eat steak? Because I make a mean tri-tip. It's been resting all day in the dry-rub."

He grins wider than his bow tie. "Only when I get out to eat on business. I'm not much of a cook myself."

"No wife at home?" she asks.

He shrugs. "Silicon Valley, you know. I don't have much time or opportunity for meeting anyone."

Suddenly, the spell snaps like a rubber band, and Kay is aware of my presence. She turns and glowers at me as if I'm intruding. She pulls her hand away from Thomas. "I need to call Matt."

Thomas slides his hand along the side of hers softly as he pulls away and she shivers slightly at his touch. Without another word, she unlocks the door and hustles into the house.

Thomas stares at me. "Did I say something wrong?"

On the contrary. Looks like you said just about everything right. "No, Kay's a bit touchy today. She's been driving all day and it's been a stressful time. She has a lot on her mind."

"Do you think I'm invited for tri-tip? Because I've morphed into Pavlov's dogs at the hint of a good steak."

"Of course you are. Kay never lets anyone leave hungry."

"So what you're saying is I'm not special. I'm just invited?"

I know what he's asking. But to give it to him is one more betrayal of Kay—and I cannot afford that. "Kay believes everyone is special."

"I can't believe she cooks and looks like that. I've never seen calves curve so beautifully." He makes a shapely motion with his hands, and then catches himself. "I'm sorry. I'm creeping you out, right? I swear, I'm not normally like this. When I saw her—" his mouth is still open. "Never mind."

"She runs."

Thomas rubs his chin thoughtfully. "I'm sorry?"

"She runs. That's why her calves are like that. Her life has really come together since I left here. I might be a jinx." I offer him fair warning.

"Right. Did you look over the preliminary prospectus?"

I shake my head. "I haven't really had an opportunity."

"Of course. You're on vacation. I should have realized—we have a shot for three more potential customers, and I think you'd be perfect for them. They've all got funding behind them, but these lawsuits could send venture capitalists running. Matt told me you're into fashion, and one of them sells designer bags."

My eyes pop. "At a discount?"

"Well, no. But their specialty is the way they work with the customer. That software process is patented, and it's being violated, but they're only two years' old. They can't afford to fight the legal battle."

"Oh my gosh. I could be like Wonder Woman saving quality handbags for everyone!" I stab both hips with my fists.

"I would have to object to a costume."

"Buzz kill." I push the half-open door. "Come on in. This idea, while intriguing, requires a lot of travel, obviously. I'm not ready to give an answer. Not even close." Considering my husband doesn't return any of my phone calls, discussing this with him isn't exactly an option.

Thomas follows me in the house, and I see him peeking around for Kay. When he spots her, I may as well have evaporated. He's speaking to me, but he's hardly present. "Sometimes," Thomas says half-heartedly, "when you don't know exactly what you want? You have to rule out all the things you don't want. I don't hear you ruling this out."

"That's profound, and far too much for me to think about on an empty stomach. Let's go see if Kay needs help with the steak." I'll admit it. Maybe I'm a bit of a matchmaker, which would be wrong with Matt in the picture. Not that I have any loyalty to Matt, but I'd like him cut from the picture before Kay moves onto the next thing.

Then again, all's fair in love and war—which seems to be Matt's own mantra.

Before we enter the kitchen, Thomas taps me on the arm, and I turn. "Matt Callaway is not dating her. I refuse to believe it." His eyes are fixed on the kitchen window where Kay is in her eagle's nest over the sink. "She's far out of his league."

I hate to burst his bubble, but it must be done. "We were nearly blown up yesterday shopping for an engagement ring. Don't you watch the news?"

"No, I don't watch the news because I'm not 70-years old." Thomas' expression falters. "Engagement? Matt Callaway plans to be engaged?"

Come on—we were almost blown up, and he leads with engagement? "There is no humanity left in Silicon Valley. I'm convinced of it."

"Wait, what?" Thomas pulls me toward the yard, away from the kitchen. Recognition dawns. "I'm sorry. You were almost blown-up and I was focused on Kay." Gone is the happy-go-lucky smile, and a cloud of darkness hangs over his brow.

"Thomas." I snap my fingers in his face twice. "Come back to me here."

"I've never felt anything like that." His jaw is set. "Kay is not marrying Matt." He looks at me with anguish. "Can't you feel that? It's wrong in every way."

I suddenly feel for Matt. Though I have no idea why. Didn't Matt once tell me that no one else wanted Kay? Isn't there the question of the orange underwear of undetermined origin? Though– though I hope to never discover its owner. *This is but an innocent flirtation. It's a universally acknowledged truth that a person in possession of a boyfriend must attract another suitor—just to make things interesting.*

As Thomas stares into the kitchen window as if he's seen a falling star and it's close enough to capture, I realize I've been here before.

The first time Seth saw Arin, I bore witness to the magic—the way he gazed at her as if she held the last piece to an impossible puzzle. It was as if I'd never existed. Somehow, I fear—if Thomas's relentless pursuit and lack of a bro-code, is any indication—Matt is about to find himself in the doghouse. Or pergola, as the case may be. Which is exactly where he belongs.

"It's your friend's girlfriend. The guy you work with—aren't their rules about that? You see, I loved a guy named Seth. I can't exactly remember why I loved him, but I did, and the second Arin appeared, that's his wife now, I faded into oblivion and ceased to exist in the world. Doesn't Matt deserve that? I mean, you don't even know who Kay is—this is just—"

"Ashley?"

"Hmm?"

"I asked you if you believe in love at first sight?"

"No. I believe in lust at first sight. Seth fell in lust, and now he's paying the price."

"Then, you don't know me very well." Thomas looks down on me with intense, gray eyes. "Sounds like Seth believed in love at first sight, too."

"I don't know you at all. I admit as much, but I do know Matt's your business partner, and I assume there's some kind of guy code that prevents this type of thing from happening. I'm not saying never. I'm just saying, maybe this needs to be put on the backburner for now."

He grins, and the innocuous, nerdy businessman disappears, and I spy a warrior in his place. I want to clasp my eyes shut, put my fingers in my ears and pretend I never heard or saw a thing.

Thomas struts into the kitchen, and I follow closely behind and nearly get tagged by the swinging door, which he's shut behind him. Kay is patting the meat with more dry-rub over the sink. Thomas stands mesmerized as if she was flying on gossamer wings, but it's not the sexiest pose—although who knows? Maybe it is. Maybe a guy likes to see a woman who knows how to handle a hunk of beef. What do I know? The kitchen has never been my natural habitat.

He scuttles past me and farther into the kitchen. "Can I help in any way?"

Kay stares up at him, and that's shocking in itself, because Kay is very tall. When she sees the intensity in his eyes, she immediately looks back down at the sink. "No, thank you," she says quietly. *Shyly.*

He mumbles something I can't hear, and her eyes meet his again. The door presses open behind me, and I grab at my throat. "Why are you standing in front of the door?" Matt Callaway pushes through the door jam, moving me out of the way with his efforts.

"No reason," I say with a crackling voice. "And could you wait rather than ram the door into me? Didn't your mother teach you any manners?"

"No, but she taught me not to stand in front of doors. What's the matter with you? You're like a scared cat on his last life."

"I—uh—" I try to keep his attention off of the kitchen. We push through the door and into the dining room.

"How's your arm?"

"No, it's fine. It's fine."

"I picked up the engagement ring," he whispers as he presses his chest twice. "You need to help me with the right way to ask. It has to be over-the-top romantic, and a complete surprise."

"Oh, I think it will be." I stall for time. "So…is that a new tie?"

He tugs at the knot. "No." His brows furrow a bit. "Who's that with Kay in there?"

I nod. "Yeah. Kay's marinating the steak, a massive chunk of beef—" My cell phone trills. "So it's not a new tie. It's a good color on you. You should wear that more often."

"Aren't you going to answer your phone?"

"Is that mine?"

"It's a Christian song for a ringtone. It's definitely not mine." He rolls his eyes.

"Matt, that's hysterical!" I say far too loud as I slap his bicep. The swinging door opens again, and I see Kay turn towards me.

Before I can see any fallout from everyone's position, I answer my cell phone. "Hello?"

"Ashley? It's Emily."

I exhale. *Like that's any better.* "Emily, is everything all right?"

"I'm in a Napa Valley mansion, what could be wrong?"

"Good point."

"I just called to tell you that Kevin says he'll call you tomorrow."

"You talked to Kevin?"

"Yeah, he called to check on me, but he had to go right back into surgery. So he wanted me to let you know that he's okay and you'll connect tomorrow."

"Oh. Yeah. Thank you."

"I also wanted to say that I think you left your underwear here. They were in a pink, lacy wad under the bathtub, and naturally, they were soaking wet. Are yours pink?"

I clutch my phone tightly and turn away from Matt. "Um—"

"You did!" She starts to laugh. "First, you fall into the pool. Then, you leave your panties at someone's house. I cannot wait to tell Mothah, she gets such a kick out of you." *Read: Mourns for her son.*

Oh. My. Goodness. I have instantly become one of *those* women, which is totally what I get for judging. When you judge, it's inevitable that life is going to bite you in the behind. You're naked, choneless, behind. "I did drive you all the way up to Napa and find you a place to live. What do you say that we keep this between us? Like a sister secret."

"But it's so delicious. I mean, you're so smart, Ashley. Everything you do is like something they give a degree or a trophy for. But to fall into a pool and leave your pah-an-tees," she stretches out the word to all its southern glory. "In someone's mansion? How can I possibly keep that to myself? It's so delicious."

"You know, you can just get rid of them. I have plenty with me."

"Consider it done. I do have to tell you that it was kind of trau-matizing to know my husband's wife wears lacy, pink panties. These are things one should keep private. Does Kehvin like that?" She stops herself. "Don't answer that. I don't want the answer to that ques-tion."

"Anything else, Emily?"

"Well, if they weren't yours, I didn't know whose they could be, and I didn't want to throw Mrs. Bowman's out by accident. I should have known they were yours. I mean, they were wet, and who else went into the drink?" She giggles again.

All I can think is that soon, there will be two of her. "Sorry to have scarred you, Emily, but yes, I do wear panties. I know, it's scandalous, but it could be worse."

"I didn't take you for the commando sort." She laughs again.

"Just throw them out." I roll my eyes, even though she can't see me. Seriously, it's a pair of panties—it's not like I left a dirty drug needle in the bathroom. They were clean! They'd just come out of the pool.

"Hmm," she miffs. "I just thought you'd want to know." She hangs up on me.

I'm standing in front of Matt with his expectant eyes, and it dawns on me that I just need to mind my own business.

"Everything all right?" Matt asks me.

"Yeah, I just left something where Emily is staying."

"So are you going to tell me what Thomas is doing here? Is he taking a cooking lesson, because it looks intense in there?"

"Kay invited him for dinner." I nibble on my bottom lip. "I think."

"Why?"

"I suppose because he was here on the front porch when we ar-rived, and that's what Kay does. She invites people for dinner. Have you two actually met?"

"What's he saying to her?" He gives a short shrug. "I've never introduced them to each other."

It dawns on me that Matt isn't remotely jealous. He never even considers the possibility that Thomas might be attracted to Kay, because he's so full of himself. I decide to test this theory.

"I don't know, maybe he thinks she's hot."

Matt laughs. He laughs!

"What's so funny about that?" I demand.

"Kay's with me," he says, as if that's the end of such ridiculousness.

"I imagine he's just making small talk while she cooks."

"He seems really into what she's saying." He's watching the two of them through the window, and it feels illicit. Almost stalkerish.

"I would imagine Thomas is fascinated by watching a woman cook in the Silicon Valley. That's not all that common, almost like an endangered animal, you know?" I open the front door and head back inside.

Matt glares at me. "She's patting a piece of meat." The way he says this, with more ego than I can stomach—like the act is disgusting—makes me want to slap him.

"Do tell, what does a man love more than a hearty steak?"

"I only meant he's supposed to be here pursuing you for our business venture, and he's in the kitchen watching my girlfriend wash a hunk of meat. You don't find that strange?"

"You really don't think she's sexy at all, do you? That's why you're questioning Thomas in the kitchen with Kay? You can't imagine that anyone on earth might find your girlfriend attractive."

"What is that supposed to mean?"

"You told me that no one else wanted her. I can't get that out of my head. Who marries someone that no one else wants? Kevin believed he'd won the lottery by marrying me."

"Well." He rolls his eyes. "Kevin."

"You don't get it. I'm not supportive of this marriage, not because you're not a Christian—which I know you want to use as your excuse. That way I'm just some religious crackpot whose opinion doesn't matter, but in all honesty that's not my reason."

"I suppose you're going to tell me. Even though you might want to take note that I'm not asking."

I let out an exaggerated sigh, jutting my chin forward for affect. "I'm worried you'll make a terrible husband for Kay because you have no idea how fabulous she is, and that makes you unworthy of her."

"So, are you trying to set her up with Thomas? Is that why you're keeping me out of the kitchen?" He lowers his voice. "Is that what this is about? Ashley's botched matchmaking schemes? Because I fail to see what would make him a better catch than me—especially considering he has no intention of marrying anyone, so maybe you should take your matchmaking skills back to Philly with you."

"I'm not matchmaking, and I'm not keeping you out of the kitchen. I'm only telling you that Kay's had offers. It's been her choice not to marry, so why would you think no one else wanted her?" My blood is starting to boil, and I'm obsessed with that line, if I'm honest. Kay may drive me nuts, but she's my girl—and no one has the right to talk badly about her. Least of all some yahoo who claims to want to marry her.

Matt takes me by the wrist and pulls me out the back door onto the patio. "Did you tell her I said that?"

I pause a minute, let him sweat it out. "Of course I didn't tell her. I'd never say something so cruel to Kay. I'd never even think anything so cruel, which is why I can't get it out of my head that you would say it. I mean, who do you think you are, Ryan Gosling?"

He drops his head, and the strut has gone out of his peacock stance. "That's why you didn't want to come with me to the jewelry store?"

"I wanted to be happy about this, Matt. Believe it or not, I did. But when you said that, you may as well have socked me in the stomach. Going to that jewelry store felt like the ultimate betrayal to Kay, because I wanted so much better for her. But I went because that's what I thought she'd want, and she's a big girl. She has to make her own decisions. You were her choice, but now that there's another possible option, am I upset by that? Absolutely not."

He scrunches his face as if in pain. "It's not what I think about Kay. I promise you on my mother's grave that it's not what I think."

I'm not convinced. I've known Matt a long time, and he is a lawyer. Lawyers know how to say whatever you want to hear. I should know, right? Where are his words of love? The listings of all of her fantastic attributes? The utter lack of intelligence and savvy thinking that falling in love brings?

"Then, why would you say it? It has to be somewhere inside your mind for you to say it." The more I think of it, the more I get incensed. "Why would you marry someone that you didn't think other men wanted? I've got news for you. There's always someone else. Even if you look like Quasimodo." I catch myself. "She doesn't look like Quasimodo. That's not what I'm saying." I look into the house, glad that Kay can't hear me "defend" her. I am definitely not helping her case.

"I was trying to psyche myself up, that she'd say yes."

"By putting her down?"

"Obviously, I don't think that, Ashley. Is that why you don't think we should get married?"

I don't know how to answer that question. He's not a believer. He had the misfortune of dating Emily. I mean, where do I even start? But if I knew Kay really loved him, it would make a difference. I know she told me that she did, but there was just something in her voice that was too desperate for me to believe it. She tried too hard to convince me, and now that I feel the desperation in Matt, I wonder if Kay has been convinced she loves him. He does specialize in persuasion.

"Matt?" Kay calls from inside, and he turns toward the house while shedding his suit jacket. "Matt?" She calls again.

"Out here!" he calls while keeping his eyes firmly on me, as if to threaten me that if I tell Kay anything, he'll be on me like white on rice.

"Were you here all along?" Kay asks.

"Uh, no. Just got here. Ashley and I had some business to discuss."

"Anxious to see your handiwork in the backyard, are you?"

"Y-yes."

"Ashley, can you come give me a hand with dinner?" This is code for something else. Kay wants my help in the kitchen as much as she wants the rat's help from *Ratatouille*. (At least the rat had mad skills.)

I walk into the kitchen and Kay appears rattled, scuttling about like a trapped rodent. *Completely out of character.* "The Tri-Tip is huge. Do you think Brea and her family might want to come to dinner?"

"With her kids?" I want to check her forehead at this point.

"It's been a long time since I've seen them," Kay says simply, as if she doesn't abhor children in her space.

"Because you don't like—"

"Ashley, can you ask them to dinner, please?"

"Yeah." I shrug. "No problem." *I mean, really. Why not make an awkward situation ten times more awkward?*

Kay steps back into the kitchen and loops her apron on over her head. Thomas tries to help and reaches for her hair, by pulling her hair off the back of her neck, so intimately, his fingers brush as light as a butterfly's wings. I feel as if I've intruded on a private moment by watching. He takes the ties and cinches it around her waist and makes a bow before placing his hands on either side of her waist. Kay turns brusquely to get away, but somehow becomes entangled in his arms, and they embrace just when Matt walks in from the living room.

Kay and Thomas don't notice either one of us as we stand side-by-side, and I'm shattered for Matt as his expression drops, though I really shouldn't be, but watching someone in pain brings me no joy. Even if they've earned it.

"That's why you didn't want me to ask her?" Matt says, a cloud of suspicion aimed at me. "You're pushing for Thomas because he's the same religion?"

Kay and Thomas turn toward us, then separate, but Thomas's arm is still at her waist.

"You're a Christian?" Kay asks Thomas, and he nods slightly.

"I'm not pushing for anything! They've only just met. Not ten minutes ago." I look at Kay for backup. I want her to tell Matt it's just a misunderstanding, but that maybe it's time he appreciated her. But she just stands there like a mannequin while Thomas has yet to remove his arm from around her waist.

"Ashley." Kay moves away from Thomas. Can you set the table for three more? I've invited Seth and Arin."

"Kay, the steak isn't five loaves and fishes. It's not going to multiply." But she's not listening.

Matt steps forward and kisses her on the cheek. "Hi, sweetheart."

I can't help but note Matt's eyes are on Thomas while he kisses Kay.

"What else can I do to help, Kay?"

"Thomas," Matt says. "Why don't you come with me out back? We'll fire up the grill," he says in a menacing tone.

After they leave, I stare at Kay. "Well, something's getting fired up and it might not be the grill."

Kay closes her eyes and puts her hand to her heart. "I'm in trouble, Ashley. Big trouble." Then she starts murmuring under her breath, "This too shall pass. This too shall pass."

We can only hope so. We hope it passes and takes Matt with it when it goes.

Chapter 21

M ATT, THOMAS, AND Kay are engaged in intense conversation, seemingly about work, but obviously subtexting deeper realms. I use this opportunity to escape unnoticed to the guest room and collapse on the bed. If I were Kay, I'd go for a five-mile run and clear my head. But sadly, I'm not Kay and my coping skills run more toward crap television and a tub of Ben & Jerry's. *I'm not exactly on the macrobiotic diet in times of struggle.*

Staring up at the ceiling, I notice how perfect Kay has the crown molding painted against the ceiling. It's absolutely straight with no paint mishaps or missed color. It's how she does everything in her life, so I don't know why I'm worried about her. The way Kay manages things, she'll probably have both men in love with her without ever having to put a ring on her finger or commit, if that's what she wants.

My cell phone rings. Wonders never cease. It's my husband.

"Kevin!" I say, half-expecting to hear his assistant's voice with another excuse.

"Why is it every time I call, you sound as if you're ready to implode? You're on vacation. You should be lounging at the beach and having pedicures."

"Kevin, you never call. How would you know what I sound like?" He is silent. "I'm sorry. Your sister told me you'd call me tomorrow."

"I had a minute," he says, like I'm nothing more than an insurance company and he's got time to check rates.

"Do you want me to come home?"

"I want you to have a vacation."

"No, I mean ever. Do you want me to come back there? Because I've got a few job opportunities here. Maybe I should stay." My stomach tightens.

"Is—is that what you want to do?" he asks.

And I don't answer. I just sit and contemplate for a full minute. "I don't know what I want."

"I'd never keep you from what you loved, Ashley. Maybe the sacrifice is too big for someone like you."

"Someone like me?" Great. He doesn't think I'm cut out to be a wife either. Not a great thought process in one's husband.

"Smart," he says. "Capable."

"Brea's capable and smart. She's a wife."

"I don't want to have this conversation over the phone, Ashley."

My chest tightens.

"Ash, you still there?"

"I'm here."

"You found a job out there?"

"Maybe," I say curtly.

He clears his throat. "So you'd prefer we moved back to California. That's what you're telling me?"

I growl like a lioness, "No, that's not what I am saying. I'm saying I can't decide—" I stop myself. "We can't decide our future in five minute increments, Kevin!"

I hear his name called over the intercom system.

"I heard. You've gotta run, right?"

"I'll call you in the morning, beautiful. I love you."

"I love you too." I hang up the phone. Never finishing a conversation is like being in a constant state of limbo. You can't move forward. You can't move back. You're just stuck.

I hang up and a text comes through from my husband. *Forgot why I called. Mom flying in. Details later.*

"Mom flying in, where? Whose mom? Not my mom!"

Kay peeks her head in and doesn't even mention that I'm talking to myself. "Dinner's ready in about 45 minutes. Did you call Brea?"

I shake my head. "She's not coming." I neglect to add that I never called her. I think another dysfunctional Reasons dinner party in the space of three days is enough fun for any California vacation.

She nods.

"Kay," I call after her.

"Yes?"

"Are you going to confront Matt?"

She steps into the room and closes the door behind her. This is happening during dinner preparation while she has two suitors in her kitchen, guests arriving soon, and a table to set. I'm reeling from the magnitude of this moment.

"Kevin sent you a bouquet of roses to thank you for taking his sister. He sent me one too."

"Good. I hope Matt is eating his heart out."

"Ash, I'm going to accept Matt's proposal."

"You're what?" I leap off the bed. "Kay, you've got to be kidding me. What about Thomas out there? What about the orange bag of lace? What about the fact that he admitted to indiscretions in your own home? Not even your home together. *Your* home!"

"Matt's told me about Thomas. He's always been jealous of Matt. This is simply another manifestation of that."

"But you don't love Matt."

"How on earth would you know if I loved Matt or not? I'm not a fairy tale kind of woman. Love looks different to a woman like me than it does to a woman like you. My mother was married—"

"Three times by the time you were fourteen. Yeah, yeah, yeah. What happened to not being the marrying kind? Not having to answer to anyone. You're an independent thinker – should I go on?"

Kay rests her hands in her lap. "I can't explain it, but my answer is going to be yes. Rest up before dinner." Kay shuts the door behind her and I focus on the perfect paint job once again.

There was a time, in the innocence of my youth, that I believed everyone who said they were a Christian acted like one, and the church was immune from the darker sins of the world. Life experience has shown me that we all have a sinful nature, with some darker than others, and innocent trust in the wrong people can have far worse consequences, because not only is your faith in humanity shaken by betrayal, but when it happens in the church, your faith in God wavers, too. Kay is the strongest woman I know. She loves God, and order, and adhering to His will, and I feel betrayed by this new, weaker Kay.

As I emerge from my room, the sun is sinking on the horizon and the dusky pink sky shows Kay's décor in the best light. Thomas Galway buzzes around Kay like an unwanted bee, and I see myself in him. How I wanted to protect Seth from a painful future with Arin, and learning the hard way that it wasn't my place to rescue him. Maybe that's my lesson here. It's not my place to rescue Kay, any more than it is Thomas's job. We're all held accountable for our own decisions, not anyone else's.

The doorbell rings, and I take my cue and get out of the way. I open the door, and Seth and Arin are on the front steps. See, this is my life. I escape one nightmare, only to enter another. Arin looks like she'd rather have a root canal than be here, and who can blame her? She must have really not wanted to cook tonight.

"Hey Ashley," Arin says without inflection.

"Hey Arin, Seth. Where's Toby?"

"He's home with my friend. She's staying with us from Brazil."

"Cool."

Arin walks past me and straight into the kitchen. Her eyes are filled with sorrow. Seth watches her go, then turns his attention towards me. "She's angry."

"I gathered. I suppose you have nothing to do with that."

"She's pregnant."

"I hope you didn't say that to her."

"Say what?"

"That she's angry because she's pregnant."

He shrugs. "Who's the new guy in the kitchen?"

I look toward Kay's small kitchen, which is crammed with people. That has to be making her crazy. "It's Matt's business partner. I guess he fancies himself a chef."

"If you ask me, he fancies Kay."

"I didn't ask you."

"No need to be so touchy. I'm just saying."

"What's wrong with Arin?"

"What isn't wrong with Arin? I can't do a thing right when it comes to her, and she's quick to tell me. I'm in trouble for texting you."

"Seth!" I pull my phone from my back pocket and there are unread texts. "I didn't read them, I guess." I study Seth and his tanzanite blue eyes, against his pale, balding head. He really is unaware that something like texting your ex-girlfriend can rile a woman—a pregnant woman. "She's trying, Seth. You can be hard to reach and you need to communicate with her."

"What? I'm there constantly for her. I don't know what she wants."

"She wants your attention."

"Seth, really? You can't stay away from Ashley for five seconds?" Arin yells from the kitchen.

At this point, I can't think of a thing that keeps me here at this so-called dinner party. I grab my sweater and handbag from the coat closet, and meet Matt's eyes. "Tell Kay, I had to go out."

"Go out where?"

"Out!" I yank open the door and some random stranger is standing there. She's tiny with golden brown hair cascading down her chest in loose, beach ringlets. Her eyes are dark and bitter. She practically snarls at my appearance.

"Hmm," she says. "This is her?" She stares behind me.

When I turn, she's speaking to Matt, who looks at me as if he has no idea who this woman is—but it's obvious he knows exactly who she is. "This is Ashley Novak. She's here visiting from Philly."

The woman crosses her arms over her chest. "Why?"

"Because I used to live here," I say, incensed.

"You used to live here with Matt?"

"Matt doesn't live here."

"Matt told me this was his house." She taps her foot on the front porch.

"No." Matt puts his hands on my shoulders protectively. "It's my girlfriend's house, Tammy. I told you that."

I gaze back at Matt to see if he's leading her in the direction he fed her.

"She's the orange underwear girl?" I ask, and Matt nods.

"I left my undies here on purpose. That's why I came to apologize. It's Step 8 of my program, and I did it because Matt had this nice house. I thought he could rescue me, but then I realized the house was way too clean for a bachelor pad and I thought I could get rid of the woman. But, I found out, I could rescue myself."

"I have no idea what's going on," I say.

"Tammy is trying to tell you that nothing happened between us. I'm not going to lie. It's why I brought her here a few months back, but then she told me about her sponsor, and that she's in for addiction. Something snapped me back to reality. Nothing happened."

"No man ever turned me out like that. Like I was a dog to be put out on the street!" Tammy's rage starts to simmer, and I'm worried she's about to go back on whatever drug she just got off. "So I left my calling card."

I shake my head. "Matt? Why weren't you honest with Kay from the start? If nothing happened, I don't understand why you chose to wait until I was pinned under you at Tiffany's to infer that I'd found something?

"Because I told you, something could have happened and I felt guilty. I thought you might have found her earring because I found the other one."

"Ahh,"

"Isn't that just as bad? It was my intention, and if we weren't in a crisis, would you have believed me?"

"It's not me who matters."

"Anyways. Sorry. Are we good?" Tammy asks.

"Yeah. Yeah," I say. "We're good. Good luck with the rest of treatment," I say quickly, trying to usher her out.

"You were first on my restitution list. I barely know you from a stick o' pigs, so I figured you were a good place to start." Tammy sighs. "It's going to get harder now, facing the people I really care about."

I look at Kay in the kitchen, but she's busily chopping vegetables and laughing with her guests. I don't think she's aware of what's happened on the porch.

A stretch limousine pulls up behind underwear chick's car, and a driver emerges. He opens the trunk, pulls out a Louis Vuitton suitcase then opens the car door. My mother-in-law, Elaine Novak, gets out of the stretch limo, and my heart pounds. I was wrong. This night could get worse. Infinitely worse.

Frantically, I try to dial my husband, but once again, it goes straight to voice mail. I text him, "911 NOW."

A man follows her out of the imposing vehicle. I can only assume it's the baby daddy, unless Elaine has suddenly gone cougar. He's tall, brimming with muscles, and he looks like Josh Lucas. "Not bad, Emily."

"Ashley, are you going to just stand there, or help me with my bags?" Elaine calls to me.

"Excuse me, Tammy," I say. "Good luck with your sobriety. I know you can do it."

Baby Daddy picks up Elaine's bag—worth more than the contents of our house—and starts up the walk. See, the world just isn't fair. *Emily gets a guy who follows her across the country and picks up his future mother-in-law's bag without being asked, and Kay gets a guy who picks up addicts and brings them back to her house.*

"Ashley!" Elaine yells at me again.

"I'm sorry." I startle out of my nightmare and jump off the steps.

"You don't have your shoes on? What are you, turning into Britney Spears?"

"Absolutely not. I can only wish for Britney Spears' sanity at the moment."

"Do you see what I mean, Josh?" Elaine snaps. "She's in her own world half the time. I don't know how my son bears it."

To give her credit, Elaine is trying to speak quietly, but on the freshly asphalted street, her voice carries across the neighborhood Josh sticks out his free hand.

"Ashley, I'm Josh Greywold. With any luck, I'm going to be your brother-in-law soon."

With any luck? I wonder if he means bad luck. "It's nice to meet you, Josh." I'd like to tell him I've heard so much about him, but it's not true. He could be a potted plant for all I know about him. For all Kevin knows about him, he's some crazy stalker who chased his sister to California.

"Ashley, you seem pale." Elaine pats my cheek. "I took an early flight. Josh has to get back to practice. Don't you, doll? My son had to text me where you were staying. It's no easy task finding you, my dear. This is really in the center of town, isn't it?"

"Kevin texted you?" I kiss her cheek and take her sweater from the crook of her arm. "Won't you come inside?" I look down at my phone, but there are no new texts.

"I'm sorry to bother you here, but I didn't have my daughter's address. It seems as if you've cordoned her off from the real world, as if she should be ashamed. It's not 1953, Ashley."

"No," I tell her. "She's actually staying in a friend's mansion. She couldn't have things more lovely. I wanted her to be comfortable." *Well, I wanted her to sail off to some exotic land never to darken my door again, but that's hardly Christian.*

"She'll be comfortable at home with me," Josh says. "Where she belongs."

I nod. "Of course. Come in, won't you both?"

As we enter the house, Kay comes out of the kitchen, wiping her hands on a towel. She reaches out toward my mother-in-law. "Mrs. Novak. What a nice surprise to see you again so soon."

"I brought my daughter's fiancé. He's so anxious to get married, and once we found out where she was, we set out straightaway."

I gauge Josh's reaction and he does seem excited to get married. Go figure.

"Come on in, there's enough dinner for everyone," Kay offers. The miracle of the tri-tip.

"We already ate," Elaine says. "We'd actually like to be on our way toward the wine country. I understand she's somewhere there, but obviously, I don't have the address."

"You didn't rent a car?" I ask her as I watch the limousine pull away.

"I thought we'd take yours."

"I don't have a car. I'm on vacation, remember?"

"You can take mine," Kay says. "I'll have Matt drive me to work in the morning." She reaches up on her tip-toes and kisses Matt. He grasps her hand on his cheek, and doesn't let go of her hand until they reach the kitchen.

"No, no. I'll rent a car in the morning. No problems."

"Who is this?" Tammy jumps back on the porch when she sees Matt alongside Kay. Her eyes slice back to me with laser precision. "I thought you were Matt's wife?" She looks at my ring finger.

I shake my head, more than a little fearful that Tammy doesn't have all the drugs out of her system just yet. I've seen way too many movies where the scary chick slides a knife out of a holster on her thigh, so I move behind Matt.

My mother-in-law is cawing. "The morning! We can't wait until morning! We flew all day to get here."

My heart starts pounding hard. "Well, you should have flown into San Francisco because you're miles away from the wine country and your daughter, and we already drove that twice for your family and we're not driving again! Understand?"

Everyone takes a step back. Including Tammy.

I take slow, deep breaths. "We've already driven that road twice in the last two days," I say to Elaine, much calmer this time.

"Third time's the charm. The third time is for love," she says this while pinching her future son-in-law's cheek as though he were nine.

"No!" I shout. "No! I'm not going anywhere. I'm on vacation. Vacation! Or do they call it *holiday* down in your neck of the woods? Regardless, it doesn't include chauffeuring your in-laws all over the third largest state in the nation!"

"Well, isn't she pleasant?" Elaine says.

I run up the steps, slam the door behind me, and clamber to my room, burrow my way under my pillow and scream into the mattress. *I'm never coming out!*

Chapter 22

MY PHONE RINGS, and I yank it out of my pocket and see Brea's name – not my husband's.

"Hello?"

"What did you do?"

"Don't ask. How'd you find out?"

"Kay told me to call you. She says dinner is starting soon and you're holed up in your room and you left your mother-in-law with the Reasons?"

I groan. "I snapped at my mother-in-law! I'm standing next to Kay, who is planning to marry this idiot, the idiot and the idiot's almost-fling, and I yell at my mother-in-law, what the heck is wrong with me?"

"I'm coming over."

I don't even argue. If anyone can save me from myself, it's my best friend. It's certainly not my husband, who has ignored my text, knowing his mother was on her way to ruin my vacation. It wasn't bad enough Kevin sent me his sister? This word *vacation*. I don't think Kevin understands it.

I hang up when there's a light rap on my door. I brush myself off, stand up straight and open the door slightly. It's Kay.

She waltzes in. "Way to make a first impression."

"Oh Kay, leave me alone."

Kay places her fingertips on her chin. "Notice something?"

I grab her hand and stare at the common chip diamond ring on her finger. "Where did you get that?"

"Matt just proposed!" she squeals.

I drop her hand. "Where?"

"You're jealous!"

"Oh gosh, Kay, I'm anything but jealous. I'm worn out. Where did he get that ring? Is it real?" I grab at her finger again and she swipes it away.

"You're such a snob! It's beautiful!"

"We picked out a two carat Tiffany's diamond. Where is that ring, Kay?"

I drop my head. I fell for Matt's baloney. Going to Tiffany's was all a ruse. He planned to buy her a piece of junk trinket all along.

"He said that you told him I wouldn't like the ring you picked out. That it was your dream, not mine, and bought me exactly what I'd like, something simple." She scoffs. "You can't even be happy for me! You're the one who told him not to buy the Tiffany's ring! You always have to be the star, don't you? You can't share the spotlight with anyone?"

To her credit, Kay doesn't rush from the room and slam the door. She waits patiently for me to respond, but I can't bring myself to be happy for her. Try as I might. I know what kind of ring Matt can afford on his salary, and seeing the bubblegum machine toy he bought her, I can't hide my disdain.

"So that's it. You have nothing to say to me. No congratulations? No, 'you'll make a beautiful bride?'"

"You will make a beautiful bride," I tell her honestly. "And I didn't tell Matt that about the ring. We picked out a ring at Tiffany's."

"You're spoiled Ashley, and your mother-in-law is out there speaking ever-so-nicely to your ex-boyfriend. Maybe you could make an appearance?" Kay slips from the room.

I fall to my knees against the bed and clasp my hands against my forehead. *"Please Lord, show Kay the truth. If I'm wrong, let me be wrong, but don't let Kay marry this man under the wrong pretenses. She has always been so faithful to you. Don't let this man corrupt her. Please, Lord! And if he isn't dark like I think he is, help me see the light!"*

The buzz from the dinner party is getting louder, and I know I can avoid my fate no longer. I step out of my jeans and put on my most innocent outfit. A cotton candy pink Houndstooth pencil skirt with a simple pink shell. I slide into nude pumps and I apply pale lipstick. Checking my reflection, I am the picture of purity as I prepare to grovel. Which is not my best look.

Before I face the wolves, my door swings open again and Brea stands before me. She envelops me in a hug. "I'm sorry you couldn't stay with us. This might have all been avoided."

I shake my head. "There's some life lesson I'm not learning. Because I keep getting the same one over and over again. I think it has to do with personal boundaries."

"Well, unless you throw the 'Boundaries' book at your mother-in-law's head, something tells me it wouldn't do you any good."

"Thanks for being here."

"It's a zoo out there. Are you ready? Pastor Max and Kelly are here. Seth and Arin. Sam is here naturally. Free meal. Kay is flashing her engagement ring around and there's that random guy with the bow tie. Then, of course Elaine is here with some hot guy with the body of Adonis."

"Adonis, I believe, is going to be my new brother-in-law."

Brea clucks her tongue. "I'll say one thing for her, Emily does not appear to be settling." She rakes her fingers through her curls to straighten them out, but they pop right back into place. "Kay on the other hand."

"She won't listen!" I say desperately.

"Don't underestimate how much can happen without your help, Ashley. You didn't marry Seth and that wasn't from a lack of your trying."

"I'm never going to live that down, am I?"

"Let's get out there. The lions are hungry. The kids are with my mom and John is with me. We've got your back."

"Unless you brought along a steel shark cage, that may not be enough."

"I'll say one thing for you," Brea says as we exit the sanctity of the guest room. "You sure know how to vacation."

It's a balmy evening on the back porch. Two tables are pushed together and covered with Kay's red-and-white checked tablecloths. She's set out white plates on gold chargers and made makeshift centerpieces out of old lanterns and candles. The fairy lights strung across the porch are lit and everyone stares up at me waiting for a reaction.

Pastor Max rises and offers me a hug. "Ashley, you look beautiful. Marriage agrees with you. Doesn't it Kelly?" he asks his perky wife. He's a burly man, the kind whose high school popularity and charm never left his side.

Kelly nods. Her long blond ponytail is gone now. Replaced by a short, blunt cut that announces she's given into the life of a pastor's wife and left her cheerleading days in the past.

"I'd like to offer a blessing over our meal tonight, and hope you'll all bow your heads and join me," Max continues.

Prayer. Yes. Let's pray. Anything to avoid actual conversation at this point.

"Lord, we thank you for gathering us here together tonight. To celebrate the return of one of our own to the Valley, and welcome new friends here with us tonight...we are grateful for the food and the laboring hands that prepared it. We ask you to bless that food and the marriage of Kay. Lord, how we will miss her in the singles' group, her organization, her amazing hospitality skills. We ask you to bless her union and her future. In His Name, we humbly say..."

"Amen," everyone says.

Matt slices up the "resting" tri-trip into thin slices, while everyone helps themselves to the myriad of salads and side dishes that would take mere mortals days to prepare.

There's a free seat next to John for Brea and one beside her next to my mother-in-law for me. When I sit, John kisses me on the cheek and smiles kindly. "We've missed you, Ashley."

His tenderness makes me want to burst into tears. I turn to my mother-in-law and grasp her hand. "I'm so sorry."

To my surprise, she grins at me with warmth. I secretly wonder if it's because she knows her son is on his way out of this marriage. "You do the best you can, darling."

Seth and Arin are sitting across from us and neither of them has stopped staring at me. Remember that childish taunt, "Why don't you take a picture? It lasts longer!" My fear of course is now everyone has a camera, and I don't want to see my weary expression plastered across social media for the world to judge.

"I explained to Josh that you tend to be on the high strung side, dear," Elaine says by way of a second introduction to Emily's baby daddy.

"It's all right," Josh says. "Emily already told me what she's like. Ashley," he says slowly, as if I might need help deciphering my own name. "Emily tells me that you used to be a lawyer."

"I'm still a lawyer," I start to explain.

"She doesn't work," my mother-in-law snipes.

"I'm trying to change that." Matt's partner Thomas stands over me. "Corn on the cob?" he offers.

"Thank you." I take a cob from Kay's red colander and he moves onto Elaine who is now whispering to Josh. No doubt about my desperate infertility issues – which do not exist as far as I know. Other than separate vacations does make pregnancy more difficult.

Elaine turns back to me. "Your friend Kay gave me the number where Emily is staying. I finally got to speak to my daughter."

"I'm glad."

"You can take us to her tomorrow. We'll find a hotel for the evening."

"You don't want to go tonight?" Excuse me if I'm fearful of her sudden accommodation.

"It seems you may have been drinking too much to go tonight. We'll go tomorrow. I promised Josh I'd take him to see the new 49ers stadium anyway. He saw it from the plane, so we may as well go tomorrow."

Josh nods as he bites into his corn.

"I didn't think you'd have time for a job," Arin says from across the table. "All that time you spend texting other people's husbands and all."

Seth's tanzanite eyes explode in size. "Arin, honey—"

"No, everyone is always giving Ashley a free pass." Arin stands up and grasps her tiny bubble belly, caressing it to make my 'sins' all the more conspicuous. "But you said it yourself, Seth, she's trying to stop Kay from getting married. I can only hope Matt isn't some rebound pity case like I am."

At this point, silverware drops, all conversation ceases and the entire table glares at me. *Can't you see? This is all hormonal. It has nothing to do with me. These two love each other! I'm the scapegoat, that's all.*

Arin plants her hand on her hip. "Don't you see? She can't keep her own marriage together, so she comes back here and ruins everyone else's!" she accuses. Seth stands up and tries to soothe her, but she is not done. "Kevin only married you because I said 'no' and you were just available."

"Arin!" Seth tries to pull her from the table.

She only laughs. "He was ready to get married and you were there! Of course you were there. You were ancient in the church! No one else wanted you so Kevin didn't even have to work at it!"

"That's enough," Seth says and pulls her from the table. "You've said quite enough. Kay, thank you for the dinner and congratulations on your engagement."

Kay's eyes are filled with tears; the liquid twinkles against the candlelight. If Arin thought I was ancient, Kay is positively geriatric, and I can see the pain in her eyes as she gazes questioningly at Matt. I swear, I'd take anything Arin had to throw at me, and more, if I could stop Kay from feeling this way. But it's my fault she does, isn't it? I put it in her mind that Matt didn't really love her by telling her about the first ring.

I stand up, and my chair falls with a clang against the brick. "Don't anyone else bother walking out. Enjoy Kay's beautiful dinner. I'll be leaving."

Seth tries to send me an apology with his eyes, but it's too late. *My husband wanted to marry Arin? Suddenly, Kevin's silence makes sense. He's finally realized his mistake.*

My mother-in-law gazes up at me with a smirk on her face and I run to my room and lift my suitcase without the slightest idea where I'm going to go.

Brea breezes in, and her face tells me all I need to know.

"You knew this?" I ask her.

"I didn't see a purpose in telling you. Kevin made his choice and I know he has no regrets. What good would it have done to tell you?"

"What good? It would have told me that my best friend trusted me enough to tell me the truth."

"I didn't want to hurt you."

I stare at Brea shocked by her betrayal, sick to my stomach that everyone knew my husband's secret except for me. "There's nowhere for me to escape. I just need to start over somewhere."

Everything I put into my suitcase, Brea takes out. "Stop, Ashley. Kevin married you. That was no accident."

"I think it was. I'm mortified." I hold up Kevin's T-shirt. "I took his T-shirt so that I could smell him when I was gone. He must think I'm such a moron."

"Kevin thinks no such thing. Kevin loves you, Ashley."

"Call him then. Call him from my phone and see how much he loves me. Better yet, text him '9-11' and see how long it takes him to answer. Go ahead!"

Brea doesn't reach for my phone. She simply offers that coddling look of sympathy. The way everyone must have felt about me on the day of my wedding.

Then, just when I think it's as bad as it can be, it gets worse. "John and I are leaving California."

"So if I move back here, you won't be here." This seems obvious after I say it, but not knowing what my future holds, Brea's absence is one more constant I've lost.

"We can't afford to stay, Ash. It's that simple. Raising two kids in the Bay Area has become next to impossible if we ever want to see John."

"No, it makes sense."

"My mom's selling her house. We're going to buy something with a granny suite. Maybe a little cottage out back."

"Unless it comes with a steel door and a padlock you control, I'd rethink that idea."

Brea grins and then, she lets me have it. "We're moving to Atlanta."

"Georgia?"

"Not actually Atlanta, but a suburb. It's got the green space for the kids, good schools, restaurants for John and me…"

"And it's got my in-laws! So what you're telling me is that you never plan on seeing me again, is that right?"

I just don't know how much rejection I'm expected to take in a lifetime.

Chapter 23

I N THE MORNING, I wait to hear Kay leave the house before I emerge from my room with my suitcase packed. There's a note on the kitchen table for me.

Ashley,

Elaine and Josh are staying at the Four Seasons. They'll sightsee today. I'll pick you up at 7:45 p.m. and we'll drive to Napa. Be ready.

Kay

I spend the day wallowing in my misery with *House Hunters* in the background. If only I'd stayed here. I had to have my insane fairy tale ideas. I'm not Brea. Fairy tales don't happen to girls like me. They happen to sweet, gentle women, not to lawyers who would spend hours debating the right way to place a toilet paper roll. Girls like me get jobs and support ourselves. We don't bake cookies and refinish darling, little second-hand furniture. We work and waste our money on pointless items like designer shoes. It's like Emily said, *own your reality.*

I meet Kay on the driveway with my suitcase. "Can you open the trunk?"

"Ashley, we're not going to have room for your luggage. I've got Josh and Elaine's to fit in there."

I stare at the car, which is basically an electric lawn mower with a roof, and I know she's telling me the truth. I lug my suitcase back to the porch, unlock the door and shove it where the landing spot used to be.

"Thank you for driving," I tell her as I get into the front seat.

"How are you feeling?"

I stare at her.

"Well, you look good," Kay says brightly. I notice her trinket engagement ring, cross my arms and turn away. It irks me to think I was taken in by the trip to Tiffany's. The manipulator! Matt knew exactly what he needed to do to win me over, and I fell for it.

"You know Arin's just jealous of you, right?" Kay asks me.

"You don't have to make me feel better. It wouldn't have hurt if there weren't some element of truth in it. Kevin and I never made sense."

"You always let your imagination run away with you. You must choose to look at the good in life!" She says this in uncharacteristic singsong tone. If by choosing to look at the good she means ignoring your fiancé is a skinflint and leaves behind other women's underwear, then I suppose that's true. As Kay grins like a cat with a belly full of birds, it obviously is working for her.

We pull up to the hotel, and my mother-in-law is ordering bellmen about in her tightly fitting icy green suit made of shantung silk.

I sigh. "You'd think she'd pick up on the whole California casual thing." Staring at Elaine, my shame is complete. Once again, I feel my presence is pointless, but I want Kevin to know, just because I'm interchangeable to him, it doesn't mean I feel that way about him and his family.

"Déjà vu," Kay says as we let the motor run in the hotel's parking circle. The bellmen reaches for Elaine's Louis Vuitton suitcase while Josh grabs his own.

I get out of the car and offer Elaine the front seat.

She waves me off. "I'm exhausted anyway. You sit up front." She slides into the backseat and looks at the bench seat behind her. "These really are like cardboard, aren't they? But I suppose that's necessary to save the environment."

I look at Kay above the car's roof. "She means to say thank you for driving her."

Kay laughs. "It gets lost in translation."

Josh grins at me and slides in the backseat next to Elaine. His knees are up to his chest. "Josh, you sit in the front. You're so tall. I should have rented a car."

He takes my mother-in-law's hand. "No, today, Elaine and I got a chance to bond. I'll be fine back here."

Another twinge of jealousy gnaws at my heart. I suppose I shouldn't be surprised. Josh has already proven capable to produce grandchildren. I'm just the second string draft choice who still has yet to prove herself on the field.

We're not on the road for twenty minutes before Elaine falls into a blissful sleep, which surprises me. Truth be told, I imagined her as sort of a vampire who didn't require rest.

Josh is nervously tapping his giant feet, and I search for some topic of conversation that doesn't include me being a home wrecker or Kevin's second string. And of course, something not as polarizing as *what the heck is wrong with you that you want to marry Emily? One too many concussions on the field perhaps?*

Polite conversation eludes me as I have no understanding of football and something tells me patent law is not his specialty. Josh is buff to the point where his stretchy football jersey is strained to the max around his bicep. He wears a military buzz cut and his eyes, while bright blue, are terribly close together, which throws off the symmetry of his face. He's a handsome guy, don't get me wrong, but he's in a daze, and it shows in his taut neck muscles and jittery big foot.

Josh notices me staring at him—I'm not exactly subtle—I'm riding shotgun and he's in the backseat behind Kay. He breaks the awkward silence, "I'm sorry about what happened last night."

I give him credit. He doesn't ask for more information, but maybe Elaine filled him in on all he needed to know. He's a southern gentleman after all. Kay hums to herself rather than partake in the conversation. The silence between us is deafening. If only I could go back in time, I'd be more supportive. At least, I like to think that I would. One look at Matt and most likely, I'd give the same heinous opinions.

"You're the reason I'm here," Josh says to me.

"Apparently, all of Atlanta is saying the same thing." I look to my sleeping mother-in-law.

"I don't want a marriage like yours where my wife is on the other side of the country and I'm home earning money. It's not how I picture my future."

"You have that in common," Kay interjects. "It's not how Ashley pictured hers either."

"Betrayal is the worst. I can't have Emily think I betrayed her. My brother went to find her at your house, but he betrayed me. He scared poor Emily and now she's run off."

That's why she told you she ran off anyway. I suppose we'll never know the full truth, other than Emily wasn't getting enough attention for her liking.

Josh's admission of devotion toward Emily is admirable, but it only serves to remind me that the man I love, the man who promised to love, honor and cherish me, won't return a blasted phone call and left me to deal with his family drama alone. Worse yet, the knowledge that his true love was Arin, only she rejected him.

Yet here are Elaine and Josh, here for Emily regardless of the games she plays and the stories she tells. They love her unconditionally and I can't help but covet my sister-in-law for the moment.

"I don't think it's ever better to find out you've been betrayed by people you trusted." Josh stares out the window, and the passing headlights flash and highlight the sadness in his eyes. "It ruins your faith in humanity. That's the real price, and once that gets into your relationship, it's too late. The end is near." He clears his throat.

"I don't want to repeat my father's mistakes. He died alone," Josh says brusquely. "After a string of women young enough to be his daughter got tired of playing nursemaid, he was by himself in a care home. Once the money ran out, so did all the women. If you ask me, that's what ultimately killed him, the lack of attention. For a guy used to having an entourage, reality was rough. He wasn't equipped to deal with the truth."

My interest is piqued by Josh's admission. "How long ago did your father pass away?"

"He left my mom and me by the time I was ten, but he called first when I got picked up for the NFL, then again when I was Rookie of the Year. I don't think he wanted cash at that point. Think he wanted to lay claim to his genetic prodigy and let me know I'd be nothing without him. It wasn't long after, he passed. A few weeks ago."

"Did you take his call?" Kay asks him.

"Not then. I went to see him before he died, so I could make my peace. Emily said I should and I didn't want to let her think less of me."

This makes me turn around completely in my seat. "Emily thought you should go to him?"

"She didn't want me to have regrets, thought it would be better to have a clear conscience, and to do it for God, not myself."

Josh, and his apparent depth, makes me question everything I've ever known about my sister-in-law. Why on earth would she hesitate in marrying this guy? Kay glances at me, and even in the dusky light, I can tell she's thinking the same thing. Emily takes *shallow* to a new level. Even if she is playing her mother's 1860 game of letting a man chase her, putting Josh through this game, especially with his history, seems unbearably cruel. Even for Emily. She may be a moron, but she's not cruel.

"How long until we get there?" Josh asks, as he taps the armrest incessantly. "I'm getting nervous."

"About ten minutes now," Kay says.

Josh taps me on the shoulder with something, and I turn to see a gray velvet box. "Do you think she'll say yes?"

I grasp the box, open it, and an enormous diamond flashes brightly in the shadows of the passing headlights. I yank at the sun visor to open it and illuminate the ring. It's a stunning emerald cut diamond, flanked by smaller emerald cut diamonds cascading down in stair-step fashion, as far as the eye can see until it disappears into the cushioning of the box.

"How much do football players make?" I lift up the ring for Kay to peek.

Josh laughs. "It's a short career. You have to look at it that way. For now, I make enough."

"Holy cow!" Kay says, grasping the box from me. "It's enormous! Is she planning to wear it or rebuild the Egyptian pyramids with it?"

"It was the biggest in the store. That's why I bought it. I knew no one else would have a bigger one. I don't want anyone thinking I'm marrying her because she's pregnant—but I know what the news rags will say."

My mouth is still agape. "Seriously, I think if you asked her brother to marry you, he would probably say yes to this ring. And he's already married!"

"Ashley!" Kay yells at me, but I notice something in Kay's expression and that she glances at her own left hand. There is recognition in her eyes. It's not the miniscule size of her diamond that upsets Kay. She couldn't care less about such trivial things.

Josh chuckles. "No, it's exactly the result I was hoping for. I knew if I could impress Ashley, Emily would be equally inspired. She thinks the world of your opinion, Ashley."

I guffaw. "Sure she does."

Josh glances over at Elaine and ensures she's asleep. "Emily is always bragging how smart you are and that she wishes she had your brains."

Lot of good they've done me.

"I think you've got the wrong sister-in-law. Is Kevin hiding another brother?" Kay asks.

I smirk at Kay and put the ring back in its box and hand it to Josh. "She'd be crazy to say anything but *yes*, Josh. And I'd say that if you brought a ring from a gumball machine."

Like someone else we know did. I smile at Kay.

It's nearly ten when we arrive at Fish and Clara's mansion. As we wind up the long drive, I can't help but wonder if I've done damage to my parents' lifelong friendship with the long-suffering Bowmans. Nothing like introducing the Ashley brand of crazy to scare normals off in quick fashion. They've had a decade's worth in two short days.

Kevin's family is wearing, like obnoxious toys that drain batteries and suck them dry. Growing up "normal" if you can call anyone's upbringing that, it never occurred to me how utterly dysfunctional seemingly successful people might be. I assumed they joined non-profit boards and organized charity balls because they had so much to share—not because their own lives might be void of genuine meaning and real connection. Kevin's world has turned mine upside down.

I step out of the car, press the keypad code and great iron gates sweep across the asphalt and reach for the vineyards.

Elaine stirs awake. "We're here?"

"Yes," I say.

"Thank heavens," she says with a thick southern drawl. "I was beginning to think you were shuttling me back to Atlanta."

Don't think the idea hadn't crossed my mind.

Josh's jaw is set as we pull into the covered breezeway. He looks as if he's joining up for active duty, which in some ways, marrying into this family, that's exactly what he's doing. The porch lights come on and all around us the centuries' old oak trees light up to share their magnificence.

Clara is at the door beside Emily. I turn to see Josh's expression light at the sight of his future bride. Emily isn't surprised at all by the sight of Josh and by his own sly smile, he's aware of this.

Elaine seems utterly clueless as though she's rescuing her misguided daughter. She doesn't greet Clara, the kind woman who has housed her runaway daughter for nothing. "Enough of these games, Emily. You're getting married and I'll have no excuses."

"Doesn't he have to ask me first?" Emily smiles coquettishly at Josh.

Elaine taps her Tory Burch flats toward Josh. "I assume you're here to ask my daughter to marry you."

"In due time. There has to be some romance to the moment."

"This doesn't require romance. You ruined that opportunity when you took advantage of my daughter's innocence."

Josh drops his chin to his chest and his regret staggers off of him like a rattlesnake shedding its skin. Emily approaches him, but pulls away when Elaine glares at her.

Josh is doing everything he can to not sweep Emily up in his arms, and she's battling the same desires. There's a sizzling chemistry between them that's like a live wire connecting them—though they're feet from each other.

Clara takes matters into her own hands and approaches Elaine. "Welcome to wine country."

"I don't drink, dear," Elaine says, and I die just a little. *Seriously? Since when doesn't she drink? I've seen her do a pretty good number on a bottle of Scotch when her son announced our wedding.* Scotch. Not some fizzy, light wine!

"Please come in the house. Is everyone planning to stay? I'll need to get a few more beds ready."

I screw up my face. "I think so," I answer sheepishly. "I'm never going to be able to make this up to you, am I?"

Clara slings her arm over my shoulder. "You'll always be welcome. No matter what." She looks me straight in the eye and I know she means it.

I make the proper introductions.

"Elaine, it's a pleasure." Clara reaches out her hands. "I've been enjoying my time with your daughter. She's going to make such a wonderful mother. You must be over the moon about your first grandchild."

"Well, you know. My son married Ashley," Elaine lowers her voice conspiratorially. "We're not sure if she can have children, so I'm grateful I'll have at least one grandchild."

Uh, standing right here!

"Ashley can't be ready to have babies already," Clara says. "She only just got married. She wants to enjoy her husband, I'd imagine. Plus," Clara grasps Elaine's wrist for effect. "Your son works so much. Surely, Ashley doesn't want to mother alone—like she's vacationing."

Can I just state that my mother has awesome taste in friends? Or is that too anti-Christian on my part, to revel in a little aimed comeback. Even without the southern drawl, Clara can give shade as dark as Elaine can cast.

"Emily, why don't you get your things together?" Elaine says. "I see no reason to infringe on this good woman's hospitality any longer. Josh assures me he's ready to do the right thing."

Josh takes the hit for Emily without commentary and I find my-self wishing I wasn't so competent. Kevin will never need to care for me in that manner. I simply don't need rescuing, which is why he must have sent me to find the answers that would extricate him from being responsible for me. He needs his freedom to work and I feel oblivious for not noticing the signs before. *Me, the girl who claims to be too smart for her own good.*

Clara grasps Kay about the waist and pulls her close. "I won't hear of your leaving this late. Poor Kay must be utterly exhausted making that trip again."

Kay whimpers slightly, loving Clara's motherly attentions. "I am worn out," Kay admits. "I don't think I could drive another mile today unless it's over a cliff."

"Well, we can't have that, can we?" Clara asks. "You're not a long haul trucker, you're an engineer for heaven's sake."

Clara is just all goodness and light. My whole life, I've wanted to be like her and Kay. Selfless. Hospitable. The kind of person where warmth, and hosting impromptu dinner parties, comes naturally, and having overnight guests is as simple as turning down the bed.

Clara never had to clear a guest bedroom of extra shoes to make a bed. It feels good to watch her and Kay together. Kay's always wanted a mother figure, and maybe that's why she's become one to a ramshackle group of single engineer Christians. Watching her alongside Clara does my heart good—it's like they sing together it's so natural. Both of them could really fill a need in each other's life. Maybe Clara wouldn't take in every stray off the street and maybe Kay wouldn't feel the need to turn a bad man, good.

Clara notices Kay's left hand. "This is new?"

Kay nods, but self-consciously covers her hand.

A look passes between them. I can't tell what it means, but something about it gives me hope. And Emily is no longer in need of my attentions.

My work is done here.

Chapter 24

BACK IN PALO Alto, life goes on as it always has. Matt Callaway shows up at breakfast time each day, Kay makes us both a lumberjack's start to the day and then cleans it all up before I'm even fully awake.

It's been two days, and not a word from my in-laws – not even a request for me to schlep up after them or find a shotgun wedding venue. Not a peep out of my workaholic husband and I find myself exactly where I was before I left Philadelphia. Only now, not only am I questioning my life's purpose, but my marriage as well.

"YOU'RE NOT PLANNING on staying through the wedding?" Matt asks me over coffee at the kitchen table.

"I was planning on staying until after the wedding," I answer. Let's be honest, I have nowhere to be. Kevin has his job to fulfill him, my mother-in-law has a grandchild on the way, and Emily has her own blissful future to plan. Everyone is fine without me, so I may as well stay on vacation.

"I can't tell if you're kidding," Matt says.

"Good." I wink at Kay. She's not the same since we got home from dropping my mother-in-law in Sonoma. She and Matt don't exchange knowing glances across the table any longer. He brings up the wedding plans, and she promptly changes the subject. She's removed her engagement ring and told Matt she was getting it sized, but the truth is, it's in her bedroom on her nightstand. The question remains, why would she lie to him? Besides the fact that he deserves it, I mean.

It's Saturday morning and Brea is picking me up for a spa day. We're driving to Santa Cruz and a spa that overlooks the ocean. Not a bad way to lick my wounds, I suppose.

"Brea's here," Kay says as she looks out the window over the kitchen sink. Her voice is quiet and lifeless.

"You all right, Kay?" I ask her.

She nods.

"Do you want to come with us?"

Kay's head bobs up. "You don't think Brea would mind?"

"No, why would she? You can take my place at the spa. I'll be happy just to read a book overlooking the ocean." I ponder this. "You don't happen to have a good book I can take, do you?"

"If you mean a beach read, no I don't."

"Take the prospectus with you," Matt says. "Thomas has been nagging me every day for an answer from you." He slides the folder toward me.

A job. I suppose I might need one of those.

Matt watches Kay take off her apron. "You're really leaving me on a Saturday? I thought we'd celebrate today."

"I need to get out of the house."

"Yeah, sure. We'll go somewhere," Matt offers.

"I think I need a spa day," Kay says, and this snaps me to attention. Kay has never needed a spa day in her life. Kay's version of a spa day is a ten-mile run uphill.

I'm willing her away from Matt and out of the house. "I'll wait in the car, Kay. Hurry up."

"No, wait Ashley, I want you here for this."

"For what?"

"Where were you yesterday afternoon, Matt?" Kay asks her beau, and his neatly-coiffed eyebrows rise.

"I was at the office."

"That's interesting because I went to your office yesterday and Thomas told me you don't pay rent there any longer. He had to sign a lease on a smaller place in the same building."

"Yeah." Matt shrugs his wide shoulders. "I thought it was a waste for as often as I was in there. Thomas prefers the office environment to meet with clients. I like to go to them, you know, their offices, lunch downtown, a coffee shop."

"Get out of my house, Matt."

His face pales, and he looks from me to Kay. "What?"

"Get out of my house, and don't come back or you'll find out just how good of a lawyer I can hire."

"Baby, come on. What's this about?" Matt rises and crosses the kitchen with his arms outstretched toward Kay.

My heart is in my throat as I see rage in a face that I didn't think was capable of feeling such an emotion. She holds up a palm. "Don't. I know what you did with the company funds."

"Kay, come on. That Thomas is full of garbage and you know it. How long have you known me? You're going to believe that worm over me? He clearly has a crush on you and he knows the only way you'd date him over me is with a bunch of lies."

It's like I'm watching a tennis match between the two of them.

"I'll get your ring," Kay says, and leaves the room.

Brea walks into the kitchen and notices you can cut the tension with a light saber. "You ready to go? I've only got so much time away from the boys."

"Ashley, talk to her," Matt says. "This is crazy."

Kay comes back into the kitchen wearing her running pants, and a bright salmon T-shirt. "Here's your ring." She smacks it on the counter and it makes a hollow, tinny sound. "Do me a favor and give me some time."

"But Kay, I love you," Matt says. "I want to spend the rest of my life with you."

"Then, you can allow me a day at the spa to think things over.

There are too many red flags. Things I can't ignore."

"I can't allow you a day at the spa if all you're going to do is obsess about my ex-business partner and his lies. Thomas wanted you from the minute he laid eyes on you. He'd say anything to break us up. How can you be so stupid, Kay? You're going to throw away two years, for the word of a stranger?"

The doorbell rings and Brea and I race for it to exit the kitchen. When we open the door, Seth and Arin are standing beside my Kevin. I rush toward my husband and he gathers me in his arms and pulls me towards him as tightly as he's ever held me. He pulls away, meets my gaze and seems to look deeply into my soul before kissing me with a passion and zeal. There is no question in my mind that my man loves me and isn't going anywhere.

"Kevin," I whisper against his neck. "What happened to us?"

I can't bear to let go of him because I thought I'd never see him again. Not in the same way. I thought there would be a table…lawyers between us…

Seth clears his throat, and I giggle as I look at him alongside Arin. "Kevin never asked you to marry him," I accuse. "Why would you tell people he did?" I look up at my husband. "You didn't right?"

"You're the only woman I ever asked to marry me."

"I'm sorry," Arin says. "I was hurt when Kevin moved on so quickly."

"Didn't you move on first?" I ask her.

"The point is, I may have said that so you didn't think you were better than me."

Seth interjects. "Pastor Max told us we were trying to harm each other rather than saying how we really feel about each other. He said we needed to apologize to you before we harmed your relationship."

"You didn't plan this?" I ask them. "To be here with Kevin?"

"Pure coincidence," Seth says. "Or maybe it's fate."

"Kevin, what are you doing here? Who is looking after Rhett?"

"You're going to kill me. Rhett is in a kennel, but my mother ordered me here."

"Your mother? She's not even here. She's in the wine country with your sister."

"When I didn't answer my cell, she called the chief of surgery and said if I didn't get to California, I was going to lose my marriage, and then he was going to lose any possibility that I would stay in Philly."

"Your mother did that for us?"

"When I called her to read her the riot act for calling my boss, she told me to get on the next plane or not to be surprised when I found you didn't return from California."

"I don't understand. Isn't that what she wants?"

"Mom said she recognized herself in in your eyes, during her early years of her marriage when my father was never around. The reason they bought us the house is because she almost left my father during his residency. I never saw them fight, Ashley. I didn't know any of this. But Mom told Dad if he only had time to be a doctor and no time to be a husband, then she was going home to her mother."

"I was thinking of going home to my mother," I admit. "Or at least Kay."

Kevin presses his lips to mine and I remember why I'd settle for scraps from his table. Kevin is the man I love, and he wants to save lives, but I need him too. And that isn't selfish. It's just a fact.

"It's time to go home, Ashley."

"I can't. There's the whole Tiffany thing—"

"You're a lawyer. You'll figure it out. I'm not leaving without my wife."

The porch gets even more crowded as Thomas Galway strides up the walk in a pair of khakis and a green button-up shirt. It seems about as casual as the formal Thomas Galway gets.

"Is Kay here?"

"She's inside. With Matt."

He nods and pushes through the front door. We all pile into the doorway behind him and stand in a small huddle, our eyes glued to the kitchen. Matt dwarfs Thomas, but it doesn't stop him from getting right in the bigger man's face. "Get lost, Matt. Or I'll tell her the whole truth."

"There's no whole truth, Kay, come on. You've known me for nearly three years."

Kay seems confused and her eyes dart back and forth between each man when Thomas gets down on one knee on Kay's kitchen floor and holds up a black velvet box.

"Get out of here!" Matt screams, lifting Thomas by the collar off the floor. Thomas bats Matt away then gets back to his knee when Matt pulls back an elbow and lets a punch fly, knocking Thomas in a lump.

Kevin rushes to the kitchen and checks Thomas. Kevin stands to his full height. "Get out of this house now, Matt, before I throw you out. Ashley, call 9-11," he shouts to me.

"I'll do it," Brea says.

Kay leans over Thomas, who still seems to be unconscious. "Thomas! Wake up, Thomas!"

It's a long time before his eyelids flutter open, and Thomas smiles widely at Kay. "Did I hit him back?"

"He was an absolute train wreck," Kay says.

"Did he see the ring you deserved?"

Kay opens the ring box over Thomas and an enormous sparkler of epic proportion glares back at her in all its tacky, ostentatious glory. It makes Emily's ring look subtle.

"Thomas, what are you thinking? We haven't even been on one date?"

"What do you think about Italy for a first date?"

"You don't even know me!" Kay says through a smile.

"A guy knows."

Kevin applies a frozen bag of peas on Thomas's left eye. "I'm afraid you're going to have a shiner, my friend."

"You knew, right buddy? When you saw your wife, you knew it

was her."

Kevin's gaze makes me go weak in the knees. "I knew immediately."

"What about you?" Thomas asks Seth.

"The minute I laid eyes on her," he says, grinning at Arin.

Thomas groans though his wide grin. "My first fight," he says with satisfaction.

"I'm not in the mood for a spa day any longer, Ash," Brea says. "I'm going home to John."

"You go, I'll see you soon."

"We'll take you and John to dinner before we leave," Kevin says. Thomas starts to get up, but Kevin stops him. "Wait right there," he says while sticking a flashlight in his eyes. "You're not going anywhere until I check for a concussion."

"I have a rule about men asking me to marry," Kay says. "They need to be free of brain injury."

Seth and Arin leave quietly when the EMT's come in and Kevin explains the nature of the injury and gives his orders. He wants Thomas checked, just to make sure there's no hidden bleeding. Kay grabs her keys and the ring box and goes along in the ambulance.

"It's just you and me," Kevin growls.

"Oh?" I take a deep breath near his neck.

He pulls me away. "Stop that!"

"What did you have in mind?"

Kevin lifts me up off the ground as if I weighed nothing, and he looks deeply into my eyes. "I thought we might prove to my mother those rumors of our fruitlessness are greatly exaggerated."

I allow my head to fall against Kevin's chest and fall in love all over again. What a girl needs is to know she matters. And whether I work or don't, whether I'm a mother or not, whether I'm married or single, I matter.

I matter because God gave me a purpose – even if I don't always know exactly what that is.

"You want to stay in Philly then?"

"I do."

"That's the second time those were the best words out of your mouth."

The End

Other books by Kristin Billerbeck

Ashley Stockingdale Series:

What a Girl Wants

She's Out of Control

With this Ring, I'm Confused

What a Girl Needs

Spa Girls Series:

She's All That

A Girl's Best Friend

Calm, Cool and Adjusted

Stand Alone Novels:

Trophy Wives Club

Back to Life

Split Ends

The Scent of Rain

A Billion Reasons Why

Swimming to the Surface

For more books by Kristin Billerbeck or to contact her, visit her website at
www.KristinBillerbeck.com

www.Facebook.com/KristinBillerbeckBooks
Twitter: @KristinBeck

Visit her Blog at
www.GirlyGirl.Typepad.com